VYOM

AND

THE ROYAL WEAPON

Tripty Bhardwaj

First published by 2018

Becomeshakespeare.com

Wordit Content Design & Editing Services Pvt Ltd
Unit - 26, Building A -1, Nr Wadala RTO,
Wadala (East), Mumbai 400037, India
T: +91 8080226699
Wordit Art Fund helps deserving authors publish their work by
providing monetary support. To apply for funding, please visit us
atwww.BecomeShakespeare.com

ISBN - 978-93-88081-69-6

Contents:

Chapter 1
Vyom: The Sky of Success

'For Vyom, its aim is paramount and we've been striving to achieve it, *every day, every time, every moment,*' Chancellor Jaywardhan Rathore was declaiming about a memorable day in *Vyom Hall* of *Vyom Institute.* 'We will die protecting our world, our country and our people and endeavouring a true victory. *Victory of peace over war, of truth over falsehood, of trust over treachery, of hope over despair, of courage over cowardice and of unity over every weakness raising hindrances to a better future.*' He gestured to a man in uniform, who had a powerful physique, sitting next to him. 'I heartedly welcome my dear friend, Major General of Vyom's army, Sagar Mittal, in our institute to celebrate this great moment.'

Vyom Hall was witnessing the presence of professors, scientists, officers and all groups of students: *Buddha, Shukra, Vasundhara, Mangal, Brihaspati, Shani, Arun and Varun.*

Jaywardhan continued, 'A century ago an organization named *Vyom, the sky of success* was founded with a sole aim. For achieving it we must realize our duties, our responsibilities towards our world and country. We must feel that the people we live among, their safety is our prime duty, their happiness is the source of ours. Today is a glorious day for all of us, as a family, as a team.'

Everyone perked up.

Jaywardhan Rathore in his early fifties, with a set of rectangular glasses and black-white moustache, had an efficacious personality. A gentle person of firm determination. He'd started his career as an Assistant Professor in Vyom Institute. His hard work and passion brought him to its highest post.

Vyom Institute was a spacious-green campus, had forty main multi-storey buildings, *Bhavans,* with three wings each, and a head office.

All the bhavans were scattered forming twelve concentric ellipses, *Parikramas,* around the head office. A group of smaller structures collectively known as *Sanrachana* situated between the sixth and the seventh parikrama included canteens, auditoriums, arenas, stadiums, sports clubs, guest rooms, cyber cafés, etc. Vyom Institute was more or less constructed like the solar system, eight planets replaced by forty bhavans, the asteroid belt by Sanrachana and the sun by the head office.

Tonight the entire campus was sparkling with decorative lights and streamers vying for attention. Open corridors and courtyards were adorned with shimmering curtains, flowers and rangoli, embellishing the ambience. Everyone was savouring the rollicking festival to their heart's content. Colourful water, dancing at melodious music, was jetting out of the fountains making every feet move rhythmically. But Jaywardhan's heartbeat had gone out of rhythm. He was in conversation with someone in *the Chancellor's Cabin* through his wireless single earphone, a concerned look on his face, 'What? But how did he branch out, Ali?'

Ali's voice came from another side, 'I'm working on it, Mr Chancellor. But he's scheming to get DTM's system for sure.'

'You take care of yourself. He must not come to know that you work for us.'

'Don't worry,' said Ali. 'I'll keep you updated.'

'*Vyom farewell.*' Jaywardhan disconnected his earphone. Ali's words had set him thinking. Murmuring to himself, he paced up and down his cabin.

His thoughts were distracted as Damini Rathore, his wife and a scientist, elegantly dressed in a beautiful cotton-printed sari and tying her black hair in a bun, entered. She asked, 'Did Ali get anything about Vikrant lately?'

'No, no-th-ing. Everything is...' Jaywardhan looked away. 'Anyway, it's time to go to the hall.'

'What's the matter, Jay?' Damini looked straight at him, his expression troubling her deeply.

'I'm fine. You don't worry,' Jaywardhan's voice grew weaker.

'So it's definitely about him, isn't it?' Damini turned him towards herself, sensing his inner turmoil.

Jaywardhan removed her hand from his arm. 'Vikrant's ambitions are exceeding, Damini. If we don't stop him now, he will ruin everything.'

Damini stood still, a great anxiety enveloping her face.

Jaywardhan took a deep breath and motioned his eyes to a framed painting hanging on a wall behind his chair showing a range of red mountains with the sun floating on a river. 'I'd made a promise to sir and I will keep it at any cost.'

A tiny flash light on a sapphire metallic belt tied on his wrist blinked green. Coming out of his memory, Jaywardhan saw a name on a small screen fixed into it, touched the screen and said through his wireless single earphone, 'Yes, Yash?

Assistant Professor Yash Chauhan's voice came through it, 'Mr Chancellor, the celebration is about to begin. We're expecting both of you.'

'We're coming, Yash. *Vyom farewell*,' replied Jaywardhan, taking a quick look at Damini.

As Jaywardhan rang off, Damini spoke, 'But our.....'

'We'll talk later.' Jaywardhan made for the door. 'You're coming, aren't you?'

After a momentarily pause, 'I am,' answered Damini.

***

'Kanak, you want to do it the whole night? You either punch your sandbag or travel on these wheels.' Kavya, an elegant and swift girl, arranging her uniform in a hanger, looked at Kanak with her large prepossessing eyes. Her long curly hair was in a pony-tail.

'And you Kavya, either interrogate people or fascinate them to get your work done,' said Kanak, speeding across the room wearing her skates, her wavy hair scattering to her shoulders. She was svelte and debonair, almost of eighteen like most of the students of Buddha group.

'That's why Kavya is *Abhyuday's* partner. Both of them collect information but with different strategies.' Paridhi was frizzling up her silky hair, standing in front of a mirror. 'Anyway, tonight I and Prithvi roistered ourselves.'

Kanak rolled her bright, dark eyes looking out of her soft-round face.

'Kanak, slow down. I won't like you without legs,' said Jessica, nonchalant, lying on her bed.

'Don't think so worse for me, Jessica.' Kanak sat on a chair next to Paridhi.

Kavya smiled tenderly. 'Well, if anything happens to you, who will toss Prithvi?'

'He's fallen only two-three times, and you're saying like I always spite him.' A niggled Kanak took her skates off while three of them tittered looking at one another.

Jessica Henriques, Paridhi Bajaj, Kanak Singhaniya and Kavya Rajpal, students of Buddha group, resided together in *Kalpana Chawla Bhavan,* a girls' hostel. Opposite to it was *S.N. Bose Bhavan,* a boys' hostel where lived Aavishkar Arora, Kabeer Khan, Prithviraj Malhotra and Samrat Chopra. Both the hostels located in Parikrama-1 were a big home to all the students of eight groups.

***

'Prithvi, Kavya was telling that we're going to Vyom Museum on Friday. I was thinking if…' Lounging on his bed, Samrat was aiming his sling shot on Kabeer's head. He was a tall and striking boy, had thick dark hair and light brown eyes.

'Don't think to try and break any rules, Samrat,' said Prithvi, giving him a wry smile. He was black haired, tall and pleasant looking with well defined oval face and almond eyes that seemed to sparkle.

'He can't do it, Prithvi. I'm sure he's never read Vyom's rule book,' said Kabeer, working on a computer.

'But you have, haven't you, *meek*?' Samrat released a paper ball from his sling shot that hit Kabeer's head.

Kabeer rubbed his head, grimacing. He was a boy having curly black hair, sharp features and two dimples that enhanced brightness of his face whenever he smiled.

Prithvi told, 'Today, Agatha was crying, telling her Nuclear Physics paper didn't go well.'

'*Really?* Because as much as Abhyuday knew, who was sitting just behind her, she did it *immaculately* with a thorough revision.' A tinge of irritation went through Samrat's face. 'Why these *brilliant students* lie I never understand? They don't leave a single page of their book, but never tell us like we're going to *rob* their knowledge.'

Kabeer jumped over his chair. 'Hurray! Now no one can stop me to read this book.'

'Why are you bouncing?' Samrat came to him, observing the computer.

'I've accessed a website. You know what it's about?' said a febrile Kabeer.

'About *your best friend. Books.*' Samrat returned to his bed. 'Only cram the books, *dab hand,* and forget the main matter,' he muttered, lying down.

Kabeer ignoring him rotated his chair back to the computer and applied himself in his work.

A lanky boy sitting on a table adjacent to Prithvi's bed was sheathing a mini speaker with a screw driver. He had a round, ingenuous face with scintillating eyes.

'Avi, tomorrow you can repair it. Get some sleep,' said Prithvi, unwrapping a blanket.

A sedulous Aavishkar said, adjusting his round spectacles, 'It's almost done.'

'So, we're going to get back our *music,*' said Kabeer, shutting down the computer. 'Thanks to Avi.'

'*A friend helps a friend*, Kabeer. I've done nothing special.' Aavishkar wiped his hands with a piece of cloth.

'Finally. We got today's lesson by *saint Avi.* Good night, everyone,' said Samrat, closing his eyes.

***

Next morning, Jaywardhan called the head of Buddha group, Professor Vijay Rajput in his cabin.

'Vijay, students of Buddha group have completed six months here. Like every year, there will be a trip to Vyom Museum for them. You talk to Dev and plan everything,' said Jaywardhan, leaning back into his chair.

'You don't worry. The students will collect their boarding pass by tomorrow evening,' informed Vijay.

Vyom Institute, a part of *Vyom Organization* was situated on *Niketan,* one of the eight islands collectively known as *Vyomdweep* in Indian Ocean. Vyom Organization primarily worked for the national security, had its headquarters in *India's commercial capital, Mumbai* and its offices in almost all the countries of the world. Every year, new batches of twelfth pass students who desired to be a member of Vyom Institute were called in Vyom Headquarters. They had to pass a rigorous but transparent multilevel selection test, *Vyom Eligibility Entrance Test- VEET,* and show their skills, capabilities and determination. If they passed all the levels, they were welcomed in Vyom Institute.

***

Students of Buddha group, first year, wearing their karate gi, were in a karate training room of *Angad Bhavan* situated in Parikrama-1.

'Prithvi, could I borrow the project you made on *Hybrid Martial Arts?*'

Prithvi sitting on a mat looked up to find Paridhi. She was pretty, looked lithe, had a bright and bubbly personality. She smiled at him completely ignoring Samrat and Abhyuday Sahni, a well-toned, average height boy, sitting next to him.

'With great pleasure.' Prithvi opened his backpack, took out a project file and extended to her.

'Thank you so much.' Paridhi flipped its pages. 'Your hand writing is pretty good, Prithvi. Thanks again.' Returning the smile, she went to her place.

'How do you feel Prithvi when you're always lionized by her?' grinned Samrat.

Abhyuday punched him in the forearm, catching the amusement in his eyes. 'Don't start again.'

'Thanks mate.' Prithvi had a high five with Abhyuday.

Yash entered the hall. '*Good morning*, children.'

Everyone stood and wished him back, 'Good morning, sir.'

'You're ready for the weekly test?' asked Yash, approaching them. 'But before it, I'd like to know something. Children, why should we learn Martial Arts? Anyone can tell? Prithvi, you?'

Prithvi said, 'Sir, so that we can protect others and defend ourselves.'

'How spanking answer he gave,' whispered Paridhi sprightly, standing behind Kanak.

'You should take his autograph then,' whispered Kanak, leaning back to her.

'Good answer,' said Yash, smiling gently. 'Vyom has the same mission. Protecting our people, our country and our world. All of you have to beaver away to acquire the know-how of Martial Arts of every kind perforce. You've to push yourself to the limit of your abilities. Let's start then.'

The students chose their partner and began practising their strikes.

'*Excellent. Well done*, students. Aavishkar hit firmly, keeping your hands up. Jessica, you've to work on your palm-heel strikes, try again.' Yash checked them pointing out their mistakes.

The students trying their best, showing their moves, worked hard for half an hour.

'After Judo and kickboxing, you all gave a good trial in karate too, but we have to toil more. That's all for today, children. *Vyom farewell*.' Yash finished the class and walked out.

'Why did you bring these wheels here?' asked Kavya, staring at Kanak who was taking a skateboard out of her backpack.

'This is our free period,' said Kanak.

'You'd said you'd help me in Organic Chemistry. Those mechanisms are over my head.'

'*Sorry*. I forgot,' said Kanak, leaving her skateboard on the floor.

Both of them made for a corner mat. They had hardly reached it when heard a terrific thud behind them. They turned to find Prithvi lying on the floor and the skateboard rolling ahead.

'Today's battle started,' mumbled Kavya.

'Kanak... you...' A wrathful Prithvi stood up. 'Did you give up attacking me by your long harsh tongue and throwing me down is your new métier?'

'You think I did it intentionally?' asked an irritated Kanak.

'Didn't you?' Prithvi gestured to the skateboard. 'Everyone knows *you* love skating, and you hate *me*, everyone knows this too.'

Samrat said, 'Let's drop the subject, Prithvi. Kanak would never do it purposely.'

'You don't know *this fighter plane*, Samrat.' Prithvi looked away.

'Like you know me, Mr Malhotra,' said Kanak, browned off. 'Why didn't you watch before you stepped?'

'So I....'

'*E-N-O-U-G-H.*' Prithvi was half finished as Kabeer shouted. 'We're saturated, friends. Do you both never get tired of engaging in your *eternal breach*? Whenever or wherever, your story begins.'

Kavya tried to be an arbiter, 'Kanak, we should team up otherwise we'll never do anything for our institute together.'

'And I've read in the stories of *Panchatantra*. *Union is strength*,' cited Aavishkar.

'*The book of morals* has just opened,' murmured Samrat.

Kanak concurred, 'Fine, I make it up with him. Truce?'

'May I help you in fighting, Prithvi?' A steady voice spoke from behind.

Prithvi turned to find his classmate Shaurya Mehra, a dashing, well-built boy with jet black hair and chocolate brown eyes. Accompanying him were his friends Urvashi Lamba, Saif Rizvi,

Lara Menon, Pravesh Vashishtha, Ujjawal Razdan and Alexander D'Souza.

Samrat said, catching a smile on Shaurya's face, 'No need of your help, *spoilsports*. We don't have crummy days yet.'

Saif snubbed him, 'No need of talking to *you*, Samrat. We don't have worse days yet.'

Shaurya said, advancing, 'We both know Prithvi that she's handful so...'

'Why should I believe you that you really want to help *me*?' interjected Prithvi.

'Shaurya likes to help *flimsy people*,' said Lara, crossing her arms.

Kabeer said, coming before her, 'But Prithvi doesn't take help from *fragile people*.'

Lara frowned. 'Your tongue is faster.'

Kabeer said sharply, 'Unfortunately, less than yours.'

'Shaurya...Shaurya...' called Narayani Reddy, a Buddha group student, her hair tied back in pigtails, from a short distance. 'Your father's in *Atithi* guest room.'

'What!' Shaurya's face glowed. 'Friends, we should go.' His eyes turned to Prithvi. 'I don't think there is anyone who really knows how to fight.'

'I don't want to fight against *you*,' said Prithvi briskly. 'I'll really feel bad if you lose.'

Shaurya smiled. 'Don't worry. I will never disappoint you.' He left, followed by his friends.

Paridhi beamed. 'Prithvi did *awesome* with that *arrogant Shaurya Mehra*.'

'But I like the way Shaurya matched his eyes with Prithvi,' Jessica totted up. Having side parting, dark brown hair, she was a rustic, cute and demure girl.

Paridhi gave her a look. Jessica raised both her hands. 'I was just telling...'

Aavishkar emerged. 'You people really do not know what peace means.'

Kanak pointed to Prithvi's hand. 'You got a bruise on the right side of your left wrist. Do something about it.' And she left.

Prithvi glanced over his grazed left wrist.

'Wow! Her eyes are very sharp,' spoke Kabeer.

'She's sharp in everything.' A smile floated on Prithvi's lips.

Paridhi going along with Kanak turned. 'When Prithvi smiles, he looks very suave. Doesn't he?'

'And when your *personable Prithvi* is at odds with me, looks very dangerous,' Kanak tagged on.

***

'Daddy, after two months you've come?' Shaurya entered the guest room.

'Too many projects were there, son.' Pratap Mehra, an officer in R & D department of Vyom Organization, hugged his son the moment he came through the door. 'How's Dhairya?'

'He's good,' said Shaurya, withdrawing from the hug.

'I know you take care of your brother very well,' said Pratap, beaming. 'So, everything is fine between you two or...?' An olive metallic belt tied on his wrist blinked green. He touched a screen on it and said through his wireless single earphone, 'Good afternoon, Mr Chancellor.'

Jaywardhan's voice came, 'Any update, Pratap?'

'I was in conversation with Vyom Museum for DTM. Everyone has thrown themselves into this mission. It'll be under control and on stream duly,' Pratap assured him.

'Meet me Pratap as soon as possible. *Vyom farewell.*'

As Pratap disconnected, Shaurya asked, 'DTM? Dhanraj Time Machine?'

'You knew about it? Then I hope you know it's the latest time machine constructed by Vyom.' Pratap sat on a sofa and turned on his laptop. 'And it's going to be settled in the institute.'

Shaurya said, confounded, 'DTM is coming here!'

Pratap asked, sending an e-mail, 'Have you decided your optional subject for the next year besides Ballistics?

'Not yet,' said Shaurya, switching to next question, 'Where will DTM be set down here?'

'I don't know exactly but may be in *Saptarishi Technology Lab.*' Pratap shut down his laptop. 'Shaurya, I've to go to the Chancellor's Office, but before that, let's meet your younger brother.' Pratap gave a radiant smile, patting him on the back.

Shaurya returned the smile.

***

'*Good afternoon, sir,*' Prithvi, Kanak and Abhyuday wished Jaywardhan walking past Buddha group coordinator's office, Angad Bhavan.

'*Good afternoon, children.*' Jaywardhan gave a gentle look. 'Mr Rajput told me that all the teachers are happy by your performances.'

'And sir, you?' Prithvi tried to catch his mind.

Jaywardhan gazed straight into his eyes. 'What do you think, Prithvi?'

'You've sent for me, Jay?' asked Vice Chancellor Zaheer Siddiqui, reaching him. Clean shaved, medium height, fine-boned.

Jaywardhan turned his attention to them. 'Off you go. You'll be late for your class.' As soon as they left, he spoke, exhaling, 'Vikrant wants to accomplish his search for *the Royal Weapon.*'

'What!' Zaheer looked taken aback. 'But Aaditya sir had hidden it in the past.'

'Yes. He knew that it was insecure in present and future as well, and no other place was safer than Ananyaakashganga for it,' said Jaywardhan.

'And to reach Ananyaakashganga, we've to go back into time in…'

'*In 1180*,' completed Jaywardhan, stepping ahead. Zaheer followed him. Both of them came out of Angad and walked to the head office.

Zaheer said, disgruntled, 'We trusted Vikrant, but didn't know that the person who procured abilities by Vyom wants to destroy it only.'

'I feel ashamed of even calling him our old companion,' said Jaywardhan, absolutely brassed off.

'He doesn't know which time the Royal Weapon is in, does he?' asked Zaheer.

'No. But once he heard our conversation stealthily and then went to sir indignantly.'

Zaheer asked, entering the Vice-Chancellor's Office, 'So he wanted to know why Aaditya sir didn't tell him about all these?'

'Yes. Sir was quick on the uptake about his horrendous motive, that's why he told him nothing, and Vikrant avenged for this.'

A harrowing accident occurred three years back in Amrit city where Aaditya Dhanraj used to stay filled Jaywardhan's mind. Jaywardhan had been honoured with the post of Vyom Institute's Chancellor. Aaditya was with him and Zaheer in his study room.

'I'd told you about the Royal Weapon and Ananyaakashganga, but not about their time.' Aaditya leaned back on his couch. 'Today, both of you are Vyom's responsible members so now I can change your lives.'

Jaywardhan and Zaheer exchanged confused looks.

Aaditya paused and gazed into Jaywardhan's eyes. 'Jay, I've awaited two years since you became the Chancellor so that you could understand your responsibilities and steel yourself for a new one.' He rose and approached a painting hanging on a wall near a book shelf. 'It's the first step to the Royal Weapon. It solves the secret to reach it,' he said, his voice calm and level. 'This location is in 1180 near a jungle. A riddle was concealed into this sun whose solution...'

A cracking sound reverberated through the room. Jaywardhan and Zaheer froze in shock to find a load of gunshots showered on

Aaditya. Jaywardhan in a heartbeat ran towards the window the bullets had been fired through. No one was there now.

'J-A-Y...' cried Zaheer, holding Aaditya.

When Jaywardhan got back, Aaditya was counting his breaths, 'The Royal Weapon... the safety of its...' But death didn't give him opportunity to speak more.

'That day we felt everything was finished,' said Jaywardhan soulfully, returning to the present.

'How much we exerted ourselves to know who put him to death, but couldn't find it,' lamented Zaheer, overwhelmed by the angst.

'And when we knew that Vikrant had hatched the plot to kill him, couldn't do anything. His man who murdered sir was killed before Samarth could catch him. We didn't have any proof against Vikrant, and he got away with it,' said Jaywardhan, broody.

Turning to him, Zaheer spoke, 'Wish we couldn't need any evidence to prove it.' He took a deep breath. 'I wish....'

***

Chapter 2

A Ride with Mandakini, the Submarine

'Why has Chauhan sir started to train us for playing football on the snowfield?' Aavishkar sounded retarded. Buddha group was in the dining hall for dinner.

'He wants us to strengthen our stamina,' said a calm Samrat. 'Such situations may come that we've to run on the snow.'

'We have enough on our plate at this time. We've just finished our first term examinations and weekly tests have begun,' Aavishkar's voice grew thin. 'And tomorrow is the theory test of *Archaic India and Archaeology*. It's more difficult than VEET.'

'Don't be hopeless, Aavishkar. You can do it.' Kanak reached for the chapattis.

Kabeer was taking note of his book more than his food. Jessica glanced sideways to see him. 'Stay away from your books. At least now.'

Kabeer was unaffected, still boning up on his topic- *History of Indian Archaeology.*

Kavya tapped on the table for getting Abhyuday's attention. He was sitting in front of her and adjacent to Samrat but engaged in gazing at Paridhi who'd been chattering to Kanak, a slight smile on his face.

'*Our sleuth* also has a secret?' said Kavya, moving her eyes from Abhyuday to Paridhi.

Abhyuday had to rearrange his expression. 'What?'

'Don't worry, partner. Your secret's safe with me.' Her grin grew wider.

He smiled gently. 'What do you want, Kavya Rajpal?'

Kavya bent forward. 'Did you ask Agatha about her Behavioural Neuroscience notes?'

'She said that she wasn't well so couldn't make them properly.'

Samrat overheard him. 'What's wrong with this girl? All she does is study, but doesn't want to help her classmates. We should've asked for Kavya's notes at the first place.' He gestured to Kavya. 'She's the best.'

'You can take my notebook tomorrow,' said Kavya, her face luminescent.

'Thanks.' Samrat, looking glad, continued his dinner.

Kavya found Abhyuday staring at her. Abhyuday tried not to smile, but it was a losing battle.

Kavya asked, 'What?'

Abhyuday bent forward to whisper in her ear. 'Don't worry, partner. Your secret's safe with me.'

***

Buddha group was in *Drona,* a mini-arena in *Sanrachana,* for its regular class of Ancient Weaponry with Assistant Professor Ambar Shetty and Assistant Professor Vaidehi Mahapatra.

'*Ancient weapons, very useful in this nuclear age,*' Ambar introduced the topic- *Utility of the Ancient Weapons.*

'Sir, we're in the twenty first century. Why are we taught about the old arms?'

'Good question, Aavishkar.' Ambar asked, 'So what will you do if you have nothing but a stone and a staff to defend yourself?'

None of the answers came to Aavishkar's lips.

'We'll be left with no option except to protect ourselves with their help only,' Shaurya's voice came from behind him.

'*Exactly.*' Vaidehi made it understand, 'You must know the art of throwing them like a spear or moving them like a sword or aiming them like an arrow.'

Aavishkar turned to Shaurya and gave a cosmic smile. 'Thank you.'

'Never do it again, Avi.' Shaurya gestured his head towards Prithvi and Samrat staring at him. 'Your cronies wouldn't like it.'

Vaidehi and Ambar started to drill the students, enlarging on the topic. Ambar suggested, 'Before attacking anyone, you must dispose your own safety. Don't be afraid to fail. *Everyone who learns from their mistakes rises in life.*'

'A bow is the symbol of balance and an arrow, of focus. If you deviate, victory will be far many miles for sure.' Vaidehi explained them how to aim the arrows at the target.

When the students shot their arrow to the target butt, Samrat, excelling himself, marked it in the X-ring.

'*Well done, Samrat.* First attempt was good.' Vaidehi looked suitably impressed.

Within a second, another arrow shared the X-ring. All of them turned to Urvashi, her light brown eyes glowing with triumph.

'*Very well, Urvashi,*' said Ambar. He and Vaidehi applauded for her and Samrat. The students joined them.

'Be careful. She may take *your* place,' Kabeer whispered to Samrat.

Samrat gave him a look.

A mirthful Kabeer found his eyes contacted with Urvashi's, but then both of them looked away.

***

After the class of Astrophysics, Applied Mathematics and Anatomy, Buddha group got its break time. Prithvi and Samrat were heading for the ground floor of *Angad Bhavan*.

'What was that in the Bio lab?' asked Samrat, loosening his azure uniform tie. 'Why do you always involve in a tiff with Kanak?'

'You don't know how many times she threw me down? Shall I tell you? *Six times.*' Prithvi showed his fingers.

'Now you're avenging them? It doesn't suit your personality,' said Samrat. 'Those were purely *coincidences.* I don't know why they happen only with *you two.*'

Prithvi asked, gauging his reaction, 'Should I seal my lips even if she clobbers me? Alright, Samrat. As you wish.'

Both of them were passing the library on first floor that Prithvi drew up. He looked into the distance through the glass window in front of them. There was a range of hills beyond the mighty *Dhaara*, a long pure river gliding on the southern side of the institute, caressing Niketan. Her gentle waters appeared to sing rhythmically in all seasons.

Samrat asked, seeing him standing quietly, 'What happened?'

'No... nothing...' said a reticent Prithvi, as though coming out of a dream.

***

Many high mountains around Vyom Institute had crowned with snow, hiding their colour, shape and texture. The white beauty vivified everything *beautifully*. The dancing cold pale streaks of late morning sun peeking behind the murky clouds tried frolicking on the field glistening with a crisp, white and shining covering. The pure, icy and fresh winds flowed from all directions. Deodar, blue pine, silver fir, white oak bowed with a cloak of snow. Their branches bending towards the ground looked forlorn. Many students of Buddha group were jumping and running around enjoying their third snowfall on *Niketan*. The navy blue and white colour of their uniform looked brighter against the pure white blanket spread on the field. They were strutting around, aiming snowballs at everyone, and their targets scattered, screaming, hiding, trying to escape the bombardment of continuous snowballs.

Kabeer, sitting cross-legged on one of the benches rimmed the field, was looking into a book in rapt attention. He asked as he saw Samrat and Prithvi walking up to him, 'Samrat, did you find the topics for our project- *How to survive in an inhospitable place*?

'I collated something from *the inhospitable place* for me.'

'You'd gone to the library?' asked an astounded Kabeer.

'I didn't get one thing yet, Prithvi. Why did Rajput sir make *him* my partner?' said Samrat, irked.

'Why don't you bemoan this to Rajput sir only?' said a displeased Kabeer, 'and what task have I ever done wrong?'

'*Task*? You call that a task?' Samrat sat adjacent to him. 'Studying lots of books then picking up explanations from them. Why do you want to put your heart and soul into this onerous task only, *aficionado*?'

Prithvi bent to find Abhyuday lying face forward beneath the bench. 'What are *you* doing here?'

Abhyuday came out, giggling. 'Because of their squabbles, Prithvi, their articles are never published in our monthly magazine- *Swaroop*. You and Kanak also have some disputes, but you both finish your task on the dot, and I and Kavya support you otherwise what would happen to the cachet of our group?'

Sarmat looked at him with a mixture of anger and shock. 'You'd been spying on us, *master of spies*?'

'I'd been in search of some *task* since morning.' Abhyuday flashed them a brilliant smile.

'Search your *tasks* somewhere else, Abhyuday. At least, don't perform your espionage knacks among...' A snowball hit Kabeer's face before he could finish.

Prithvi turned to see Urvashi covering her mouth in shock and a ducked Alexander a few feet away. Kabeer brushed the snow off his face. Alexander straightened himself. Urvashi removed her hands, rearranging her expression. Alexander whispered something in her ear. She shook her head in *no,* staring at Kabeer and signalled to Alexander to leave.

'Didn't they know how to say sorry?' said Samrat, looking up at Prithvi.

Kabeer didn't react, still gazing at Urvashi going away.

Abhyuday's eyes caught Paridhi talking to Kanak and Kavya on the field's edge. They sparkled blissfully.

'What did you feel by looking at that hill, Kanak?' asked Paridhi.

'I can't tell. I just felt something as never did before,' Kanak sounded clueless. 'A kind of vague memory of some war flooded in my mind.'

Paridhi made neither head nor tail, 'What?!'

'That hill is in *Amrit city*, Kanak,' told Kavya. 'We haven't gone there yet.'

Kanak motioned her eyes to the same hill Prithvi had noticed. This time she couldn't take her eyes off it.

Kavya and Paridhi exchanged floundered looks, not so competent to grasp her thought.

***

Eventually the day came Buddha group was bargaining for. The students were ready to have a trip to Vyom Museum. At 7.00 a.m., they were dropped at an edifice *Vyom Mandal* in the north-west of the institute, a magnificent fifteen-storey V shaped red-yellowish building, a verdant square garden surrounding it. Vyom Mandal was a collection of offices of different departments like finance, defence, home affairs, HR, health, environment, transportation, communication and many more. It was the only waterway to enter and exit Niketan for a port was established to its east.

The students entered the lobby by opening the glass doors. The luxurious furniture contrasted sharply with the ceiling and walls painted white-yellow and floor made of blackish-brown marble. Within a minute, the place was nearly packed with students, officers and security guards, their noises high and low.

A lady's voice came through ceiling speakers, 'Welcome to Vyom Mandal. Buddha group has to reach *the Aquarium Hall* after boarding an escalator to the left. Be ready. *Vyom farewell.*'

The students proceeded to the escalator. The officers allowed them to move into the Aquarium Hall only after scanning their boarding pass.

Samrat asked, taking a seat next to Kabeer in the hall, 'Where is Prithvi?'

'Busy in his *most* favourite work,' said Kabeer, gesturing his head towards right.

Samrat turned, and his confused expression was replaced by a galled one.

'I'd been calling you for a long time, but you didn't bother to turn your neck,' said Prithvi, glaring at Kanak.

'And why should've I done so after what you did in the Bio lab?' grouched Kanak. 'You know what your problem is Prithvi that *you're* problematic.'

Prithvi erupted, 'Really? Then I shouldn't have paid attention *to your dulcet voice* in the Bio lab. When are you going to kick your habit of being a fighter plane every time?'

'Why don't you amend yourself, Mr Malhotra?' Kanak blew her top.

'I was calling *an eccentric girl* to apologize, but just now I realized that I made a mistake. I am going, *Miss truculent.*' A furious Prithvi left.

'I am not enamoured of *talking* to an *eeriest boy,* too. Good bye, *Mr Crackpot,*' said Kanak, seeing red.

A third witness of this brawl Kavya, visibly peeved, said, 'When are both going to leaven *their* tongue?'

Kabeer raised his hands in surrender. 'Please, don't look at me for answers.'

***

The rectangular Aquarium Hall was structured by high white walls from three sides. A giant aquarium formed its fourth side, the water more blue than any sea. Aquatic reptiles, plants, amphibians, fish, invertebrates were streaming, flying and dancing making the aquarium a complete ocean. Colourful fish of different species were coming out of their home to look at the students watching them eagerly while inquisitive turtles didn't want to be disturbed. Freshwater sharks were turning sharply to avoid the sides of the aquarium. The ceiling was double height. Hazel marble floors complementing luxurious cyan carpets greeted everyone.

'You said you wouldn't fall out again with Kanak, didn't you?' Samrat said to Prithvi. 'I should've got *Prithvi Promise.*'

'This is the only thing in the world I cannot promise about.' Prithvi was still apoplectic.

Samrat whispered to Kabeer, 'I think both of them were the sworn enemies in their last life.'

'Then nothing has changed,' Kabeer whispered back.

At the other end of the hall lay a dais with a lectern, a man in a black suit in his late forties stood behind.

'Good morning, children. I, the head of Vyom Mandal, *Devraj Solanki* welcome all of you,' the man said, his voice brimmed with geniality. He gestured to two persons in uniform standing beside him. 'Let me introduce my wise comrades. Lieutenant commander Prayas Patel and Lieutenant commander Samriddhi Gujral. You'll go to Vyom Museum with them only.' He said through his wireless single earphone, 'We're ready.'

Within two seconds, the aquarium divided into two parts with a thump. It opened as a sliding double door revealing a commodious port stretched in thousands of square feet, crowded by large cargo-handling equipments, beautiful ferries and magnificent ships. The enchanted and excited students were led out by Prayas and Samriddhi. They clustered near a ferry. Many eyes flickered with curiosity; many glimmered with interest to see an enormous submarine surfaced the water around one kilometre away from the shore.

'This is *Mandakini*. Vyom's class two passenger submarine, constructed in 1955. She can accommodate hundred passengers at a time,' Kabeer laid on the facts.

'And she has *Veg* torpedoes having monopropellants,' added Shaurya, standing behind him.

Samrat said, 'So, you're interested in war-weapons.'

'And you're interested in shooting, want to be a sniper,' reacted Shaurya.

Samrat's eyes dazzled with wonder. 'You know a lot about me.'

'And you do not know anything about me.'

Samrat riposted, 'After what you did in Science fair, we actually came to know who you are.'

'Saif and Lara had made that project...' Shaurya couldn't finish.

Samriddhi announced, 'Students, do heed. You've to board *Varun-the ferry* to reach *Mandakini-the submarine*. Start moving in.'

'You believed in *your* friends, not in Abhyuday and Kabeer who'd actually made that model. After spending one month with us, you should've known we're not like what Saif and Lara portrayed us,' said Samrat with a sharp tone.

Shaurya bent forward to whisper in his ear, 'We'll see who's right.'

'You'll see we're right,' Samrat whispered back.

***

Prayas, Samriddhi and students reached Mandakini by Varun and boarded it.

'Everyone, take your seat. Miss Vyoms on the left side, Mr Vyoms on the right,' said Samriddhi, moving through the passageway.

After keeping his side bag in an overhead bin, Kabeer sat next to Aavishkar, opposite to Prithvi and Samrat.

Mandakini's interior was like a business class aircraft, comfortable and beautiful. She had started her journey, bustling at her full tilt. About five hundred square metre area around her was illuminated so that the students could experience the world under the ultramarine water. The excitement in their heart was beyond compare.

Aavishkar's eyes twinkled with eagerness watching a shoal. 'Look friends, golden fish...'

'In fact, they're golden in colour, but...but...' Kabeer broke off.

The fastest jet of the cosmos got disrupted.' Samrat laughed for good measure.

Kanak, sitting to the left side of the aisle with Kavya, Paridhi and Jessica, said, 'But they lose their colour as go into the dark.'

'Right. I forgot.' Kabeer hid his embarrassment with a soft smile.

Some students were exuberant seeing the shoal, some engaged in the calculations of aquatics. Some amazed by the clusters of sea shrubs, some busy in describing about the mosses and some, *beyond all these.*

Kabeer taking his eyes off a book looked at Paridhi. 'It's *too late.* Prithvi's fan's not talked to him yet.'

'And Prithvi's mind is elsewhere. He rather wants to fight Kanak right now.' Aavishkar was using a screwdriver on a small metal box.

Samrat grinning slapped Aavishkar on his arm. 'You caught my mind, *machinist.*'

'Prithvi...Prithvi...' called Paridhi, waving her hand. Her face gleamed with delectation.

Samrat chuckled. 'Here she is. *Our friend's biggest fan.*'

'Hello, Pari.' Prithvi returned the smile. 'How're you doing with *your friends*?' His eyes motioned to Kanak.

Kanak rolled her eyes, ignoring him.

'Prithvi, NO,' Samrat muscled in. 'Do you want to pick up a fight with her again?'

'We're good, thanks.' Paridhi's face lit up. 'I forgot to thank you for helping me in the practical period of *Modern Weapons* class.'

Prithvi reacted, 'Pleasure is mine, Pari. I'm not one of your friends who after taking someone's help in Bio lab turns red in fury.'

'Prithvi, stop. Not a single word now,' mediated Kabeer, as always.

You're right, Kabeer. I really don't desire to get my life plane crashed.' Prithvi was unable to hold back his smile.

'Did he *really* help you, Paridhi?' asked Kanak, gazing at Prithvi. 'I don't think so. He doesn't know anything but fighting.'

'*Oh no.* You shouldn't have said this, Kanak,' murmured Samrat.

Prithvi stood up, sounded offended. 'What did you say?'

'I say anything. You have any concern, Mr Malhotra?' Kanak stuck out her tongue at him.

It inflated Prithvi's anger. 'I have always concern with you, *fighter plane.*'

A Buddha group student Shikhar Bhutia, sitting in the row behind Kanak, peeked at them. 'Prithvi is again disturbing you, Kanak?' His eyes narrowed in irritation. 'You want me to handle him?'

'Thanks, Shikhar. She's the only one who can handle Prithvi,' said a cool, calm and collected Aavishkar.

Everyone turned to Aavishkar. Some confused, some embarrassed but mostly amused.

'He meant that she didn't need you here. So why don't you back off?' said Prithvi confidently.

Kanak said, 'Why do *you* always have problem when Shikhar is on my side?'

'What?!' Prithvi felt awkward. His eyes caught Shikhar with half a snigger. 'I don't even care...'

'Could you two not quash your *Mandakini battle*?' shouted Samrat, trying to get around the matter.

Kanak and Prithvi looked daggers at each other, turned their face and eventually sat down.

***

'I've been watching these lights over and over, but don't understand what they are?' Kavya was looking out of the window.

Paridhi lifted her finger to Prithvi's window. 'They're also visible from that side.'

They were passing a series of flashlights seemed to be coming from a distance. When Kanak watched those lights attentively, her smiling lips shrunk. In her eyes developed blurry scenes of a fierce and horrid battle. The ground was wet with blood, throngs of arrows were showering, shrilly noises were everywhere and were a gory battlefield obliterated by embers. Combatants and large bodies of horsemen and elephants-warriors by hundreds were hurling spiked bludgeons at one another resulting in their mutilated bodies, well-trained horsemen surrounding the footmen, striking and slaying them with swords and spears and lances.

'Kanak... Kanak...' Kavya jiggled her.

Jessica asked, 'What happened?'

'Nothing...' A scrambled Kanak somehow handled herself.

'These could be light houses?' Aavishkar noticed the same lights. 'But light houses *inside* an ocean!'

'Not possible?'

Aavishkar turned right to find Prayas smiling. Prayas divulged, running his eyes over the students, 'These are light houses in fact. Tight securities are into this immense Indian Ocean to navigate safely to Sangrah Island or Niketan. All facilities of our protection are inside this ocean only.'

Everyone favoured him with their soft smile, but Kanak couldn't. She tried to push away those traumatic images.

Prayas told, 'Be prepared to disembark. We're about to reach Sangrah.'

After ten minutes, Mandakini decelerated. The students left their seat, took out their bags and headed for the exit. Prayas and Samriddhi led them out, and then they boarded a ferry to reach a port similar to Vyom Mandal. It was a fifteen minute ride by a bus for Vyom Museum from the port. They were dropped in front of a huge metallic gate where they could catch the facade of a building looked like an ancient monument. Four guards carrying their weapons standing on either side of the gate, two in the security booth and a lot of CCTVs welcomed them.

'Good morning sir. Good morning ma'am,' said a security guard from the booth with a slight bow, forwarding a tablet to Prayas.

'Good morning, Abhay.' Prayas placed his left palm on it.

As soon as it was scanned, the gate opened revealing *the palatial, splendid and stupendous Vyom Museum*. All the students looked up, awed and mesmerized.

Eight main multi-storey buildings and a few smaller structures formed *Vyom Museum*. The buildings were named after *Gargi Vachaknavi, Aacharya Chanakya, Samrat Vikramaditya, R.N. Tagore, Sardar Bhagat Singh, Munshi Premchand, S. Chandrashekhar and Swami Vivekanand*. The entrance corridor housed their grand white marble statues.

When they entered the reception area found a lady in her late forties, attired in a beautiful floral-print sari, awaiting them. 'Students, I am Dr Siya Barua, the curator of Vyom Museum.' Her round face bore a calm and welcoming smile. 'Are you ready to experience a new avatar of the museum?'

Siya started with the ground floor of the *Vikramaditya* building, the storage of ancient and modern armaments and munitions. All the halls were packed with swords, lances, guns, rifles, tanks, cannons and missiles. Having visited six halls, Siya led the students to the last one having built-in wall shelves.

Siya told, 'This is the best arsenal in the whole world, used to protect our Vyom. You're taught its complete usage when you'll be in *Vasundhara* group- third year.'

'Ma'am, the carbine number nine in shelf-3 is V-K-97?' a voice asked. All eyes turned to see Shaurya standing beside Kabeer. 'Its pièce de résistance is that it can aim its target inside the water.'

An impressed Siya said, 'Absolutely right. That's it.'

'He's becoming cynosure,' Samrat whispered to Kabeer. 'Be careful. He may take *your* place.'

'Now we'll move to the *Chandrashekhar* building,' said Siya, directing them to the exit.

While leaving Prithvi's eyes caught the ceiling of the foyer painted in a scene of a war. He opened his eyes wide. A series of voices buzzed in his ears. He was distracted by Kanak tapping him on the shoulder. '*Prithvi...*'

Prithvi seemed as if came out of a thought. He looked at her with a face full of confusion, questions and amazement but without saying anything, he left. Kanak couldn't catch the emotions run into his eyes.

***

Chapter 3
Dhanraj Time Machine

Chandrashekhar building housed an astronomical observatory. The students were thrilled to witness celestial events of the solar system and its nearby space. In *Premchand* building, they got an opportunity to explore the world of Indian literature, culture and civilization. Siya showed them models of various kinds of submarines, fighter planes, fighter ships, satellites and their launch vehicles, rockets, probes, etc. stored in *Bhagat* building. The students were manifested several robots, androids and electronic devices in *Vivekanand* building.

Exhibiting a microchip, Siya told, 'This is *Manasvi-55*, a system coupler. It connects the systems of two time machines.'

'Ma'am, how's that?' asked Kabeer.

Siya answered, 'If it's fitted in a time machine or a connector, the information about the desired time machine can be received.'

'If we're in a time machine and it gets lost, this chip won't find us, will it?' asked a flapped Jessica.

'Manasvi -55 can assure the presence of that time machine in a particular time...'

Jessica exhaled noisily, but Siya wasn't finished, '...but it cannot track its location unless it somehow gets access to its security system.'

After the lunch, Siya and the students reached *Tagore* building where they enjoyed a play and a 4-D movie.

'Ma'am, when are we going to see *the time machine*?' asked a high-spirited Aavishkar, coming out of the theater.

'Let's go then.' Siya led them to the first floor of the last building-

Gargi, where a large metallic figure was kept. 'This is *Dhanraj Time Machine* aka *DTM* after the name of Vyom Institute's former Chancellor, Professor Aaditya Dhanraj.

DTM was a seven by five by eight feet brown-silver cuboidal structure, had two medium sized glass windows at its lateral sides and one small window at its front. Siya opened the door at its back side, displaying several buttons, touch screens and electric panels. It could occupy not more than ten people at a time.

Siya added, '*Mrityunjay Time Machine, MTM,* constructed by Mr Dhanraj had been destroyed partially in an accident. MTM's retrieved system is needed to be transferred in a time machine and that's why DTM is being constructed.'

Kabeer said fervently, 'I know a lot about DTM.'

'Really? Be sure you don't forget anything this time.' Samrat punched his shoulder.

Kabeer grimaced, rubbing it.

***

The remaining hours passed swiftly. It was 7.00 p.m., time to return to the institute. After the bus and the ferry, Prayas, Samriddhi and the students boarded Mandakini.

'Today was tiring. I need a break,' said Samrat, slouching next to Kabeer.

'You don't have to prepare for Electronics practical test?' Kabeer turned a page of his book.

Samrat closed his eyes, ignoring his words.

Mandakini was cleaving through the blue water of Indian Ocean, continuously heading towards her destination. Some of the students were relaxing over each other shoulders, one or two trying to get some sleep. Suddenly Mandakini suffered a vigorous stroke. Most of the passengers were thrown against their seat belt, the others crushed against their seat, body bounced, hands-legs flung. Their breath nearly terminated, an angst falling upon them. The entire submarine had shaken.

'What was it?' Prayas entered the control room, almost rushing.

Samriddhi told, looking at a collection of screens, 'A torpedo had passed near the propeller shaft. It didn't harm Mandakini physically but gave her a powerful shudder.'

Prayas mandated one of the officers, 'Annihilate it.'

The officer switched a torpedo from Mandakini, which destroyed its opponent instantly. 'Target's incinerated, sir,' she told, her face flushing with victory.

After a quick investigation, Samriddhi informed, 'It was HH4 heavy weight torpedo travelling with 250 knots, similar to Vyom's torpedo, *Astra*.'

'What?!' said Prayas luridly. 'No any torpedo is match for Astra.' His eyes widened. 'It was ours?'

'I think it's over, Kabeer. Now you can let go of my hand,' said Samrat with childlike glee.

'Yes...yes, why not?' faltered Kabeer, leaving Samrat's squeezed hand. 'Because of *me* you're safe.'

Everyone was *not* certain of feeling safe, their head was still spinning.

'Students, no need to perturb. It was an accident. We're out of danger now,' Samriddhi's voice spoke through the wall speakers without a hint of worry and confusion.

***

'There is someone wants to disturb us, sir,' said Prayas with his large, confident eyes. He was standing in Jaywardhan's cabin, accompanied by Samriddhi.

Jaywardhan asked, 'What do you mean?'

Samriddhi told, her voice confident, 'We don't think the person who switched the torpedo wanted to kill us. If it was Astra, it wouldn't have missed its target.'

'Why did someone do it? We know very well that no outsiders can enter Niketan and attack us,' said Zaheer.

'What if it'd been done?' Prayas found it a possibility.

Jaywardhan said, his eyes narrowed, 'Or what if one of us has become *the outsider*.'

***

Next day, Buddha Group was heading back towards the hostels after finishing its Swimming and Diving lessons.

Samrat questioned, 'Do you know anything about some royal weapon, *studious boy*?'

'Royal what? asked Kabeer inquisitively.

'Royal weapon,' repeated Samrat. 'Four-five days ago, I'd overheard Mr Chancellor and Zaheer sir. They looked very disturbed and worried. This weapon's been hidden in 1180, and a man *Vikrant* is after it.'

Aavishkar wondered. 'In the past! Is it possible?'

Shaurya's friend Ujjawal's interest suddenly captivated, who was walking behind them.

'There was one more thing…what was it? Yes… *Ananyaakashganga*, I guess its haven,' added Samrat.

'*Ananyaakashganga*?!' Prithvi's face abruptly changed colour. This word enveloped his mind. '*Why does it sound familiar to me?*' An inner voice whispered to him.

***

'Mr Chancellor, a central fact has turned up about the torpedo tried to strike Mandakini. Our doubt was not erroneous,' informed Prayas. 'It was triggered from one of our submarines. Firstly, we didn't believe but when we followed up, we had a finding that an Astra torpedo was missing from *Jaltarangini*.'

A meeting was going on in Jaywardhan's cabin.

'That torpedo was Astra?! How could it possible?' asked an incredulous Zaheer. 'If anyone wanted to attack us, why were our submarine and torpedo used?'

'Because someone wants us to doubt our companions or whoever has done this is around us,' said Jaywardhan, leaning back on his chair, smelled a rat.

Damini said, 'Prayas, find out the whereabouts and activities of the officers, professors and commandos especially the members of the institute and museum on the day Buddha group went to Sangrah.'

'This incident must not affect our incoming plans. We have to think faster and sooner than the assailant,' Jaywardhan's voice sounded serious and acute, his face creased with concern.

**

Buddha group was enjoying the class of *Innovative Arts and Handicraft*. A group of students was busy in covering piles of books with brown paper, the other group was stitching small pieces of flowers, leaves and buds on a fuchsia pink bed sheet. Each month, Vyom Institute donated clothes, stationery, food and many other useful things to seven under-privileged schools run in Amrit city. This time, Jaywardhan asked Vijay to take Buddha group with him.

'Have you all got this news?' Kanak walked in, swinging with gladness. 'Kavya told me that we'd be going to *Jyoti Vidyalaya* on Saturday and...,' she said with a flourish, 'after that we'd be allowed to visit the great *Amrit city*.'

'*Hurray!*' Paridhi leapt to her feet, leaving the work of packaging food items.

Prithvi, Kabeer and Abhyuday entered the classroom. 'Good that you all have come. I'm telling about something *important*,' said an ebullient Kanak. 'Abhyuday, did you tell them?'

'She's acting like the head of *Vyom Information Bureau*,' Prithvi whispered to Kabeer.

'Prithvi, you wear your red blazer when we go to Amrit. You look very hand... I meant good in that,' said Paridhi, her face aglow with euphoria.

Prithvi asked, 'Amrit city? Are we going?'

Abhyuday revealed, 'Kanak was telling about it only.'

'I don't wish to become the head of VIB, Mr Malhotra,' Kanak said to Prithvi, her eyes narrowed in anger, 'but I want to shoot you. Let me know when you're free.' She turned around and took herself off.

Kabeer said, mildly startled, 'Her ears too are very sharp.'

'You missed her tongue,' added Prithvi.

***

'Vikrant wants the Royal Weapon badly only to trounce *us*,' Damini's loud and full-toned voice almost echoed through Jaywardhan's cabin. 'He asked you to gang up, wanted to entice you, but you did the best by sweeping him out of here. We're his biggest foe, and his hatred for us fuelled his ambition.' She took a deep breath to compose herself. 'It's good that he doesn't know the real meaning of the Royal Weapon otherwise...'

'When he'd come here to meet me six months ago, he wanted to know about the location of the Royal Weapon and Ananyaakashganga,' told Jaywardhan, sat on a sofa.

Damini said, a surprise frown on her face, 'But you don't know about it. That's why we're transferring MTM's system into DTM for finding their time out. You just know the way to reach Ananyaakashganga.'

'He wanted to satisfy himself...'

'I knew this felon would try to do something wrong and he did. He's the only person behind the attack on Mandakini,' Zaheer scowling flounced in. 'He always wanted to sully his hand in our blood, started with Aaditya sir so that he couldn't help us.

'Ali is there, Zaheer. He'll definitely get something about his movements,' said Jaywardhan, rising.

A knock on the door attracted their attention.

Jaywardhan said, rearranging his expression, 'Come in, Arunima.'

Arunima Raghuvanshi, an attractive young woman in her late twenties, working in the Technical Department of the institute, entered carrying a laptop. 'Mr Chancellor, we've transferred Mrityunjay Time Machine's system into DTM,' she informed in a joyous voice.

Jaywardhan was happy beyond limits. *'Well done, Arunima.* Is DTM functioning properly?"

'It'll take at least two days to see whether MTM's system will work in this latter-day time machine or not,' said Arunima, placing the laptop on Jaywardhan's table.

Zaheer enquired, 'How much data can we retrieve from MTM?'

'90%,' replied Arunima, moving her fingers on the keys. 'As you know sir, MTM had been mangled, but when Mr Dhanraj constructed it, he made all the efforts to secure its central system. That's why *it* remained intact, and we could recover the data.'

'MTM was destroyed to an ambit. In that case, it was difficult to overhaul it and collect the data from its parts. 90% is pretty good.' Damini looked impressed.

A tiny light on Zaheer's sapphire wrist belt flashed green. He touched its screen showing a name and said through his earphone. 'Yes, Siya?'

'Sir, could you and Mr Chancellor come to museum?' imparted Siya, her voice sounded urgent.

'Is there something important?'

'It's more than important, sir.'

'Okay. *Vyom farewell.*' Zaheer hung up and said to Jaywardhan, 'Siya wants to talk about something, but you stay here. I'm going.' He took himself off.

'Arunima, now you keep tabs on the Supernova robots and ask Kushal to stick to his work,' said Jaywardhan.

'I'll let you know all the reports, *Vyom farewell.*' Arunima turned to leave.

Jaywardhan said, a smile of contentment on his face, 'Arunima, you did a great job. Keep it up.'

'Thank you, Mr Chancellor,' said Arunima, returning the smile.

***

'*Marvellous*, Kushal. I asked Sagar to send word to Mumbai. Our

S.T.F. will be here soon. Make all the preparations for the mission, son. *Vyom farewell.*' As soon as Jaywardhan rang off, the green light of his wrist belt flashed. He connected himself, 'Yes Zaheer, why did Siya call you?'

Zaheer sounded disturbed, 'Is there any end of our problems, Jay?'

Jaywardhan rose from his chair. 'What happened?'

'Manasvi-55 has disappeared from the museum.'

'*What!*' said Jaywardhan, stupefied. 'Why did the alarms not turn on?'

'I also am not getting this. Siya investigated and came to the conclusion that it happened on the same day Buddha group came to visit here.'

A shocked Jaywardhan asked, 'She has doubt on the students?'

'No, Jay. You know that no any students can get Manasvi out of the safety glass wall. There is a cipher to open the casing, and only few people know about it.'

'Including that person who's stolen Manasvi.'

'Don't worry, Jay. We'll get it by fair or foul means,' said Zaheer, determined to get to the bottom of the matter.

***

Aavishkar was fixing a small tyre in a mahogany metallic structure of size of a shoe box with a screw driver. He was sitting next to an asleep Kabeer on the same double bed. His tool boxes were open lying in his reach. Pliers, wrenches, drills, levels, rasps were scattered on his quilt, many nuts and bolts resting on his pillow.

Kabeer's eyes opened. He looked at the wall clock, blinking his eyes to get rid of the blur. 'It's two a.m., pal. You're still working?' He sat up. 'You always spend your pocket money on these tools?'

Aavishkar showed him the metallic box. 'It's not just a tool. I'm constructing *a detective car,* and it has a name, *Tez.*'

'*A detective car?*' asked Kabeer, slightly surprised. 'Abhyuday's birthday's coming?'

'It's for us. I'll fit a camcorder into it,' Aavishkar sounded excited.

'And a CCTV jammer, I'd suggest.' Kabeer took the box in his hands. It looked like a two-seater miniature car with headlights, tail lights, windscreen and side windows. 'Will it run?'

An unsettled Aavishkar said, 'I'm working on it. I don't want to make Tez a workaday mechanical car.'

'We can connect the car, I meant Tez, to our computer. It'll operate it.'

'Then we'll need specific software, don't we?

'Don't worry. It's the least I can do for you, Avi,' said Kabeer, keeping Tez next to the computer. 'Now get some rest. We've to get up early in the morning.'

'I can sleep peacefully now,' said Aavishkar, content.

***

'What about DTM?' Jaywardhan made an appearance in *Revati Technology Lab* situated in the basement of *Gagan Bhavan* in Parikrama-2.

'After transferring MTM's system into DTM, only half of its system has been in function for last four days. We're trying our best. It will surely activate,' informed Kushal Rathore, showing him DTM on a big LED screen. He was tall and muscular, had a fit body and a delightful personality like his father.

'Get your work done as fast as possible, son. We don't have much time. On 20 December, DTM will be going on its first journey.' Jaywardhan seemed to be assessing something in his mind. 'And be very careful about its central system's protection. *DTM must not be hacked.*'

***

Shaurya, Lara and Saif were leaving the dining hall as Saif saw Kanak entering. 'Coming alone tonight?'

Kanak replied, wearing a smile, 'I'm enough for you, I believe.'

Saif turned on her, 'This is your problem, Kanak. Your tongue... faster than light.'

'You got scared?'

'You think...'

'Saif...' Shaurya interrupted him, refusing to be drawn into a debate. 'She likes to give tart replies. Don't waste your time.'

'Why are you doing so, Shaurya? You know she's more dexterous than your friend,' said Prithvi arriving on the scene with Samrat. 'Why don't you ask *him* to leave his habit of masterful...'

'Why do you care?' said Shaurya before Prithvi could finish. 'You're our well wisher?

Samrat's face seemed to convey anger. 'Mind your attitude.'

'If Kanak wants to prove something, why doesn't she do it before us, but not by her speedy tongue?' Saif continued in his antagonistic tone.

'We should leave now, Kanak.' Prithvi found no need of further conversation.

Lara snarled, 'Why doesn't she fight alone?'

'There is...' Samrat couldn't finish for Kanak had made up her mind, 'Fine. I'll prove myself... against Shaurya.'

'What?!' said a startled Samrat.

Shaurya's eyes widened.

Kanak said, 'Tomorrow we're going to Amrit city, and *Eklavya Sports Club* is there only.' She met her eyes with Shaurya. 'We both love sports, don't we? I hope you'll be ready.'

'You really want to do this? I don't...'

Saif, overweening, interrupted Shaurya, 'Cocksure. He's born ready.'

'And what are we going to do there?' asked Lara.

Kanak replied, '*Sports car racing.*'

Strong lines of worry began creasing each face belonged to Shaurya's team. Prithvi and Samrat looked at her with unmentionable expression.

'Then see you tomorrow.' Kanak cleared out.

A tensed Samrat said, 'This girl has gone insane.'

'You're mistaken. She's already been insane,' corrected Prithvi.

***

'I don't know why Kanak has done this?' said Paridhi, applying a yellow cream on her face. 'And where is she anyway?'

Kanak said as entered the room, 'I was in the cyber café, playing some car racing video games.'

Jessica said, 'I hope without thinking you...'

'Kanak does nothing without thinking, Jessy,' spoke Kavya.

'Saif and Lara have been nuisances for us. We have to do something,' said Kanak, reaching Kavya.

Paridhi asked, 'But why Shaurya?'

'You've to get the better of the king if you want to win his army. As Abhyuday found about him, he doesn't like all these racing sports.' Kanak had her stratagem. 'Don't worry. I know very well what I'm doing.'

***

Chapter 4
The Mask Disappeared!

Next day, after having a good time with the children of Jyoti Vidyalaya, Buddha group was visiting Amrit city by a bus with two officers. They were passing high buildings and beautiful monuments and green gardens. Amrit was a beautiful city built and developed upon a massive land of almost fifty thousand hectares in size, one of six biggest cities on Niketan, a good hour away from the institute. It was located on the western banks of *Dhaara*, meandering her way into the Indian Ocean, at the foot of *Giriraj* Mountains, stretching as far back as the eye could see.

'We have six hours to do the city,' said an exuberant Kavya.

Abhyuday informed, 'Rajput sir told that he'd join us by 4 o'clock at *Vihangam* and then take us to *Dhyanchand stadium*, our last visit for today.'

'Thanks Abhyuday for asking Rajput sir to allow us to go to *Eklavya Sports Club*,' beamed Paridhi turned to him.

'It's my pleasure, Pari,' blushed Abhyuday, continued gazing at her even when she started talking to Kanak next to her. He turned his neck to the window to find Kavya, sitting on its side, staring at him. Her face lit up in a brilliant smile.

'What?' His expression seemed to convey embarrassment.

Her eyes caught his yellow jacket. 'So you knew this is her favourite colour,' she said, smiling a little broader.

Abhyuday winked at her, lowering his voice to a whisper, 'I do my homework.'

Aavishkar asked Kabeer sitting behind Kavya and Abhyuday, 'Have you thought anything about that special software?'

'Prarthana di will give it by tomorrow.'

'Prithvi's sister, Prarthana di?' Aavishkar's countenance changed. 'How will *she* get it?'

'Do you know her friend Aaryaman? His father develops such special programmes. *He'll* give it to Prarthana di,' said Kabeer, looking outside excitingly and lively.

Aavishkar tapped his shoulder. 'Didn't she ask why *you* need it?'

'I told her that you wanted to do research on it. Now, I guess you're going to quit asking.' Kabeer seemed galled.

'As you wish, mate.' A grin spread across a sated Aavishkar's face.

'Shaurya, you shouldn't have agreed for this nonsense,' said Urvashi, perplexed. 'Can you do car racing?' she and Shaurya were sitting at the back.

'Don't worry about me. I'll handle,' answered Shaurya, looking away.

Soon the bus arrived at its second stop, *Eklavya Sports Club* dedicated to more than twenty sports such as hockey, cricket, racing, boxing, track and field athletics and others. The officers asked the students to meet near the entry gate in one hour. After getting their permission, Buddha group reached the grandstand in the east of the main office.

'You two are ready?' Abhyuday asked Shaurya and Kanak.

'He's ready,' answered Saif presumptuously.

'We're using the GT cars not the open wheel,' continued Abhyuday. 'After ten minutes, we'll start the race.'

'Fine.' Shaurya left for the track.

Samrat said to Kanak, 'Prithvi wants to tell something.'

Kanak looked at Prithvi with questioning eyes.

Prithvi said, 'I just wa... I want to tell you that your car may have good downforce, and you think it can go faster around the corners, but even then be a little patient to find the balance and the limit with it. Adjust its traction control system. Its loss will make your car more difficult to handle when turning into and out of the corners.'

'Thank you,' beamed Kanak though slightly amazed.

***

Shaurya and Kanak got in their cockpit and put on their helmet. Their friends stood excited but on pins and needles in the grandstand. 5, 4, 3, 2, 1, and the race began. Kanak kept her speed slow while Shaurya revved his car's engine.

'Why's she picking up speed so slow?' asked a nervy Aavishkar.

Prithvi was in his element. 'No race can be won on the first lap. She's just saving the tyres.'

Kanak wasn't a past master of racing, but was trying her best. She accelerated her car sharply and switched it from one lane to another not giving Shaurya a chance to overtake. He oversteered his car, but got hit to the boundary of the track. An annoyed Shaurya veered left, managing to maintain control over his car. He pressed down on the accelerator and tried to overtake swerving widely away from her. He took five seconds to gain a few feet on her, and now he was leading. His friends broke into applause.

Last seven laps were left. Kanak engaged the throttle stepping hardly on it that allowed her to transfer more power through the wheels and push the car to its limits. Soon she caught up Shaurya's car. Car racing wasn't Shaurya's forte so he was struggling to keep control. As she passed him, his car skidded right, about to hit the boundary, but somehow he escaped. With his retarded speed, it took around ten seconds for him to gain the required pace to pass it.

Kabeer hold his breath. 'This is the last but the shallowest curve of the track.'

As soon as Kanak reached at the distance of five metres from the curve, she turned the traction control on only for five seconds and then immediately turned it off. Her car made a sharp turn around the corner resulted in an increase in downforce that stuck the tyres to the track more readily. Now it took her a moment to win the race. Her friends let out whoops of victory.

Kanak and Shaurya came out of their car. Her friends approached, jumping, leaping, running, rejoicing while his straight to him, their face fell.

Kanak said to Saif, 'Your friend should've practised more especially in the sports he doesn't like.'

Shaurya's eyes narrowed. 'You knew that.'

'She'd come well-prepared,' said Samrat ecstatically.

Saif yelled in fury, 'That's not fair.'

'You shouldn't talk about what unfair is. You did all this, Saif. *You're* the reason,' said Kanak.

'What do…?'

'Stop it,' Shaurya interrupted Saif's words and turned to Kanak, his eyes showing the hurt he felt. 'I'd expected something more and different from you.'

Kanak's smiling lips shrunk.

'We should head back.' Shaurya cast an angry glance at Kanak and buzzed off, accompanied by his team.

Aavishkar said, 'Today, Shaurya would've definitely realised that fighting Kanak is not easy.'

'Ask me,' mumbled Prithvi.

***

Amrit city was well worth a visit, a utopian amalgamation of past and future, culture and modernization, spirituality and materialism. The third stop was *Umang,* an amusement park where many amazing rides thrilled the students. Having been entertained by a beautiful play written by *Mohan Rakesh* in *Rangmanch,* a theatre, they attended a musical concert where their feet danced, and lips sang. Everyone had a whale of a time with their friends.

Time elapsed, and it was three o'clock. Buddha group took a tour of *Vihangam,* the highest natural point of Amrit city located at the southern edge of Amrit Hills. From the point, the students could see a panoramic view of nearby crowded markets, gorgeous gardens and magnificent monuments to its west and a vast plains landscape with snow covered Giriraj Mountains in the eastern distance. By 3:45 p.m., the students started gathering up near their bus.

Kanak asked Samrat, 'Where is Prithvi?'

Samrat ran his eyes across the crowd. 'He must've come back yet.'

Kabeer told, gesturing to Vihangam point, 'He'd forgotten his satchel in the restaurant. He asked us to move and went up there. It's been more than twenty minutes.'

Jessica said, 'I think he got lost.'

'It's out of the question, Jessy,' said Kabeer, riled.

'I should go up there,' said Samrat and turned around to leave.

'I'm coming with you.' Kanak followed him.

On their way, they found Abhyuday returning. He asked, 'Where are you two going now?'

Samrat replied, 'We're looking for Prithvi.'

'I saw him going to that side fifteen minutes ago,' told Abhyuday, pointing to the right.

Both of them turned to see a range of hills at a distance. An unmetalled road curved smoothly up one of the gently sloping hills.

'Why did he go there?' asked Sarmat, muzzy.

'You saw him and let him go?' said Kanak, her voice conveyed anger. 'Why didn't you stop him?'

Abhyuday opened his mouth to reply but Kanak continued, 'Then let's do some *search*, Abhyuday Sahni.'

Following the same unmetalled road, Prithvi descended the hill reaching its base on the other side. The clouds were floating across the reddish-orange sky, parting to reveal the evening sun. He, confused and lost, moved forward watching far and near. He suddenly happened on something. He looked into the distance towards a grand palace appearing to be built of white marble. He got staggered. A golden symbol was brightening on its largest dome. As he stepped ahead to stare hard at it, his eyes widened. It was a golden sun. He lifted his right leg to move that something hit it. He looked at his foot to find a brown metallic mask shaped exactly like a human face. He bent down to pick it up.

Kanak, Samrat and Abhyuday were climbing the same hill.

'How do you know he would've come here?' asked Samrat, racing behind Kanak.

'I just pointed you to this side,' said Abhyuday.

Kanak said, speeding up, 'I just felt that he should be behind this hill.'

Samrat and Abhyuday exchanged confused glances.

Prithvi had brought the mask close to his eyes. His pulse quickened. Once he looked at the palace and then wore it. A bright red light dazzled, flashing before his eyes a disastrous and bloodcurdling war. He saw large bodies of cavalry and infantry, horsemen ready to crush foot soldiers, war-elephants smashing horsemen around him. He could categorically hear their commotion. Babel had enveloped the ground. Bloodshed and massacre was everywhere. It was just havoc.

His horrified eyes fell upon a warrior looking no more than eighteen fighting another one of around twenty, muscular and well-toned. Both of them, seemed well-trained at sword handling, were wearing the same brown metallic mask on their face.

Prithvi could hear the younger warrior say, 'I never thought of raising arms against you even in my dreams, brother.'

As soon as the words came out of his mouth, the older one made him unarmed. He was about to lash him out, but an arrow instantly wounded his hand. It belonged to a girl, her face and body protected by armours, her left hand clutching a bow.

'Make a blitz over an armless person isn't the rule of the battle,' she said, preparing her defense.

Finding himself unarmed, the older boy gnashed. 'Now it's time of *the real war*.' He turned around, removing his own mask. His head bore a jewelled golden circlet with the sun in the centre.

A sudden jolt of fear went through the girl. 'How many rules will you violate? First this war instead of the duel and now *this*.'

Her words were left unheeded. The older boy moved forward. 'Today, the earth will be drenched in your blood, *little brother*.' As soon as the words left his mouth, a purple ray emerged from the sun of the circlet. Before it could harm the younger warrior, the girl leapt in front of him. The purple ray slammed her chest, and she fell motionless.

The younger boy's cry resounded loudly, 'R-A-K-S-H-A....'

Again a bright red light flashed. The mask, putting off Prithvi's face, fell down. Everything recovered its original state. No war. No blood. No warriors.

Kanak's voice came, calling him, '*Prithvi...*'

Prithvi's attention was elsewhere.

Samrat complained, 'What are you doing here?'

'Do you know how worried we were?' said Abhyuday.

Prithvi seemed lost in his thoughts for a few moments.

Kanak asked, holding his arm, 'Why did you come here?'

Prithvi reacted, slowly gathering his wits, 'I've been imbuing for a few days that I should come over here.'

Kanak stared hard into Prithvi's eyes trying to assess his thoughts.

'Okay. We'll thrash it out later. Now we have to get back,' said Abhyuday.

'I want to show you something...' Prithvi turned to pick the mask up, but it wasn't there. 'Where's it?' he astoundingly whispered to himself.

Samrat asked, 'What's it?'

'That mask,' said Prithvi, still shocked. 'That one I'd worn..., and there was a palace...' he attracted their attention towards a direction. They turned their eyes.

'Nothing is there,' said Abhyuday. Prithvi stood dumb-struck.

Just then, a gem in Kanak's metallic ring flashed yellow. 'Rajput sir is waiting for us,' she told.

Three of them turned to leave, but Prithvi was still watching towards he'd seen the palace.

Kanak spoke, 'Let's go. We can talk about this later.'

Prithvi somehow shook his head.

They rushed towards their bus waiting for them near Vihangam. When Vijay saw them approach, his face rapidly regained its colour. 'Where had you all been?' he asked in his composed voice.

Kanak replied, 'Sir, we were getting about and couldn't catch the time.'

Four of them apologized.

Vijay said, 'You all are good students. I hope you'll understand your responsibility.'

They together said in their most earnest voice, '*Yes sir.*'

Prithvi told his experience when he'd worn the mask to Samrat, Kanak, Kabeer, Aavishkar and Abhyuday while returning to the institute. No one believed it first except Kanak, but when they realized the gravity of the situation, they were momentarily taken aback. Kanak also shared her feelings when she was with Kavya and Paridhi and got attracted towards the same hill. Prithvi didn't ready to leave the thought about it and decided to go to Amrit city once again on next Saturday.

What was that war where one brother wanted to kill the other? Who was that girl who sacrificed herself to save someone? What was that mask, and how did it disappear? Why did everything appear so realistic to Prithvi? So many questions hung in the air waiting to be answered.

***

Chapter 5
Dhairya's Birthday?

It was late in the evening. Everyone had left the common room for students in Parikrama-1 and headed for the dining hall except Shaurya and his friends.

'Kanak shouldn't have done this,' said Saif churlishly, 'and I know Samrat was the one who gave this *sports car racing brainwave* to her.'

Urvashi cut in, 'So now what? It's better that we go on our separate way. No confrontation, no clash.'

'You meant we should hide ourselves scared of them?' said Lara, fused with wrath and embarrassment.

'That's not what she meant,' countered Pravesh. 'This is our mistake that we let Shaurya compete.'

Alexander said, 'Pravesh is right. We're his friends. We should've stopped all this in the first place.'

'Why don't we let *Shaurya* decide what he wants,' said Ujjawal.

'It's too late, Alex,' Shauyra broke his silence after absorbing every logic and argument. His stoic features gave no suggestions of what was on his mind.

***

'Thank you for coming, my friends,' Jaywardhan accompanied by Zaheer welcomed Devraj and Sagar at the entrance of B-Wing, *Rohini Bhavan*.

Sagar said, shaking his hand with him, 'The S.T.F. will reach here with full preparations by tomorrow evening.'

'What've you thought, Jaywardhan?' asked Devraj.

Four of them moved forward.

'As only few people know about our mission of the Royal Weapon,' said Jaywardhan, 'Sagar, I want you, Samarth and four more commandos to go to the past through DTM. Ali told that Vikrant has prepared a team of experts to send to the past.'

'Why four commandos? If you want to do it, send the full force,' Sagar put his view forward boarding an elevator with three of them.

'You know we don't have such machine that could tell us about a particular time. We can only reach there through time machines. And we don't know what Vikrant will do there. To know his mission, we've to follow this plan, and at the right time after trouncing him, we will find out the Royal Weapon,' told Zaheer.

The elevator opened on the fifth floor. As they entered *Kshitij*, a conference hall, found Damini, Kushal and Arunima awaiting them.

Jaywardhan gestured them to sit and continued, 'Vikrant, in his whole life, has made fewer friends. He's not given value to anything before his ambition. We didn't help him when he needed us, and that's why he execrates us.'

'Although he's been working for a research center in Mumbai, he has his own teams and own labs for his secret mission,' said Devraj.

'As long as our agent is in his center, it's impossible to hide anything from us. We'll soon get word from him regarding Vikrant's plan,' Damini talked about Ali.

'But we have a problem now,' said Jaywardhan. 'Lately, Vikrant's come to know about 1180.'

Everyone was too stunned to react.

Jaywardhan continued, 'And it might be possible that someone has *told* him.'

Damini said, 'Someone is betraying us?'

'We can't say anything now.' Jaywardhan turned to Kushal. 'I want you to shift DTM from Revati to Saptarishi. Get ready everything by tomorrow.'

The preparations for the past mission had been started so was begun the search for the betrayer of Vyom, helping its enemy.

**

'You'll have to do this for me,' Shaurya was in conversation with his younger brother and a Buddha group student, Dhairya. An average height, thin boy with clean cut features.

Dhairya's scrupled, his peaceful face frowned, '*No.* I'm not giving anyone a drugged cake. It's not fair.'

'You're not to decide it,' Shaurya's tone sounded commanding. 'Ujjawal was telling that Pari has one of Prithvi's projects. First and foremost, get it by hook or crook. Above all, you're going to celebrate your birthday tomorrow.'

'*My birthday?* Tomorrow?'

'I know it's difficult for you to choose between your big brother and your friends, but it's up to you,' said Shaurya, trying to convince him.

Dhairya stood silent. He had to back up his brother's demand.

**

Next day, Buddha group students gathered in the dining hall for the lunch.

Samrat asked, taking his chair, 'Avi, when are you going to give us your surprise?'

'Very soon, mate,' answered Kabeer dished out some rice onto his plate.

'Today's my birthday.' Dhairya stood next to Prithvi's chair offering a plate full of pieces of chocolate and pineapple gateau.

'*Happy birthday*, brother.' Prithvi rose from his chair and gave him a tight hug.

'Thank…thank you,' faltered Dhairya, withdrawing from the hug.

Prithvi was about to take a piece of cake.

'Take this one. Special pineapple cake for *you*.' Dhairya gave him a specific piece of cake and then distributed the remaining pieces among rest of his friends.

Aavishkar complained, 'What's this, Dhairya? You gave your special pineapple cake only to Prithvi and Kabeer?'

'No, Avi... no... That's only...' Dhairya struggled to find words to respond. 'I...I need to go to Shaurya.' He took leave of him.

'I don't like pineapple flavor, but Dhairya offered me so lovingly I couldn't refuse.' Kabeer scanned Kanak's cake. 'I like the chocolate one.'

'Nice try,' said Kanak, smiling, and exchanged her piece of cake with Kabeer.

'Listen, friends. I forgot something... *usually*...' Mayur Ambedkar, belonged to Buddha group, came on the scene, accompanied by his best friend, Ibrahim Mirza. 'Someone told me that in our Physics lab, Rajput sir had called Prithvi and K... Ka... who was the second one?' He tried to recollect.

'Kabeer?' asked Ibrahim.

'Not me. Kanak, definitely,' affirmed Kabeer.

'Kanak? Yes... maybe she was...' said an unsure Mayur.

Kanak showed mild surprise. 'Both of us? *At this time?*'

She and Prithvi left the dining hall in *Angad Bhavan* to move to *Aryabhatta Bhavan* behind it.

Licking his index finger, Prithvi spoke, 'My cake was delicious.'

'Next time when you want to talk to me, kindly choose a good line for the start.' Kanak was stomping up the staircases.

'I'm not telling you.' Prithvi was behind him.

Kanak chuckled, 'Are you talking to the walls?'

'Why are *you* so concerned? I was... I was... talking to her... this girl.'

Kanak turned around sharply, looked so eager. 'Which girl?'

Prithvi gave her a smug look. 'You are so concerned of *me*.'

'Don't waste my time. Let's go.' Kanak strode to the second floor.

'For now, I'm wasting my time with *you*.' Prithvi hopped after her.

After reaching second floor, C-Wing of *Aryabhatta Bhavan*, they entered the Physics lab but didn't find Vijay.

'I don't understand why sir called us now?' said Prithvi, coming out with Kanak.

'And he hasn't shown up yet.' Kanak ran her eyes from one corner of the corridor to another.

Both of them were unknown of seven pairs of eyes peeking from a room adjacent to the lab.

'*Kanak*... is with Prithvi? How could it happen?' hissed Shaurya.

'Mayur blighted our game.' Saif looked disappointed. 'We'd given those drugged cakes for Prithvi and Kabeer so that when we lock both of them in the store room, we can disturb Kanak and Samrat.'

'Doesn't matter. I hate *that speedy tongue, Kabeer*,' said Lara with rancour.

A worried Ujjawal spoke, 'But Kanak didn't eat the drugged cake.'

'What's...?' Kanak's head started spinning. She held her head, trying to keep her eyes open.

'Cake's done its work,' said an exhilarated Lara.

'Why is she passing out? Kabeer's had the cake,' Saif's voice was a mixture of euphoria and surprise.

'Are you alright?' Prithvi supported Kanak but not too long for his vision became hazy. He too was getting fainted.

Ujjawal said, 'Let it be. *Everything* is supporting us.'

'Right. *Sharing* always supports,' spoke Pravesh.

Shaurya said, 'Get back on the track, Pravesh.'

Pravesh touched his ear. The hearing-aid had come out of his ears. Apologising, he fixed it.

Prithvi and Kanak didn't take much time to be unconscious. Shaurya and his friends immediately carried both of them to a store room in front of the lab.

'We'll have great fun.' Saif bolted its door.

'I've done this for you Shaurya, for our friendship,' spoke Alexander in a frail voice.

Urvashi said, her eyes studying Shaurya intently, 'Is it right what we're doing?'

'They've started, Urvashi. We have to only finish it.' Shaurya didn't exhibit even the slightest hint of repentance. 'If someone's good to me, I'll best to them. But if someone's bad to me, I'll worst to them.'

***

Aavishkar was busy in making a snow figure on the institute's snow covered field between Parikrama-2 and Parikrama-3. 'It's been two hours, but Prithvi and Kanak didn't show up,' he said. 'What do you say Samrat they would like my car?' He and Kabeer had showed *Tez* to Samrat.

'Quit making of your bear. They'll automatically come,' said Samrat, playing football.

Aavishkar gave his snowman a final touch. 'He's not a bear. He has a name, *snowy*.'

Kabeer sitting on a bench looked up from his book. 'Why are they getting late, anyway?'

'Before a while, I asked Abhyuday about Rajput sir. He told that he was in the Chancellor's Office, but both of them weren't with him. I thought they would've gone somewhere,' expressed Samrat.

'*They've really gone somewhere*,' a voice spoke.

Three of them turned to see Dhairya, standing at a distance.

Aavishkar asked, 'Do you know where they are?'

'In the past.'

Samrat laughed, 'We really don't...'

'I know... it...it's hard to believe... but...' Dhairya struggled through the sentence.

'What are you talking? *How's it possible?*' asked Kabeer.

Three of them were completely taken by surprise.

'Through a t-ime machi-ne,' a tone of agitation was in Dhairya's voice, disappointment visible on his face.

Kabeer spoke, 'Are you talking about that *time machine...* that is here... *DTM?*'

Dhairya nodded nervously. 'I don't know how they reached it. They told me that they'd go to the past by dint of it. Prithvi mentioned about any royal weapon and Ananyaakashganga. They didn't tell thoroughly, but wanted to scout and protect them from any Vikrant,' he said in one breath.

'*What!*' recoiled Samrat.

'They were in hurry so dropped you all a line.' As Dhairya took a folded paper out of his pocket, Kabeer lunged forward. He took and unfolded it.

'It's Prithvi's handwriting,' said a concerned Kabeer. '*We're sorry, friends. We couldn't tell you anything as we didn't have time. We're going to search the Royal Weapon, but we'll need you. Please come to the past through DTM as soon as possible. We don't hope but believe that you'll come for us and for Vyom, but yes, don't tell anybody about it. Your friends, Prithvi and Kanak,*' he completed his reading of the letter.

Dhairya spoke, 'Don't know whether it's good news or...' he broke off.

A discomfited Samrat asked, 'What?'

Dhairya continued, 'DTM is back, but I don't think they've returned.' He turned to leave, regret smothered his face. 'Let me know if you need my help.' He left with heavy steps.

'Prithvi and Kanak...? How could they... without telling us?' said Samrat as anxiety gnawed at his heart. 'If they wanted to do it, could've told us before.'

'You think they could do it?'

'Dhairya wouldn't lie to us, Avi. He's our friend, and this letter, it's Prithvi's handwriting. A solid proof we have. We cannot ignore it,' said Kabeer.

'We must ask everyone about them.' Samrat went like wind towards the hostels. Kabeer and Aavishkar accompanied him.

***

Chapter 6

The Time Travel

It was early in the evening. Speeding down a stairway leading to the ground floor of S. N. Bose hostel, Samrat spoke, 'Everyone was telling that they didn't see them after lunch. So, they might've gone to the past when Rajput sir called them.'

'He or Mr Chancellor might've sent them,' conjectured Kabeer.

'I don't think so,' replied Samrat. 'We're going to the head office only to confirm that they'd met someone there or not.'

'We should ask someone there...'

Samrat interrupted Aavishkar, 'We're not sure that anyone knows about them. Prithvi has mentioned in his letter that *no one* should be told about it. If Mr Chancellor comes to know, they will definitely be in trouble. We agree that they didn't share their plan with us, but if they've stepped for it, wouldn't have done without considering the consequences.'

Kabeer estimated, 'You're right. They might not get chance to tell us. Prithvi would've told Kanak about the Royal Weapon, and when they were going to Rajput sir, they took this step.'

'Anything could be possible, but we've to help them,' said Samrat with a perturbed expression.

They were at a distance from the head office entrance that Shikhar's voice came from behind. 'Avi, where had you been? Ma'am S. Imran needs you in her cabin regarding New Year programs. You've given your name for a show on Robotics, haven't you?'

'But I...'

Before Aavishkar could finish, Samrat spoke, 'Avi, you go. We think about it.'

Aavishkar said, 'You...'

'Don't worry. You go,' repeated Samrat. 'We'll meet you in our room.'

'Okay.' A reluctant Aavishkar left with Shikhar.

A confused Kabeer asked, 'Why did you do it?'

'You know him better than I do. He surely wants to help Prithvi and Kanak but not in the way I want.'

Many questions struck Kabeer's mind. 'What're you thinking?'

'We have to learn DTM's location.' Samrat stepped back to the hostel.

'We're not going in?' Kabeer ran behind him. 'Kavya told that it's been shifted today in the morning to Saptarishi lab. If Prithvi and Kanak had used it, it must've returned there only.'

'We need to enter Saptarishi to be sure.'

***

'So, you wanted to know my plan?' said Samrat, entering his room. 'We're going to do what Prithvi and Kanak want.' He opened Aavishkar's closet and took Tez out of it. 'Kabeer, you know Tez's functions and how it's operated by your computer. You told Avi about its system, didn't you?'

'What have we to do with it?'

Samrat said, coming to him, 'Rathore sir and Raghuvanshi ma'am have been working on DTM. When Shikhar had come, I saw both of them entering the head office. They might be still there.'

'Okay. So?'

'Listen to me carefully. You have to follow both of them through Tez so that we could get DTM's exact location,' specified Samrat.

'What do you...?' Kabeer's eyes widened in realization. 'Samrat, no.'

'Yes. We're going to travel through time.' Samrat turned on the computer. 'You'd read the letter. They need us.'

'I too want to help them but not with this option. I mean if Mr Chancellor comes to know...'

'Our Vyom is more important than everything. I'd seen Zaheer sir when he heard that Vikrant's name. His face had lost its colour. We'll have to do it, Kabeer. We don't have any option left,' said Samrat, his face veiled by distress. 'Although it's a cursory decision, I know it'll be right. After all, we must know *what this Royal Weapon is* which has disturbed everyone.'

The room fell in silence.

'Okay. I'll help, but I want you to say one line for me,' said Kabeer with a particular sense of seriousness.

Samrat asked, flustered, 'What...what line?'

'*Kabeer, you're the best partner I've ever got.*' Kabeer's lips pulled back in a grin.

Samrat for a moment couldn't react and then laughed loudly. 'Nice timing, Kabeer.'

'I'm with you *till the end*,' said a determined Kabeer. He pressed a key on the keyboard and initiated Tez's engine.

Tez turned towards the door, came out and ran along the walls of the corridor. A camcorder fitted on its front glass kept an eye on the surroundings, and Kabeer and Samrat followed it through the computer.

'Turn on the CCTV jammer.'

Kabeer did as Samrat suggested.

Their room was on the second floor so after passing the corridor it was wheels within wheels for Tez.

'Now what?' said a worried Samrat, seeing the staircase going down.

'I knew such problems would come sooner or later. I'd advised Avi about it.' Kabeer pressed a key on the keyboard. Two silver wings of ten centimetres each came out of Tez's roof. As he pressed another key, it started flying.

Samrat said deliriously, 'Our Ingenious Avi made *a matchless car.*'

'I've contributed significantly to *this matchless car,*' bragged Kabeer.

Samrat was on the alert. 'Get it a bit lower. All the students have gone for the dinner even then we can't make a single mistake.'

When Tez crossed the staircase reaching the ground floor, Kabeer made its wings in. As it rode to the corridor along the edge of the walls, it halted.

'Who's this?' said Kabeer, clearly vexed.

'Cock the camera,' said Samrat.

When they saw a boy standing in front of a door through the camcorder, Kabeer's muddled expression was replaced by an angry one. 'It's our *spy boy*, Abhyuday Sahni. He'd certainly be busy in trying to get what's going on inside by putting an inverted glass tumbler over the door.' He smouldered, 'What does he think of himself?'

'Like you said. Our *spy* boy,' said Samrat, mollifying him.

Kabeer had to take Tez away from the walls. 'Let me finish my business, detective Abhyuday. I'll get back to you,' he said, still heated.

Tez exited the hostel and after crossing a quadrangle sped to the head office, away from everyone's eyes and reach, blended into the darkness. It took it about five minutes to reach outside the head office entrance, into the shadow of a tree.

After waiting for a long when no one came out of the office, Samrat doubted, 'Have they gone?'

Just then, Arunima and Kushal turned up. Samrat and Kabeer got activated. Tez began to chase them, following Kushal's legs closely. Arunima and Kushal walked past Angad Bhavan and Aryabhatta Bhavan to enter Gagan Bhavan situated in Parikrama-2. As Kushal reached B-Wing, he halted to take a call through his wrist belt. A panicked Kabeer had to pull Tez up.

Samrat said, exhaling, 'It was a close shave.'

After finishing the conversation with Zaheer, Kushal accompanied with Arunima moved ahead and after them, Tez. They boarded an elevator to reach third floor while Tez winged passing stairways stealthily and perfectly to do the same. It turned left to progress towards its final destination.

A specific door had to be passed to enter Saptarishi Technology Lab. Kushal touched some numbers on a screen to the right of its metallic gateway. Saptarishi's gate opened. No sooner both of them and Tez did enter than it shut behind them.

As Tez's camcorder caught DTM standing ten feet away, Kabeer said, 'It's here only.'

Tez turned right and hid itself under a wooden rack.

'The meeting after a while is very important for us, Arunima. Zaheer sir will brief us on the mission.' Kushal pressed a button on DTM's door to open it.

'Everyone is helping us. No matter what Vikrant plans, we'll definitely find the Royal Weapon,' said Arunima, operating many supercomputers together.

Kabeer asked, 'What does ma'am mean by *everyone*? Prithvi and Kanak?'

Samrat only shrugged.

Saptarishi's gate opened again, and Zaheer appeared. Tez was waiting for this opportunity. It apace got out and then very discreetly came back to the room.

Kabeer shut down the computer. 'I guess all the senior professors, scientists and officers will go in the meeting sir was talking about.'

'Let's go now.' Samrat left Tez on Aavishkar's bed.

'And Avi? What about him?'

'We can't take him with us.'

'*What*? Samrat you…'

'If Mr Chancellor comes to know about our plan, someone must be here who can prove us innocent, who would explain what we did was for good intention or if we trap in the past, someone should be here who can tell everyone where we are,' said Samrat.

Kabeer said, 'He doesn't know about our plan.'

'That's why I didn't keep Tez back into his closet. His memory is superior. When he finds it out, he'll know. By the way, when DTM evaporates, everyone will come to know.'

'Then why...'

Samrat spoke before Kabeer could finish, 'We should not while away our time. We've to improvise.' He walked out.

'I think it was important.' Kabeer ran behind him.

***

Shaurya and his friends were in the dining hall for dinner.

'Three of them are not here,' said Pravesh, straining his neck to get a better look of the hall.

Ujjawal said, exulting at the success, 'They must be busy.'

'I guess they didn't doubt that the letter wasn't written by Prithvi but you.' Shaurya gave Alexander an encouraging look.

Alexander's lips broke into a very faint smile.

Urvashi asked, 'How did you get this idea?'

'A week ago Ujjawal overheard them discussing about some royal weapon and Ananyaakashganga,' told Shaurya.

'What will they three be doing now?' Urvashi's tone was thoughtful.

'They'll be disturbed, trying unsuccessfully to find them out. If they take any big step thinking that Prithvi and Kanak can search any royal weapon, they'll face dire problems. And during this confusion, both of them, being locked, will enjoy in the store room.' Shaurya seemed gratified.

Saif warned, 'We can't believe those blockheads. They can take very big pace.'

'Let them do whatever they want. A single blunder and they'll be caught. Then Mr Chancellor will never forgive them,' grinned Lara.

Alexander asked, 'What about Avi?'

'It's just a *payback time,* Alex. We aren't going to harm anyone.' A pacific smile swung over Shaurya's lips.

***

'The students have started to return. Hurry up.' Samrat asked, 'You've taken the suggested requisites?'

'Avi will kill us if he learns that we've taken the CCTV jammer out of Tez,' said Kabeer, walking to keep pace with Samrat, a five-centimetre black device with a blinking green LED light in his hand.

'I hope you've turned it on.'

Kabeer shook his head. 'And I've perused about time machines from a book Avi has. I didn't know that book would be useful *here*.'

Both of them left the hostel and made their way towards Gagan Bhavan.

'And I didn't know that overhearing Mr Chancellor and Zaheer sir would be handy for us. We've to reach 1180. Prithvi and Kanak will be there.'

They rushed into Gagan and hurried up the steps. After reaching third floor, they stood quietly against a wall near Saptarishi Lab.

Samrat peeked at its doorway. 'All clear. Let's move.'

Both of them raced to the lab. They had hardly reached the halfway when saw Damini and Zaheer exiting from Saptarishi. They rushed back and hid behind a big statue at the corner of the corridor.

'Vikrant always creates jeopardy for Vyom, Zaheer. We have to do something,' said Damini, sighing deeply.

An upset Zaheer said, 'Jay is crest-fallen. The only way to reduce his discomfort and consolidate Vyom is to protect the Royal Weapon. I want Vikrant never to approach Ananyaakashganga.'

Kabeer whispered, 'Ananyaakashganga?'

'Shhh...' Samrat put his hand over Kabeer's mouth. 'Mr Chancellor also took this name. The Royal Weapon might be there.'

'Thank God, Vikrant doesn't know how important Professor Dhanraj's painting is to us,' said Damini.

Zaheer added, 'Like he doesn't know how important DTM is to us.'

Both of them walked on and disappeared.

Samrat let out an audible sigh of relief. 'Let's try again.'

He and Kabeer emerged from behind the statue and broke into a sprint to reach Saptarishi's gate.

Samrat gestured to the screen on which 0 to 9 numbers were displayed. 'Do your job.'

Kabeer touched 2, 1, 0, 3, 6 and 9. The gate opened, and they whipped in.

Dr Venugopal Subramanian, working in the lab, turned back. 'Anything else, sir?'

No one was near the door. A surprised Venugopal came to it and looked around. In a bemused state, he went back to the supercomputer he was working on. Kabeer and Samrat had secretly slipped behind a cupboard near the door. They steamed towards DTM stood to the left. As Kabeer pressed a button on its door to open it, a notification flashed on the supercomputer.

Venugopal was confounded. 'What…!' He turned to DTM. As he saw Samrat and Kabeer inside it, shouted, 'Who are you… and…?'

After closing DTM's door, Kabeer had touched some symbols on one of the screens.

'CLEAR OFF,' cried Samrat.

In the nick of time, Kabeer pressed four buttons followed by a white one on one of the keyboards. A shell shocked Venugopal ran towards them, but it was late. As Kabeer pushed a thrust lever next to the keyboard, DTM disappeared.

'*God!*' Venugopal immediately got back to the supercomputers. 'How could it be?' he said, scrambled. 'It's not in 2018 now. Only after half an hour, we can connect with it.' Several times, he tried to access DTM, but every time it looked as failures. 'I have to inform Mr Chancellor.'

***

As Aavishkar entered the room, he found no one there. He turned back to leave, but then decided to wait. He was going to have a long wait for those of his friends who had left 2018 to travel through time but not for them who were locked.

Lying in the dim-lighted store room, Prithvi began to revive. He stood up, rubbing his eyes and stepped. 'What's...?' He tumbled down stuck by Kanak's leg. 'She's also here! She didn't stop dropping me down even out of her sense,' he said with a frustrated gesture. 'Kanak...Kanak...' He splashed some water from a tap of the store room on her face and tried to make her restore. She slowly came to her consciousness.

'Do you recognize me?' Prithvi asked with raillery.

'I can never forget this ugly face.' Kanak stood up, holding her head with the hand. 'Is this Physics lab?'

'You meant conspicuous face,' reacted Prithvi. 'And it's a store room I guess.' He set eyes on all around.

'But we were outside the lab. I was...getting swooned,' she recalled.

'The same thing came about with me. Anyway, first let's move out.' Prithvi got the door and tried to open it. 'It's bolted or locked.'

Kanak frowned, clearly surprised. 'Someone locked us in here or we got locked by mistake?'

'Someone is out there? Open the door.' Prithvi knocked on the door heavily. Continuously, he and Kanak tried to get some help. In the long run someone unbolted the door. They were Kavya and Abhyuday.

'What are you two doing here?' marvelled Kavya. 'When you didn't return to the dining hall, we thought you'd come later directly to the hostel.'

Abhyuday added, 'But when it was too late we came here to find you two. You know, it's 8:30.'

Kanak's hand covered her mouth in shock. 'What!'

'We came here after lunch,' said Prithvi, seemed to be in daze. 'Samrat, Kabeer and Avi would be looking for us.'

Kavya told, 'Yes. They were asking about both of you.'

***

'Everything is according to our plan. DTM will leave at 10:25 for

1180…' Jaywardhan stopped in mid sentence as Venugopal knocked on Kshitij's door.

'May I come in, Mr Chancellor?'

'What is he doing here?' thought Jaywardhan, then allowed him to enter.

Venugopal sounded urgent, his face pale, 'Sorry, but I had to come.'

'What's the matter?' asked Zaheer.

'Sir, sir…'

Worried, Damini said, 'Why don't you tell us, Venugopal?'

Ma'am… that…that DTM has… disappeared from Saptarishi,' faltered Venugopal.

Everyone's jaw fell open. They were too stunned to react. Venugopal found them gaping at him in arrant awe.

***

'I can't see anything,' Kabeer's voice broke the silence of the dark night. The flare of a white light lit up his face.

'You'd pressed the right buttons?' asked Samrat, holding a torch.

Kabeer saw one of the screens. 'Yes. We're in 1180.' He pulled back the thrust lever.

'How will we know about them?' said Samrat, coming out of DTM.

'I guess it's a jungle.' Kabeer was behind him. 'A horrible jungle.' He quickly took a flashlight out of a backpack he was carrying. 'Since we didn't enter any location, DTM has landed within a radius of one to two kilometres of its last time location.'

'It meant we're one to four kilometres away from the place they've come. Good.' Samrat lolled down under a tree, resting against it. 'By the way, they know we'll come so we should wait. We can't move without them otherwise we might get lost in this *horrible* jungle.' Looking up at an appalled Kabeer, he struggled to dissimulate his smile.

***

Chapter 7
The Last Painting

Aavishkar came downstairs to find Prithvi, Kanak, Kavya and Abhyuday nearing him. 'You... here!' His reaction was a combination of shock and happiness.

'Where should've we been?' said Prithvi. 'Where are Samrat and Kabeer?'

'I...I don't know. I was going to looking for them.'

The assembly bell rang before Prithvi could react.

Kanak said, confusion fogging her brain, 'Why are we being called in Vyom Hall at this time?'

'It never happened before,' said Prithvi.

Aavishkar rearranged his expressions. 'You go, I'm coming. I've turned on the computer.'

***

'Did any tragedy happen?' Jessica took a seat.

Kavya kept her eyes turned towards Jaywardhan, Zaheer and Vijay standing on the stage. 'Some pressing issue is there. Something is wrong.'

'We couldn't get anything from CCTV footage. Neither their image nor how they did all this. They'd used an advanced jammer,' Vijay whispered to Jaywardhan.

Jaywardhan said, surprised and fretful, 'Then I say Vijay, our students' technology outran ours.' He addressed when all the students reached the hall, 'Students, lend me your ears. We have a momentous announcement to make.' The murmurs died instantly. 'DTM has disappeared from Saptarishi Lab and...and our two students rode it to the past.'

Whisperings of dismay filled the hall.

Zaheer said, 'We want to know about those students not present among you at the moment. We hope a complete cooperation from you.'

Jaywardhan asked after a moment, 'Did anyone come to know who they are?'

Someone answered the troubling question. 'I know,' two words boomed across the hall.

Many curious eyes fell on Aavishkar, standing at the door. '*Samrat Chopra and Kabeer Khan.*'

'*What! Samrat and Kabeer?*'

'*What was the need to do this?*'

'*Were they out of their mind?*'

All of them were dumbfounded, bewildered, in a state of fear and tumult.

'Come with us, Aavishkar.' Vijay bid, '*Vyom farewell,* students.'

***

Aavishkar was in Jaywardhan's cabin. He told about his car, and how Samrat and Kabeer reached DTM through it. When he saw Tez on his bed, he was quite surprised then went through the video recorded by its camcorder.

'What put them up to reach DTM?' asked Zaheer, his voice firm.

A hesitated Aavishkar replied, 'We came to... know that... Prithvi and Kanak have gone to the past through it and didn't come back. Samrat and Kabeer might've wanted to get them back so...'

'...so *they* travelled through time,' Damini completed his sentence angrily. 'And you're telling this now?'

'Ma'am, we thought if you knew about it, Prithvi and Kanak would be in trouble,' Aavishkar put across.

'Now, *Samrat and Kabeer* will be in trouble, Aavishkar,' said Vijay. He turned towards Jaywardhan. 'They could do this I'd never thought.'

Jaywardhan asked calmly, 'How did you come to know about Prithvi and Kanak?'

'Mr Chancellor... actually...,' said Aavishkar, downcast, 'we were informed by a letter.'

'And you believed it?!' said a fuming Damini.

Aavishkar told that they scouted for Prithvi and Kanak, but didn't find them. Samrat and Kabeer would've thought that they really went to the past. When they got to know that DTM was in Saptarishi, they understood that it returned without their friends. That's why they took this step he did know nothing about.

Damini said, her anger abated, 'How could these students bring this misery upon themselves, Jay?'

'Their act was reckless, but I know they are not. They reached DTM and operated it. That was not easy at all. I think our students won't do anything amiss. And what if there is something more to tell?' Jaywardhan looked at Aavishkar who was unable to see in his eyes.

***

Kanak, Prithvi and their friends in a quandary were waiting for Aavishkar outside the hostels. When he turned up, Kanak asked right away, 'What is this? Kabeer and Samrat are in the past?'

'Why didn't you tell us?' asked Prithvi.

Aavishkar gave them the full story of what he knew. 'I didn't say anything about Dhairya. I knew he would've done it under some pressure,' he finished.

'But he must've thought about its repercussions,' said Abhyuday, outraged.

Kanak said, her tone urgent, 'It's our time to think. We have to meet Mr Chancellor.'

Prithvi agreed, 'Right. We cannot leave them in the history.'

***

Jaywardhan, in Saptarishi lab accompanied by Zaheer, Sagar and Kushal, asked, 'When did it return?'

'Ten minutes ago,' told Kushal, standing inside DTM, looking at one of the screens.

Jaywardhan said, 'We have to improvise now. DTM will go to the past after midnight. First, we'll search out Samrat and Kabeer and try to know about Vikrant's strategies, but this time Sagar won't go. When both of them return safely, we'll decide something.'

Everyone shook their head in consent. Jaywardhan exited from the lab and strode to the head office. He found Vijay, Prithvi, Kanak and Aavishkar waiting outside his cabin.

Kanak initiated, 'We want to say something, Mr Chancellor.'

'Come in, children.' He entered the cabin followed by four of them. 'If you want to know about your friends then don't worry.'

'They'd gone there because of us…' blurted Prithvi, '…and the main reason was that royal wea…'

'Prithvi…' interjected Aavishkar.

'How do you know about it?' asked a flabbergasted Jaywardhan.

Prithvi looked at Aavishkar signalling him not to tell anything.

Jaywardhan repeated, 'Prithvi, how do you know?'

Kanak asked, 'About what?'

'About the Royal Weapon and Ananyaakashganga.' Prithvi told everything then.

Jaywardhan's eyes widened in realization. 'That's why I wondered how my students could do it impetuously. I appreciate their love and valour, but it's not easy to reach the Royal Weapon. Vikrant is our enemy, and evidently if he gets it, most of the things we know may be ceased.' He paused for a while and said, 'As far as your friends are concerned, we're trying our best.'

'God! They laid themselves open to a venture,' said a jumpy Kanak.

Vijay told, 'You need not to be worried. We're sending our commandos for them.'

'Then we'll help,' Prithvi put up his wish, 'we are the part of Vyom. We must help it.'

'What do you want, Prithvi?' asked Jaywardhan.

Kanak replied, 'We want to bring them back.'

'That's why we're sending our Special Task Force,' said Vijay.

'Then we can help your commandos. We're taught to protect and help others, aren't we?' said Prithvi, his tone firm.

'If we're together, we can find them sooner. Samrat and Kabeer don't know your commandos. It could be possible that they'd think them strangers or Vikrant's men, but we're not strangers to them.' Kanak gesticulated, her voice steadfast, 'We must be given an opportunity to help our friends, Mr Chancellor.'

Jaywardhan looked at them for a second and said, 'I have no doubt on your spirited abilities. I'm happy to know that you care of your institute and friends. But when we come to a real mission, it's easy to say than to act. The consequences may be beyond your imaginations.'

'Those consequences will be in *our* favour, Mr Chancellor. *I promise*,' Prithvi's voice was brimmed with determination.

Jaywardhan flashed him a quick, admiring smile. He said, 'Vijay, three of them are going, too. Do the preparations.'

'Very well, Mr Chancellor.' Vijay walked out.

Aavishkar wasn't involved in the conversation as he was busy in noticing the framed painting behind Jaywardhan's chair.

'What are you doing there, Aavishkar?' asked Kanak, looked embarrassed.

Aavishkar did not blink. 'Why is this painting so strange?'

'Avi, you started here. It's Mr Chancellor's cabin,' said Prithvi.

Aavishkar's eyes still glued to the painting. 'I should've asked him only,' he continued without turning to them. 'Mr Chancellor, could you please tell me about it?'

'Why not, my child.' The smile returned to Jaywardhan's face. 'This painting belonged to our former chancellor, Professor Aaditya Dhanraj. He was blessed with a great mind to observe Science and

Art simultaneously, to construct extraordinary machines and make marvellous paintings as well. It was his *last painting.*'

Jaywardhan turned to see three of them looking excited and interested. 'Whatever he did for me, for Vyom, it is irreplaceable. The day we lost him, we'd lost a teacher who taught us how to stand for your country, we'd lost a dreamer who prayed for a peaceful future, we'd lost a genius mind and a brave person who never gave up no matter how many times he failed, and he was the same till his last breath.' Tears broke through his proud eyes. He tried to hide them behind his warm smile, but Prithvi, Kanak and Aavishkar caught the emotions on his face.

***

'I'd said these blockheads could do anything,' spoke Saif, enraged. He and his friends were in the common hall.

An irritated look was on Ujjawal's face. 'What were those idiots thinking? How to prove *an everlasting friendship*?'

'This shouldn't have happened,' said Alexander, controlling his rising consternation. 'Their life is in danger, Shaurya.'

Lara overruled his objection, 'Not theirs but ours. Avi's in the Chancellor's Office. If he says anything against Dhairya...'

'He won't. I know that,' said Shaurya, hiding the confusion and agitation he felt inside.

Urvashi said, 'So what next?'

'We've to wait to know *what next.*' Shaurya's serious expression was restored.

***

'I really didn't know we could collaborate like this besides those projects,' said Kabeer with a playful grin. He and Samrat were still reclining under the tree, waiting for the ones who hadn't actually arrived 1180 yet.

'Could you please skip this topic?' An indifferent Samrat looked away.

The smile left Kabeer's face. 'Why do you do it?' He stood up. '*You* said that I'm the best partner you've ever got.'

'No, I didn't say this. All I said was *nice timing, Kabeer.*'

Kabeer opened his mouth to say, but then something dawned on him. He stared blankly at Samrat.

Samrat stood, giggling, and patted Kabeer on the shoulder. 'Try next time, brother.' As he turned around, he was stunned into immobility not finding DTM. 'What…!'

Kabeer's heart skipped a beat. 'Where's DTM? We'd left it here only!'

'Where can it go?' Samrat's head spun. 'We should've been around it.'

'We didn't know it'd be disappeared itself,' said Kabeer, trying to control his breathing.

'We have to dig it out, Kabeer,' said Samrat, his face filled with horror. 'Take Avi's book out and see if anything is written about this *weird kind of behaviour* of a time machine.'

***

'Commandos, I know they're good enough to take care of themselves but still…,' said Jaywardhan to the S.T.F. in Saptarishi lab.

'Don't worry, Mr Chancellor. They'll be safe. *Vyom farewell,*' said Samarth Sen, the commandant of the Task Force.

Prithvi smiled gratefully. 'Thank you, Mr Chancellor, for believing in us.'

Jaywardhan put his hand on his head. 'Don't burden yourself that you have to prove something, Prithvi. This is an opportunity to learn. Learn to stand again whenever you fall.'

'We will not let you down, Mr Chancellor,' reacted Kanak, an imperishable shine in her eyes.

Having entered DTM with Samarth and three more commandos, Prithvi, Aavishkar and Kanak looked at Jaywardhan. He smiled fondly at them. Samarth activated DTM, and as he pushed the thrust lever, it disappeared.

***

The time machine Kabeer and Samrat had been hunting for had

returned to 1180, next to a lake, near the same jungle but beyond their reach.

Vice-commandant Divy Kashyap came out of DTM and looked all around, listening intently for any sound. 'All clear, sir.' Everyone came out at his signal.

'They should've been within a range of one to four kilometers,' said Samarth, 'but under the circumstances, they might've left the place they'd arrived. We have to be quick.'

Out of four crowns- red, yellow, green and blue, two on the left and two on the right of his digital square wrist watch, he pressed the red one. The glass of the watch opened like a single door pivoted on its right edge. Below its LED screen showing *0.0016 Km, NE,* was a small black button. He pressed it. Then he pressed the red crown again to close the case.

Kanak put her hand on a lost Aavishkar's shoulder. Her eyes seemed to ask, '*What happened?*'

Aavishkar coming out of his thinking shook his head in *no*.

'This is *Aavriti*, acts as a remote control for DTM, but it'll work only in 1180,' told Samarth, showing his watch to three of them. 'Now keep your distance from DTM.'

When Samarth pressed Aavriti's yellow crown, a titanium shield enveloped DTM. As he pressed the green crown, a kind of metallic rotary excavator emerged from DTM's bottom. Its bucket wheel rotated about a horizontal axis and set about digging the ground, spreading the soil over an area around. DTM had begun landing down. When it fitted wholly inside the pit, Samarth pressed the blue crown, finishing the excavation.

'It's one of the methods to protect DTM.' He turned to see Prithvi, Kanak and Aavishkar, their eyes conveyed excitement.

Divy with his two assistant commandos moved to the pit to hide DTM's top with the soil.

'Your friends didn't have Aavriti, that's why DTM was insecure. Thank God, it returned to lab safely,' said Samarth.

As the commandos finished their job, everyone moved into the jungle led by Samarth.

Prithvi asked, 'Now, how will we get to know about DTM?'

'Aavriti's LED tells its location as it's now 25.5 metre in North-East.' Samarth showed his watch to him. 'And when we press the crowns in reverse order, blue, green and yellow, it'd come out if it's inside.'

Kanak opened her eyes wide. '*If* it's inside!'

Prithvi and Aavishkar were behind her and at the last were the accompanying commandos, holding their torch, looking all around scrupulously how the land lain.

'This is DTM's unique mechanism. Every time we'll connect it to its supercomputers as soon as we land in the past or future for its safety. After half an hour, it'll itself return to its original time and be sent back according to the protocol,' recounted Samarth. 'If we don't connect it to its supercomputers, even then it'll return, but it's not safe for its central system.

'That's what happened with Samrat and Kabeer. They couldn't connect DTM as they didn't have Aavriti,' said Kanak. 'So whatever happens, DTM will return.'

'Unless or until it's disconnected from its supercomputers,' spoke Samarth without turning to her.

Aavishkar whispered to Kanak, 'Could the sun be amid a river?'

A surprised Kanak looked at him. '*What!*'

'But in that painting…'

She said, taking no notice of his impatience, 'Move on Aavishkar. We'll talk later.'

'So if we want to ride *along* with DTM, we've to push the thrust lever so we've to go inside it, but if we want to send it to the past or future, we do what you did?' asked Prithvi, just behind Aavishkar.

Samarth said smilingly, 'Exactly.'

'When DTM disappears, the ground will go deep down? I meant there would be nothing beneath it then,' asked Aavishkar finally.

'The titanium shield protecting it doesn't vanish. The ground remains the same, and nobody has any doubt,' completed Samarth.

***

Chapter 8

A to Z 18 15 2 15 20 19= 26

'But Dev, this… how did it happen?' Zaheer had a dead blow. 'Siddhant is investigating,' said Devraj. He and Zaheer were heading for Kshitij Hall.

A great sadness fell upon Zaheer. 'Jay will be devastated from his death.'

Both of them looking broken entered Kshitij to find Jaywardhan and Damini standing.

Damini asked impatiently, 'What's the matter?'

'Damini… that Ali…' Zaheer couldn't find the strength to speak.

'What about *him*?' asked Jaywardhan agitatedly.

Zaheer turned with a display of emotions on his face. 'Ali…Ali is no more.'

Jaywardhan and Damini froze at his words.

Zaheer continued, 'Before dying, he sent an e-mail to Dev that Vikrant had learnt about him. He mentioned about a truth also he discovered lately.'

'I didn't read the whole message at that time. I was worried about him,' said Devraj. 'I immediately informed the Headquarters, but it was too late.'

There was a dead silence pervaded the hall.

A dejected Jaywardhan broke it, 'Ali knew it was full of danger to work with Vikrant, but still he took a leap in the dark.'

'It's enough, Jay,' cried Damini wrathfully. 'There will be a direct fight now.'

Zaheer said, 'If he's here.'

'What do you mean?' asked Damini.

'He's gone to 1180.' As Devraj finished, a man in black suit, looked to be in his late twenties came in.

'Siddhant, how did it happen?' asked Zaheer.

The man was Siddhant Deshpande, an agent of Vyom Information Bureau and Ali's associate. He informed, 'Sir, Ali has revealed in his mail that someone is among us informing Vikrant about our plans, about the S.T.F.'

Damini asked, 'Did Vikrant know about our changed plan that we didn't send the S.T.F. as it was scheduled but after two hours?'

'We're not sure, ma'am,' replied Siddhant. 'If he'd left 2018 before 8:30 p. m., then *no*. But he might know the coordinates of the place the S.T.F. was supposed to reach.'

Zaheer said, 'Around 8:15, Samrat and Kabeer went to 1180. After that we'd to change our plan, and then Vikrant can't get any information of present through any of the connectors. We cannot make call through time.'

'I want that person duping us behind the bars.' Jaywardhan was in high dudgeon. 'Our commandos and students might be in danger.'

'VIB is doing its job. We will hunt it up through thick and thin,' Devraj was stout, expressing his enthusiasm.

'There is one more thing, Mr Chancellor,' added Siddhant. 'Ali has warned us about Vikrant's one more covert mission having a code, *A to Z 18 15 2 15 20 19=26 UNCONTROLLED*. There was a line in his message over and above it, *Diamond cuts Diamond*.'

Every mind was filled with chaos, disquietude and uncertainty. Every troubled heart desperately searched for answers. There was hope but it felt a million miles away.

***

Samarth and his team had reached the upland of the jungle. 'The forest is becoming denser. We have to be on our guard more effectively,' he alerted.

Kanak spoke, 'How desolate and grisly this place is. No one is appearing high and low.'

Prithvi laughed in his sleeve. 'Someone is with *me* who's more desolate and grisly.'

'I'm in no mood to fight, Prithvi.' Kanak rolled her eyes.

'You never understand, Kanak. Fighting you energizes Prithvi,' revealed Aavishkar, walking alongside her.

Kanak glared at him while Prithvi couldn't help smiling.

Frantic, Aavishkar turned to Samarth. 'Sir, may I have Aavriti for a while?'

'Handle it carefully.' Samarth gave it to him. 'You must also know about this.' He showed the black button below LED. 'By pressing it, DTM...' he couldn't finish for three bullets struck Divy.

An unsettled Samarth rushed to him, 'Divy...Divy...' and found him dead. He stood up, drawing his gun. 'Turn off the torches. Children, stay back.'

They couldn't have enough time to think as discharging started from all the sides. They swiftly hid behind a hedge.

'Who's having guns in 1180?' thought Samarth. 'Vikrant!' He ordered the commandos, 'Start the counterattack. They won't stop.'

Both the sides were involved in the cannonade for two minutes.

'We haven't left with enough bullets,' said Samarth, checking the magazines. 'We have to save the children,' he enjoined the rest two commandos. They gave him an encouraging look. He took Aavishkar, Kanak and Prithvi and did a bunk followed by them.

The opponents were keeping pace with them. Another commando became the hunt of gunshots. They turned back dismally to see their dead friend but they had to move on. They weaved through trees and bushes, trying to outpace their opponents.

At once, Aavishkar tipped. Aavriti was released from his hand. He instantly groped for it and fortunately found it.

Prithvi helped him up. 'You're okay?'

Aavishkar nodded. 'What to do now?' he mumbled as found Aavriti's glass open. 'This might be...' he pressed the black button below LED but nothing happened. Then he pressed the red crown. Aavriti's glass covered its face. He pocketed it in his sweat-shirt. His speed had decelerated. Two shots could make him their target, but the third commando blocked them to save him.

'Go away...' He breathed ultimately.

The firing didn't stop. Scratching trees, bushes, climbers, it wanted to continue hunting more humans.

'This way,' Samarth gestured his head towards right, and they changed the course. He glanced back and saw some shadows giving chase. Four of them put everything into the running, but there was no escape.

Samarth halted having paid attention to a swamp around six feet away. 'Prithvi, you and Aavishkar go right and follow its edge. We go left. It will distract them. We'll meet along its perimeter.'

Prithvi protested, 'We're not lea...'

'You are. Now go,' argued Samarth, frayed. 'Take care of yourselves.'

A reluctant Prithvi nodded. The two groups parted.

Hardly had Samarth and Kanak ran for thirty seconds when two bullets hit him. He staggered.

Kanak recoiled in horror. 'S-I-R...' She helped him up. 'You're okay?'

Samarth gathered his wits and tried to search out a place to set up a counterattack. After a forty-metre run, he held Kanak's arm and immediately hid behind a tree trunk. 'I hope you know how to use it.' He gave her a gun, gasping. 'You have only four bullets.'

'I can try,' said Kanak, seizing it.

Samarth and Kanak, staying hidden, opened fire. When he finished three opponents off, her shot hunt its first target.

Samarth had an admiring grin on his face. 'They've trained you well.'

'Drop your gun, Samarth,' said a man, standing only five feet away, levelling his flashlight pistol at Kanak's head. 'Or I drop *her* dead?'

Both of them put their gun down and raised their hands in surrender.

'What's Vyom's S.T.F. doing with these kids?' said the man, stepping forward.

Samarth hid his expressions of surprise appeared on his face for a moment.

The man continued, 'This is our war, Samarth. Children are not allowed.'

As soon as he pulled the trigger, Samarth leapt in front of Kanak. The bullets shot him and he fell. The man was shell-shocked.

Samarth didn't give up. He lifted his gun and fired on him. The man was dead.

'Sir...sir...' Kanak sat down, cradling Samarth in her trembling arms.

Samarth was hemorrhaging, losing his breath. 'Look girl, I don't have much time... listen to me...' His final moment had come.

'Please... no...' Kanak couldn't hold back her tears.

'Take it with you...' Samarth put a haversack off his back. 'Take great care of it and Aavriti. I...I couldn't do anything... for my ... but... you all... can...' he said with his dying breath.

'Please sir, don't... you... you...'

'Go away... Kanak. RUN... You have to protect this bag. You have to protect yourself, for Vyom, for your friends...' Samarth breathed his last. Death had taken his life away.

'Sir...? SIR...' Kanak's eyes streamed. She could hear the paces getting louder. *She had to decide.*

***

'Ma'am, we got something from Ali's mail.' Siddhant was in Damini's cabin. He kept a photograph on her desk. 'It's of three days back.'

'In Mumbai?' As soon as Damini saw it, she was momentarily taken aback. She looked up suddenly at Siddhant, her face distraught, 'Have you shown...?'

'No, ma'am. You're the first.'

Damini let out a sigh of relief. 'Thank you. I'll take care of it now.'

It took one look in her eyes for Siddhant to know what he'd to do.

***

'*Now we have to find Samarth and get DTM with his help. Let's go.*'

Kanak, blended into the shadows of a tree around a hundred metres away from the spot, listened some voices in rapt attention, hanging on every word. 'They want time machine!' she mused.

The sound of the footsteps gradually died away. She shut her eyes devastated with tears of sorrow and terror. She wanted to accept whatever happened to Samarth as a nightmare, let this terrible moment pass, cry aloud but she couldn't.

A voice pierced through the silence, 'Thank God, you're okay.'

Kanak spun around to see Prithvi accompanied by Aavishkar. A small tear escaped her eyes. Prithvi caught her wiping it quickly. She turned about, her hand covered her mouth.

'What're you doing here? You should've met us on the other side. And sir? Where is he? He was with you, wasn't he?' Aavishkar asked a barrage of questions.

'What happened, Kanak? Look at me.'

Kanak felt Prithvi's soft touch on her shoulder. She stayed rooted. Tears welled up in her eyes.

Prithvi continued to hold her shoulder. 'Kanak, *please.*'

She somehow told about the terrible supervened calamity.

Prithvi and Aavishkar were beside themselves with grief, disoriented at this rapid accident which had cast them in a chasm of hopelessness and uncertainty.

'I'm sorry I'd to leave him there to save this bag,' said Kanak, tears rolling down her cheeks.

Prithvi said, '*Don't be*. This was his dying wish.'

'They wanted DTM. That's why they turned on us so that we couldn't reach it again.' Logic ran through Aavishkar's mind.

'Aavishkar, tie Aavriti. It'll be safer.' Kanak carried the haversack on the back. 'Now we have to find Samrat and Kabeer by ourselves, but before it, we have to reach sir. We can't leave him there,' she said with a long face.

'By the way, they won't get DTM. It'll already have returned to the institute,' said Prithvi.

It took hardly five minutes for Kanak to find the spot, but Samarth's body was missing. 'Wha…?! He was right here...' she said, reeled.

Aavishkar said, 'Those people might've taken him with them. After all, they did want to reach him.'

Kanak looked at Prithvi. 'But now, why? He's dead.'

***

'I've gone through this whole book, but didn't get anything,' told Kabeer with a look of despair, a thin book in his hand.

'It's dawn. We neither got DTM nor both of them,' said Samrat, perplexed, walking with Kabeer.

'Before a while, I heard bizarre sounds like gunshots. At once, they died away.'

Samrat couldn't gulp down what Kabeer said. '*My melodious music*, don't forget, we're in the past.'

'What next?' Kabeer sat down heavily, giving a long, weary sigh.

'It's enough. Now, we'll look only for both of them,' decided Samrat. 'I can see some structures.' He strained his neck to see into the distance beyond a cluster of trees. 'Get up, Kabeer. We have to move.'

***

A large group of tents stood in the jungle glade. Around forty men with weapons were watching over far and near. A big-beefy, hawk eyed man with long stubble beard, standing outside a tent, was deep in thought.

'Vikrant sir, we've investigated Samarth's clothes but found nothing,' said a man with a disheartened voice.

Vikrant turned, narrowing his eyes in irritation.

A tall, well-toned man, Vikrant's chief assistant, Aashutosh Shinde raised the curtain of the same tent to come out. 'How's it possible, Prateek? You've searched him thoroughly?'

Prateek shook his head.

'What if he didn't have anything, sir?' Aashutosh asked Vikrant.

'No, it cannot be. He was scheduled to come here after ten last night, but don't know why he arrived late. Perhaps, Jay changed his ploy, but I know he'd surely sent him to search the Royal Weapon. Our information can't be wrong. Samarth must have something regarded it,' said Vikrant, his brow began to wrinkle.

'What to do with his body?'

'Whatever you want, Prateek. I don't care. I hate who are loyal to Vyom.' Vikrant's eyes flashed fire. 'And Samarth has showed his fidelity with it.'

***

Prithvi, Kanak and Aavishkar had been looking for Samrat and Kabeer with no success in the same jungle. Kanak, trudging, had been quiet for a long time.

Prithvi knew how to break her silence. 'Avi, how could this beautiful forest be a desolate and grisly place to someone?'

Kanak did not react.

Prithvi whispered to Aavishkar, '*I silenced Kanak Singhaniya!*'

Kanak turned to him. 'What do you want?'

'He just wanted to talk to you but never knew how to start,' said Aavishkar, an intelligent and amused look in his eyes.

'What?' Prithvi turned scarlet from embarrassment. 'It's not...' he couldn't finish. He fell face forward as he stepped.

Kanak had to force herself not to laugh. 'Nor he knows how to walk.'

Out of the blue, the same apocalyptic fray Prithvi'd witnessed in Amrit city flashed before his eyes. He saw those two warriors assault each other. The older boy continuously showed his knacks, overpowering the younger one. Triumphing over fear and pain, the younger warrior effortlessly manifested no signs of exhaustion. But ultimately the older one's jab hunted his jaw. He staggered and fell down, his eyes blurred. His rival was about to stab him. A terrified Prithvi turned about swiftly, his heartbeat quickened.

Before Kanak was standing, extending her hand. 'I wasn't responsible. So you like to get up or what?' She helped him stand. 'You're okay?' she asked as if reading his face.

Prithvi said, dissembling his emotions, 'I'm… fine.'

'Friends, you better come see this.'

Both of them saw Aavishkar crouch, staring the ground.

Kanak squatted down. 'A mark? Crushed grasses? What's it?'

'It's an imprint of any massive object, covering a large area.' Prithvi touched the mark.

'It's approximately seven by five by eight feet. It may be…' Aavishkar employed his grey matter, '…*DTM?*' A smile reached his eyes.

Prithvi and Kanak's face brightened.

***

Chapter 9

In the Dungeons

'It's 7:00 a.m. Why has DTM not returned yet?' Jaywardhan was in conversation with Kushal in his cabin.

'It must have. Samarth made any mistake?'

'No. He knows it is very important for us.' Jaywardhan rose to leave the chair. 'Vikrant is there, Kushal. We cannot risk commandos and students' lives.'

'I go and try to find out. *Vyom farewell*, dad.' Kushal headed for the exit.

***

The sun was high up in the sky. Prithvi, Kanak and Aavishkar were still following the trail.

'We couldn't get another trace yet to find both of them,' said Aavishkar, gasping.

'Will this forest end?' Prithvi sounded exhausted. 'Are we lost?'

Kanak wiped her sweat. 'I wish they hadn't gone far.'

'And I wish they hadn't encountered any trouble,' said Prithvi with a sense of foreboding.

***

'Where are you taking us? What did we do?' shouted Samrat.

Kabeer was behind him. Their hands were cuffed behind their back, their face mildly bruised. Ten soldiers were around them, swords in their hands. Having stepped down a long staircase, they turned right to pass an underground corridor.

'You shouldn't have touched us. You don't know…'

The man leading the troop turned to Samrat before he could finish. 'Yes. I should've *killed* you,' he growled, clenching his fists tight.

Samrat did not leave the eye contact.

'Brother, calm down,' Kabeer whispered to Samrat. He asked loudly, looking all around, 'What's this place?'

'This is your first time in dungeons, *boy*?' said the leader and turned to move.

Kabeer muttered under his breath, 'I knew that, *stupid.*'

They passed oil lamp lighted cells. Many eyes followed them. Many faces sneaked a peek from behind the bars to welcome the new members.

After throwing both of them in a dark cell, one of the soldiers locked it. They left as fast as they came.

Samrat was in a temper. 'You can't leave us behind. We'd just asked you about our friends, and you imprisoned us here in this... *whatever you said.*'

'Dungeon,' reminded Kabeer.

'Yes, in dungeon.' When Samrat saw Kabeer silent, burst out, 'Why don't you say something?'

Kabeer asked calmly, 'Should I waste my breaths like you?'

'I am doing *what*?' Samrat's expression showed fury rising through the frustration.

Kabeer said, touching his jacket. 'This is the reason why we're here. Their clothes or *costumes* are different than ours. We aren't like them. They might've thought us impersonators or spies and locked us here.' He had the historic culture at his finger tips.

'If you have *PhD in History*, why didn't you tell me earlier? I would've thought *plan B.*'

'What plan B? Traversing that jungle and not coming to this dominion?'

'*Anything*,' said an exasperated Samrat. 'So what do they do with impersonators or spies?'

'You'll really not want to know.' Kabeer's reply filled Samrat with a cold chill from head to knees.

***

'I'm dead tired, can't walk anymore.' An enervated Aavishkar slumped down. 'I'm having a wolf in my stomach.'

Kanak peered from behind the bushes. 'We're near the edge of the forest, I guess.'

Aavishkar's eyes were somewhere else. 'And these trees have many fruits.'

'Let's look for a water body,' said Kanak, casting a glance at all sides. 'Aavishkar?'

'You two go. I feel like sitting here.' As yet, Aavishkar had started having a mango plucked from a tree.

After a five-minute hunt, Kanak and Prithvi found a pond.

'It's so clean.' Kanak dipped her hands in water. 'It's too frigid. Such clean pond is impossible in our time.' She drank it, cupped in her hands.

Both of them freshened themselves by cold and pure water.

'Nature is so merciful Kanak, isn't it? She provides us everything we need.'

'But unfortunately, we've been forgetting her kindness. We don't respect her, don't understand her. Actually she doesn't need us. *We're* the one who need her.' Kanak watched the pool in rapt attention. 'Many forms she has, showing us the other forms of life, and they're pristine here in the past rather than the present.'

Prithvi listened patiently without saying a word. 'Sometimes, you talk awesome. You've refined your tongue?'

'That's all you wanted to say?' asked Kanak with a weak smile. 'I don't know why those things are happening with you, but you have to ignore them, Prithvi. We'll surely talk about it once we're back to Vyom.'

'You're right. It'll be better for me,' said an upset Prithvi, gazing at his reflection into the water. A prolonged silence descended on him.

Kanak's voice brushed his distressed thoughts aside. 'See Prithvi, that valley is looking so different, isn't it?' She showed him a gorge located two-three kilometres away. 'I've never seen vermilion massif.'

Prithvi looked up at it, his eyes flashed admiration.

Kanak continued, 'And that river skimming along its bottom, so vivacious. It just looked like Dhaara.' She bent down her eyes. 'Where are you, boys?'

'We'll find Samrat and Kabeer very soon,' assured Prithvi, tried to lay his hand on her shoulder, but then quit this thought.

Kanak slowly nodded but didn't look at him.

Prithvi's serious voice suddenly turned into a chirpy one, 'So it's been around thirty hours, and I couldn't see myself in a mirror.' He ran his hands through the hair. 'How am I looking, Kanak? Handsome?

Kanak looked at him with a raised eyebrow. 'I'm not Paridhi.' She turned to move. A hint of a smile hovered on her face. 'We should go.'

Prithvi crooked his eyes together in a frown, going along with her. 'You've just insulted me, haven't you?'

'No. As I'm busy thinking if someone catches us in these clothes here in 1180, then? We...'

'HELP...HELP ME...' A noise tore through the ambience.

Prithvi turned about. 'What's it?'

'Anyone... please...' A loud plea for help emitted from the same jungle. Two men at arms were chasing a girl of about eleven, her long-straight hair flying behind, her dark eyes filled with horror.

Unexpectedly, two hands lugged her into a clump of trees. They belonged to Prithvi.

The girl tried to release herself. 'Who...'

Kanak's hand covered her mouth. 'Keep quiet, and don't move. We're helping you.'

The terror-stricken girl stilled, gasping heavily.

'How could she vanish?' One of the soldiers set his eyes on. 'If General learns about it, you know what he'll do with us.'

'She won't be too far,' another one spoke. 'Let's go.'

They sped away as fast as they could, disappearing into the jungle. No sooner did Kanak withdraw her hand from the girl's mouth and Prithvi loosen his grip than she made a distance.

'Who are you and...?' asked a frightened and surprised voice. She was an adorable girl, dressed in an amber lehenga covered in dirt, had pale skin and a small pointed nose.

'Don't be scared. We...' Kanak's eyes suddenly fell upon her arm. 'You're hurt?'

Prithvi observed the wound. 'Not a gash but it's bleeding. Let's go. We do something.'

Prithvi and Kanak stepped to move, but she didn't. She was standing, afraid and confused.

'You can go down with us. We won't harm you.' Prithvi extended his hand to her. The girl once glanced at them up and down, then lifted her skinny hand slowly and grabbed Prithvi's.

***

Aavishkar had been awaiting Prithvi and Kanak for a long time. As he saw them coming, asked furiously, 'You both care about me? It's behind time.' His sight caught the girl. 'Who's she and why's she wearing a costume?'

'Two soldiers were after her. She's scared and hurt,' told Kanak.

'Why were they chasing her, and how was she hurt?'

'We don't know, but...' Prithvi ran his eyes over the trees around. 'Yes, come on.' He gestured towards a tree at a distance. 'We've to bring some neem leaves.'

Aavishkar didn't get his answers, but he went along with him.

Having applied the paste of neem leaves Prithvi and Aavishkar had brought on the girl's wound, Kanak said, 'I need something to bandage it.' She and the girl were seated on the ground, Prithvi and Aavishkar standing closely.

Prithvi said, 'Avi, you always keep a hankie with you?'

Aavishkar placed his hand on the back pocket. 'I won't give it. This is my favourite.'

'Aavishkar, she needs it,' Kanak tried to coax him, 'you never want anyone to be in pain, do you?'

'Fine.' Aavishkar took a hickory handkerchief out of his pocket and begrudged it.

Kanak tied it over the neem paste on the girl's arm.

'Now you'll be fine. Neem is a very good antiseptic.' Prithvi's cheeks were wide spread.

The girl didn't react. Her eyes conveyed a profound sadness.

Kanak asked, 'You're alright?'

'I shouldn't have escaped the dungeons... I shoul...' The girl was at low ebb, her eyes moist.

'Why are you in tears? Keep quiet,' Aavishkar tried to pacify her.

'Calm down,' said Kanak. 'Why were you in a dungeon?'

'And why do you think you did wrong by breaking away?' asked Prithvi.

The girl grizzled. 'Because now that varlet General will oppress my parents.'

Aavishkar asked, 'General? What bad blood is between any General and your parents?'

'If you tell us your whole matter, we can help you,' said Kanak.

The girl wiped her tears. 'Really?'

Prithvi spoke, '*Absolutely*. So why don't you share?'

The girl stood up. 'My father is a farmer. Last year, there was a drought in Shivnagar, the capital city of my realm Mahendragarh. He needed seeds for cultivation, and for seeds, he needed money.'

She breathed deeply.

'What did he do then?' asked Aavishkar.

'He betook himself to our monarch Karnaveer who asked his General Bhanuday to give some money from the exchequer as debt to my father. It facilitated my father's job, but crops weren't even reaped that General's soldiers came to collect the tax. My father made them aware of the situation, but that General's devilry...' she began sobbing narrating her anguish, 'when he came to know about my father, got furious and ordered him to return the whole amount with interest. My father refused and wished to go to our monarch for railing against him. Bhanuday didn't ready to accept my father's rebel. He locked me in a dungeon to stop him. My father couldn't do anything. He loves me so much...' Her tears ran amok.

Kanak said angrily, 'This is a raw deal. *That swindler, imposter* General...' She looked up at Prithvi. 'We must do something for this girl. We can't leave her in the lurch.'

'What about Samrat and Kabeer?'

Kanak said, 'We'll surely find them, Avi, but we should help her too.'

'It's late. As the dawn breaks, we'll go to Shivnagar. You don't need to worry. Your parents won't have a single problem. *I promise*,' said a determined Prithvi.

'You definitely don't need to worry now. You've got *Prithvi Promise*,' beamed Aavishkar.

***

As Prayas accompanied by Samriddhi walked out of Devraj's office in Vyom Mandal, encountered Lieutenant Tushar Kesarwani. He asked, 'Where had you been?'

'Sir, I...I... went to meet someone,' hesitated Tushar.

'Who's in the institute you needed to meet?'

Samriddhi's question paled Tushar's face. 'Ma'am...ma'am... Siddiqui sir called me. He wanted to ask about the assault on Mandakini,' he replied. 'May I go now?'

Prayas permitted him to leave. Then he asked Samriddhi, 'How did you know that?'

'He didn't receive my calls, then I tried to locate his wrist belt and got the coordinates of the institute,' told Samriddhi. 'Above all, he lied to us. How could he meet Siddiqui sir? He's gone to Sangrah to meet Dr Barua.'

'We'll have to get the truth then,' said Prayas, exchanging a determined look with Samriddhi.

***

Kabeer was lying on the floor, staring at the ceiling. He said to Samrat who was peeping out, 'Can I ask something? I've been think...'

'It isn't time of questions but to worry about Prithvi and Kanak,' hissed Samrat. 'But how can I blame *you*? This is Avi's company what dented you. *Childhood friends.*'

'Just listen to me,' said Kabeer, sitting. 'When we fled with DTM, all would've learnt about it because Subramanian sir had seen us. According to Prithvi's letter, it seemed no one knew that they'd come here. *How's this possible?* I meant no one told us about them. Not even Kavya and Abhyuday. Except...'

'Except Dhairya,' completed Samrat.

'Exactly. Were we misled or Mr Chancellor knew about all this and made it covert?' supposed Kabeer.

'No. Mr Chancellor would never send them alone,' said Samrat. 'And the Royal Weapon is not any *run-of-the-mill* instrument, I guess. If Mr Chancellor wants to search it, he'll employ someone more efficient, not the students. It'd be Prithvi's decision to try to find it.'

As Samrat finished, a warder with two assistants made an appearance. 'Boys, your dinner.'

One of the assistants slid two plates in, each having one dry chapatti and a piece of onion.

Samrat grimaced. 'Do you also have it?'

'Stop your baloney. You'll be getting nothing instead,' said the warder, his face contorted in rage. 'You're lucky that tomorrow is our prince's coronation. Before it, General wouldn't like to do anything worse with you.' He gawped at both of them from head to bottom. 'And your outlandish clothes are not allowed here. General doesn't want you to come before people in *this* condition.'

The other assistant threw some pieces of clothing to them.

'Put them on if you don't want to be chastised *severely*,' said the warder and stormed away, followed by his assistants.

'What do they think of us? *Aliens?*' said Kabeer, irked.

Samrat said, briefly looking at the warder, 'Who's this *General*? I think these people obey *him* more than their king.'

***

Chapter 10
A Girl in Twinkle Apparel

Kanak slowly opened her eyes. Breathing in the fresh morning air, she sat up glancing over Prithvi and Aavishkar. They were asleep on the grass floor as she had. The sun had risen with its soft-orange light, gradually disseminating over the entire jungle. The birds were up chattering away. The pleasing cool breeze brought a calm smile to her face, which suddenly vanished. She watched around her, perturbed. 'Get up, Prithvi,' she cried, yanking Prithvi's arm.

Rubbing his eyes, Prithvi woke up. 'What happened? Why do you always yell?'

Aavishkar too woke up, yawning.

'Come out of your awful dreams, Prithvi,' said Kanak, rising. '*The girl has disappeared.*'

A very much awake Prithvi let out a gasp of shock, '*What?!*'

'Let's go. We have to find her. Take the bag, Aavishkar.' Kanak sped away.

'Those soldiers mightn't have caught her,' said Prithvi, running behind her, followed by Aavishkar.

'This girl's been plaguing me. First, she took my favourite hankie and now this. I barely got any sleep.' Aavishkar was off mood.

Kanak turned back, refusing to pay attention to his rising rage. 'If you walk with this speed, Aavishkar, *2018* will come.'

Aavishkar had to step up his pace.

They looked for the girl far and near for ten minutes. At once, she appeared standing, joining her hands in the center of a small clearing. Three of them breathed long.

When the girl saw them, she smiled sweetly. 'You all came *here*. I was just doing *Surya Namaskar*. Lord Surya wasn't visible there clearly in view of shrubs and trees.'

'You're doing your Surya Namaskar, and we couldn't sleep because of you,' Aavishkar flushed angrily, heading towards her.

The girl stepped back, befuddled and panicked.

Prithvi attempted to placate him, 'She was just praying, Avi.'

Kanak hid her tiredness behind her smile. 'If you wanted to go somewhere, should've told us.'

'You… you were asleep. I thought not…not to disturb you,' the girl faltered.

Prithvi placed his hand on her shoulder. 'It's alright. Let's go now.'

The engaging smile returned to her lovely face.

***

'Jay, Samarth hasn't sent DTM back yet. What does it mean?' said Damini.

'We've been trying to figure it out. You don't need to worry about the children. Samarth is with them.'

Jaywardhan's cabin fell in a fraught silence for a while.

'Ali's death weighed heavy on my soul, Damini. I couldn't do anything for him,' said Jaywardhan, his face wearing a thousand sorrows.

'Why are you talking like this? You're not responsible for his death, but whoever is, we'll certainly punish that person.' Damini's frowned eyebrows settled. 'And I think we got something. I'm not sure, but we should look into it. *Someone lied to me, Jay.*'

***

After leaving the jungle behind, Prithvi, Kanak, Aavishkar and the girl turned east following an unpaved road to Shivnagar. The north-western boundary of Shivnagar was terminated by the same ridge of red mountains Prithvi and Kanak had noticed. The same sparkling river meandering gently through the meadow caressed the land, gliding along the foot of the mountains and then vanished into the same jungle they'd exited.

Kanak asked the girl, 'How did you escape that prison, and why did you come *here*? You could've gone your home.'

'In the dungeon, I pretended to be fainted. A warder came to see me. On getting opportunity, I bit his hand and got away.'

'My God! This girl is a *maniac*,' Aavishkar whispered in awe.

The girl continued, 'I knew one of the secret underground tunnels of Shivnagar. I tried to elude the soldiers by sneaking through it, but they followed me. I didn't get where to go. I was just throwing them off and luckily reached here.'

Kanak seemed impressed. 'You gave the slip to those soldiers by getting into this forest. *Brilliant*.'

'I do not merit this compliment but thank you,' said the girl courteously.

Prithvi asked, 'What's your name, dear?'

'*Sitara*,' she told.

Aavishkar mumbled, 'That's why she's wearing this lahenga with so many stars.'

'May I know your good name?' asked Sitara.

'We're five, by the way.' Prithvi introduced, 'I'm Prithvi, she's Kanak, and he's Aavishkar.'

Sitara asked, lifting her index finger to Aavishkar, 'What's it? Resting on Aavishkar bhaiya's nose?'

'These are glasses... used to correct... defective eyesight,' Kanak tried to explain.

Sitara looked at three of them attentively. 'Have you disguised yourselves? I meant your clothes are very much different than ours.'

'Yes.' Kanak's face broke into a nervous smile. 'We've come here to find our two friends.'

Sitara's expression conveyed dissatisfaction and confusion.

Prithvi said, 'We...we are... princes, and Kanak's princess. We don't want anyone to recognize us otherwise they'll complain to our parents. Then we won't be able to find our friends.'

Kanak and Aavishkar marvelled at his reply.

'You all are gallant I believe. You don't need anyone else.' A sweet smile was back on Sitara's face. 'You told that you are five. Your lost friends wear clothes like you? I remember when I was in the dungeon, soldiers were locking two boys clothed like you.'

Kanak said buoyantly, 'Samrat and Kabeer?'

Prithvi asked Sitara, 'Could you tell us where that dungeon is?'

'Absolutely, but today your friends may not be there,' conjectured Sitara.

'Why?' asked Aavishkar instantly.

'Our prince's coronation will be celebrating today. It's a tradition of Shivnagar that in any great carnival, fights between slaves are organized in the stadium which is to the right of the palace. Your friends will be brought there only.'

Kanak asked, panic-stricken, 'What fight?'

'It's General Bhanuday's way to punish slaves. His warriors beat them while people think it a gala. He'd done the same thing with my uncle. He was innocent, even then... ' told an agonized Sitara.

Kanak patted her hands, her eyes filled with commiseration.

'This is your Shivnagar, Sitara?' asked Aavishkar in complete awe.

Staring them in the face was the beautiful fortified city, *Shivnagar,* protected by the city walls, supplemented with towers, which could only be crossed by an elephantine metallic city gate.

'We've to reach the stadium flat out. They can force Samrat and Kabeer to fight,' said Prithvi worriedly. 'Let's go in.'

'What are you doing, bhaiya? If you go there in this raiment, you'll be caught. I understand you, but those soldiers will not,' elucidated Sitara.

'We'd forgotten about it,' said Kanak. 'We'll have to change our clothes.'

'This girl is very intelligent,' said Aavishkar. First time Sitara noticed an admiring smile for her on his face. 'But where will we get the royal garbs from?'

Sitara said, 'You'll have to reach the royal wardrobe I guess. Since the function's being celebrated, the city gate will remain opened for guests.'

Aavishkar asked, 'And where will that wardrobe be in the palace?'

'I'm sorry. I don't know this,' answered Sitara.

'It's okay.' Kanak smiled gratefully. 'Thank you for your help.'

'We'll have to rescue our friends. Then that despot and Bhanuday...'

'No, Prithvi bhaiya. Our monarch Karnaveer is very gracious, but that General is the root of all problems. Monarch relies on him hence we suffer. No one can protest him,' said an upset Sitara.

Prithvi put his hand on her shoulder and pressed it gently. 'But today, it won't be the same. We'll meet our friends because of you. It's the least we can do for you.'

'If you weren't with us, we would've done nothing,' affirmed Kanak.

Prithvi spoke, 'Sitara, since you're in your regular clothes, you may go in easily. So, bring your parents and the people, victims of Bhanuday's atrocities *but* verily believe in their king, to the stadium. Okay?' Prithvi had devised a scheme. 'Now, go.'

Sitara nodded vigorously and then raced to the city gate.

***

'How long will your team take to finish the construction of *Yatra* series of time machines?' asked Jaywardhan. It was late in the morning. He was walking with Kushal on the field just outside the staff canteen in *Samrachana*.

'We've completed level six, dad. Only level seven is left,' told Kushal. 'After that we'll send them for trial...'

'We don't have time for that,' Jaywardhan interrupted him. 'We can't wait for DTM anymore. Prepare those five time machines as soon as possible.'

'I'll give my best,' said Kushal, his eyes mirrored his cast iron determination. 'Samarth might be in any trouble otherwise he would've surely sent DTM.'

'I think so,' said Jaywardhan. 'I've asked Arunima to try to get access to Aavriti. Where *it* is, Samarth and DTM will be there.' He stopped and turned to Kushal. '*One more important thing*. We're transferring *Yatra* time machines from *Revati* lab to Vyom Mandal's *Megh* labs. You and your team will be staying there only. Devraj will take care of everything. You'll leave by tomorrow afternoon.'

***

Prithvi, Kanak and Aavishkar reached at a distance of twenty-five feet from the city gate of Shivnagar.

Prithvi asked both of them to be on their alert, 'We have to move very carefully.'

Aavishkar indicated to one of the bullock carts stood outside the gate. 'Why is a large container on that bullock cart?'

A light bulb just went on in Prithvi's brain. He said, gesturing to that cylindrical wooden container. 'Just tell me, Avi. Will we fit inside it?'

Kanak's eyes widened as the brilliance of the idea struck her. 'You meant by sitting into it...'

'It's about five feet high, four feet in diameter. Maximum four people can fit.' Aavishkar quibbled, 'But I'm not going in.'

Kanak ignored Aavishkar's complaint and suggested, 'We've to do our work before its cartman comes.'

The cartman was taking permission from one of the city guards to get his vehicle in.

'Let's start.' Prithvi made for the bullock cart, followed by Kanak and Aavishkar, steering clear of any attention. He climbed over it vigilantly and opened the lid of the vessel. 'It's filled with some kind of oil.'

'Pour it down,' said Kanak, mounting on the cart. 'Aavishkar, you hold it, staying down.'

Both of them together tipped the vessel down, making the oil flowing out.

Aavishkar kept his eyes at the cart man. 'We must hasten.'

No sooner did the container get emptied than they began to move into one by one.

'He's coming. *Hurry up*, Aavishkar,' said Kanak.

They nestled inside the vessel and fitted its casing over it before the cartman reached there.

Aavishkar grouched, closing his nostrils, 'How weird this reek is? Was it compulsory to sit in this *odoriferous drum*?'

Prithvi hushed him, 'Lower your volume. If someone hears you, you'll be turned into *odoriferous*.'

The cart had entered Shivnagar. It passed piazzas, gardens, well-protected houses, entertainment centers, and ultimately arrived at the palace, a beautiful building made up of pure-white, yellow and blue-grey marbles.

***

'Kabeer and Samrat are still in the past. I don't know why Mr Chancellor sent Prithvi, Kanak and Avi there?' said Kavya, playing tennis with Abhyuday on the tennis court of *Maharana Pratap Sports Club* in Sanrachana.

'We even don't know whether they will be back or not,' said a worried Jessica, sitting on the first tier of seating.

Paridhi, next to Jessica, gave her a punch on the arm. 'Please, Jessy. Prithvi is there.'

Abhyuday and Kavya stopped playing to catch their breaths.

Paridhi asked, 'Kavya, you or Abhyuday got anything?'

Before Kavya could react, Abhyuday replied, 'Not yet. But we're trying our best.'

Paridhi had an admiring grin on her face. 'I know, Abhyuday. You will definitely find something.'

Abhyuday blushed at the unexpected compliment.

Kavya stared at Abhyuday with a forced smile. '*Absolutely.*'

***

Four servants brought the vessel to a storeroom of the palace. One of them said, panting, 'It's very heavy. What's inside it?'

'Vegetable oil for dinner,' answered the other one. 'Let's go. We have boxes of fruits to bring here.' He left, followed by the others.

Kanak slowly opened the lid of the container and peeped out. 'All clear.'

'Dear God, if you wanted to keep me inside it, I should've got cold,' carped Aavishkar, coming out, followed by Kanak and Prithvi.

'Seal your lips, Avi, like your nose,' said Prithvi.

'Here's the passage.' Kanak walked out.

Three of them searched for the wardrobe, avoiding the guards cautiously.

Mesmerized, Prithvi stared at the utter elegance and resplendence of the architecture, passing a corridor. 'This palace is really stupendous. A prince's life is very comfortable. No work, only rest.'

'Why don't you stay here? We four will return, fine?' grinned Kanak.

'You won't stay with me? Who'll be my bodyguard then? And if you don't like this offer, you can be a princess.'

Kanak glared at Prithvi. 'I do not want to be *your* princess, *prince Prithviraj.*'

'*My princess*! I didn't mean that.' Prithvi appeared tickled. 'But I appreciate your choice.'

'It isn't time for scuffle, friends.' Aavishkar turned back. 'Someone is coming.'

They immediately hid behind the long curtains hanging along the walls. Two maids carrying some clothes were passing through the passageway.

'You know, these taffetas are for our prince. A present by the king of Sakhipur,' one of them told, holding some packets.

Prithvi peeked from behind the curtains. 'We should go after them.'

They chased them, laying low. The maids walked into a room in the end of the corridor. After a minute, they came out without the packets and went away. Three of them silently entered the room.

'Not a few dresses are here. What should I wear?' A confused Prithvi glanced over the storage of clothes.

'You'd said you're a prince. So, dress up like a prince,' tittered Kanak, culling costumes for her. 'Get dressed fast, Aavishkar. You'll wait for Sitara outside the stadium and lead our back-up plan.'

***

Chapter 11

The Rescue Mission

In the oval stadium of Shivnagar, the public in stands around the ground were acclaiming the king, the queen and the prince. Their shouts rent the sky. The king sitting in the central, well-decorated and protected stand, accompanied by his family, greeted the guests.

The central arena had been prepared for the fight. The guards brought the slaves in chains through internal corridors, which connected the stadium directly to the dungeons. Both Samrat and Kabeer were dressed in light blue short kurtas, maroon pajamas, white belts-*cummerbund* and mustard-yellow sleeveless vest jackets.

Samrat looked beyond the guards towards the crowd. 'It looks like a stadium.'

'In ancient times, people used to gather here to watch athletic contests, dramatic events or fights…,' a thought struck Kabeer. A sudden jolt of fear went through his nerves. 'They can't do this to us. We're not fighters.'

'So, what are you? *Spies*?' The chief guard of the troop who had brought Samrat and Kabeer to the dungeons stood behind them. 'Our General hates frauds. You deserve a punishment.'

'What's your name?'

Samrat's words snatched his grin. He edged closer to him, barely suppressed his anger. 'What does it matter to you, boy?'

'You want us to fight. Fine. I like to fight against you. I should know the name of the loser.'

Hardly had Samrat finished when his face suffered a severe blow. His mouth bled.

'SAMRAT,' cried Kabeer, holding him with his chained hands.

'Send him first,' the chief snarled.

A guard next to him responded, 'Yes, chief.'

The chief threw an incandescent gaze at Samrat and headed for the central stand.

***

Prithvi, worn a cherry-red embroidered long coat, a white chudidar pajama and a royal blue belt, and Kanak, dressed in a peach long straight cut kurta, a violet chudidar pajama and a lime-green full sleeves jacket below the knees, were descending the stairs to reach the lower zone of the stadium.

'Samrat and Kabeer should be here,' said Prithvi, weaving through the crowd, craning to see the field.

Kanak, lost and nonplussed, continued to stare at the field and multitudes. Her ears resounded with a girl's voice, *'What happened, Yagya? Are you ready to lose? If I win, you have to give me whatever I want.'*

'Kanak...Kanak...' called Prithvi, intruding into her thoughts. 'You're okay?'

'Yes...' Kanak looked up at him. A word reverberated through her mind, *'Yagya...?'*

***

'You all please be seated. I am highly obliged that you graced this occasion by your presence,' said Karnaveer loudly, rising. He gestured to a man in his early twenties, sitting adjacent to him. 'I hope you shower your blessings upon my son, Sarang, which will help him to fulfil his responsibility judiciously.'

An average sized but brawny man next to Sarang stood, his voice powerful and lucid, 'I, the chief of the armed forces of Mahendragarh, General Bhanuday on behalf of our monarch, Karnaveer, give permission to inaugurate today's ceremony with the grand fight.'

'Where are they?' Kanak's worried face lit up as she saw a guard bringing an unchained Samrat to the arena. 'There he is.'

'Hold my hand,' said Prithvi, cautious. 'This place is dangerous.'

'As you say.' Kanak firmly grasped his left hand.

'I'd never heard these three words from you,' said Prithvi playfully and raced down to the last tier of seats.

'Where are you going?' asked a guard stood near the boundary, stretching out his right hand.

Prithvi said politely, 'He's our friend, not a fighter. We need to meet the king.'

'You're with him?' The guard called his associates, 'Arrest them. They're spies.'

A wide-eyed Kanak said, 'What! No, we're not spies. We are...'

Four guards rushed to besiege them.

Prithvi continued in a firm but respectful tone, 'Please, listen to us.'

Two guards moved to chain them, refusing to pay attention to his words.

'I really did not want to do this.' Prithvi gathered himself to make a move. 'NOW.'

Playing his cards well, he grabbed a guard's right hand holding a long chain, wrenched it around his neck and sent him falling on the field.

Kanak threw a series of aggressive jabs at the other guard. The rest three guards drew their sword instantly.

This conflict attracted many eyes to them including Samrat, Kabeer, Karnaveer and Bhanuday's. Samrat's eyes widened in surprised ecstasy. Kabeer's pale face blossomed. He stepped but was pulled back by a guard.

The guard bringing Samrat hurried away to help his fellows. Samrat caught his neck from the back, twisted it with enough force, sending him to the ground and sprinted to Prithvi and Kanak, facing the guards.

'What're you two doing *here*?' asked Samrat, standing back to back to both of them in a defensive position.

An astounded Prithvi asked, 'You *killed* him?'

Samrat bristled at his reaction. 'You care him more than me? For your information, he's only blacked out.'

'Who are they?' ranted Bhanuday. 'CAPTURE THEM.'

Four more guards charged at them with their weapons, including the chief.

Kanak said to her opponent, 'We're not your enemies. Leave us.'

He wasn't ready to believe her. He got dangerously close to her, swinging his sword. She dodged and gripped his hand behind his back, twisted it to make it swordless.

Prithvi's rival attacked him, swinging wildly. He stepped back, avoiding the strike. He deftly went behind him, clubbed him on the back of the head and knocked him unconscious.

Samrat was engaged with the chief. 'Your bravery allows you to fight an unarmed boy?'

The chief glared at him, releasing his sword. Samrat gave a half-smile and prepared his defense. The chief's fist aimed Samrat's chest, but he managed to dodge and catch it with his right hand. Samrat kneed him in the stomach and punched him in the face. 'That's for ruining my attractive face,' he said.

'They're not being controlled by our guards, Bhanudaya!' said Karnaveer, surprised. '*Call the army.*'

Bhanudaya nodded. A soldier behind him ran down with his message. Within a minute, fifty soldiers armed with sword and shield marched into the stadium. It took them a moment to besiege Samrat, Kanak and Prithvi, forming three concentric circles around them.

'We've not come here to battle against anyone,' said Prithvi, raising his hands in surrender.

'Why have you come then?' a composed voice spoke from beyond the multi-tier defensive formation. 'I'm eager to hear the reason.'

The soldiers stepped aside, leaving their position to reveal the king, Karnaveer. Accompanying him were Bhanudaya and Sarang.

Kabeer shouted, 'They're here for us.'

'Your majesty, both of them are our friends, not combatants. They've been forced to fight here,' said Prithvi, responsive, bringing Karnaveer's attention to him.

Bhanuday hissed in wrath like an angry snake, 'What is this balderdash? Who are you?'

'We belong to the royal family of *Vyom nagar*, a dominion in the east of Mahendragarh,' Prithvi cooked up.

Samrat and Kanak exchanged floundered looks.

Bhanuday impugned his words. 'Why do we believe you?'

'Do you have a single reason not doing so, *General*?' said Prithvi with an intriguing smile.

Sarang spoke, 'We should at least hear them out, General Bhanudaya.'

Karnaveer nodded to Prithvi to continue, leaving Bhanudaya to seethe.

Prithvi said, 'We'd come to Shivnagar's forest for hunting, but unfortunately both of them got separated,' he gestured to Samrat and Kabeer, 'and reached your capital. We request you to release them.'

'*What a fantasy*!' thought a mentally glad Kanak. She put her side. 'Your majesty, our friends are innocent. Your General's mistaken them for spies, and they're being punished like this.'

Karnaveer seemed a little doubtful. 'What is this, Bhanudaya?'

'They're lying, your majesty. They're shams. Since they've been caught so are making stories.' Bhanudaya snarled in mock anger, '*Cowards*.'

'Truth spawns courage, General, and I can see courage in their eyes,' said Sarang discordantly. 'Cowards don't fight the way they did for their friends.'

'And this fight is not only to save *them*, your Highness,' said Prithvi with conviction, pulling back his shoulders. 'This fight is for justice.' He turned right and ran his eyes across the crowd to see Sitara and Aavishkar standing among the people in a stand. He nodded them briefly.

Aavishkar and Sitara came down to the ground, followed by a group of people including her father. Aavishkar wore a lavender chudidar pajama and an off-white embroidered long coat with a maroon belt.

Kanak told, 'This is Sitara, a girl from your kingdom, your majesty.'

Samrat and Kabeer were shocked to see Aavishkar, but they didn't say anything.

Bhanudaya's face lost its colour rapidly. 'We're celebrating our Prince's coronation,' he said, horrified. 'This is not a place for…'

Karnaveer cut in, 'What do you want to say, Sitara?'

Bhanudaya looked appalled. He groaned but inwardly.

Sitara valiantly revealed all the atrocities' Bhanuday had committed with her family. Her bravery won over the people. They stood for her. Bhanuday's brutal and dastardly acts were made known to everyone.

'Your majesty, we are so sorry. We couldn't protest because of this vile General, but my Sitara stood against him,' said Sitara's father, his eyes shining with pride.

'You are accusing *me*?' said Bhanuday, a belligerent tone in his voice. 'And your daughter, she…'

He couldn't finish as Sarang punched him in the face. 'Not a single word, Bhanudaya,' he said, incensed and turned to Karnaveer. 'I'd requested you father not to lean on him more than a limit.'

'Yes. You already had a qualm about his actions, but I didn't give any attention,' Karnaveer's expression conveyed his rue. 'Today, I don't need any evidence. My people have given me the proof of his and his men's crimes.'

'Your majesty, I did nothing. These people are framing me. I know they're with these tricksters.' Bhanudaya, aghast, glared at Prithvi, Kanak and Samrat.

Karnaveer turned away from him in anger. 'I never expected you to stoop to such levels, General.' He called his reliable guards to incarcerate Bhanuday and his faithful companions.

A wicked Bhanuday fell at his feet, acclaiming himself loyal and true. He begged for his life, but he was granted only life imprisonment.

Karnaveer commanded the guards to release Kabeer. 'We will be highly grateful to all of you. Our people will live peacefully now because of you.' Two guards brought two swords, a dagger, a bow and a quiver full of arrows, a crossbow with quarrels and five shields at his behest. 'These will be the best accolades for you all, won't they?'

Prithvi said, 'We didn't do it for any...'

'Kindly accept them as the gifts from Mahendragarh,' insisted Sarang.

Five of them appreciatively received the presents.

Karnaveer approached Sitara. '*You* are exceedingly brave, my daughter. Mahendragarh is proud of you.'

Kanak said, 'It's time for us to leave, your majesty. Our family is awaiting us.'

'You will come to meet me, won't you?' asked a lugubrious Sitara.

'We really don't know but don't wait for us.'

Prithvi's reply was enough to bring tears to her eyes. She bent her head down.

Prithvi sat on his knees, held her chin and raised her head. 'Look Sitara, we're from a different world. It's hard to explain. You just take care of yourself and keep smiling always,' he said with an encouraging smile, looking into her dark eyes.

Sitara hugged him tight. 'People like you who help others selflessly are rare in this world. I wish I could always be with you.'

'People you love always stay within you, *deep inside*.' Prithvi wiped her tears, his eyes showing a hint of dampness.

'Aavishkar bhaiya, I will not give you back your hankie,' said Sitara. 'I want a souvenir.'

Aavishkar had to fight so hard to keep back his tears. Prithvi and his friends bid farewell to all of them with a heavy heart, gave a tender look at Sitara and left. Sitara kept looking at them until they melted into the crowd, vanishing from her sight.

***

'I'll miss Sitara. I scolded her uselessly.' Aavishkar was still emotional, returning to the jungle, accompanied by four of them.

Samrat asked, 'What are *you* doing here, Avi?'

Prithvi replied, 'He came with us to find both of you.'

'But you two had come here first, and we followed you,' said Kabeer astonishingly.

'Whatever you were told about us wasn't true. Dhairya lied to you, and that letter wasn't written by Prithvi.' Kanak told them everything. About the ambush. About Samarth.

Samrat was in daze. 'Why did Dhairya do it to us?'

'He's *Shaurya's* brother. And why Shaurya did it, no need to tell,' said Kanak. 'The entire matter will be in light after asking Dhairya only.'

'Where did you get these costumes from, anyway?' Samrat noticed Kanak from head to toe. Kanak stared gravely at him. 'I meant… you're looking very…very…beautiful,' he faltered.

Prithvi chuckled. 'Why do you hesitate, Samrat? Say it what you want.' He ignored Kanak's eyes roll. 'Okay, I do it for you. *Prithvi and Avi look like princes, Kanak. Why did you not wear a lahenga or sari?'* He modulated his voice, deadpan. 'Good question, Samrat, and luckily I know its answer,' he continued, amusement twinkled in his eyes, 'I've heard that princesses are very delicate what Kanak is not. Princess like dresses won't suit her. She's looking very nice in her costumes, and it'll be easy for her to fight in them what she is, *fighter plane.'*

'I did not want to be dolled up like those exquisite princesses, Mr Malhotra,' Kanak talked up. 'I didn't have time in the wardrobe to ornament myself like *you*.'

'I'm famished, friends. Last night, Samrat didn't let me take dinner. I think I'll get along with these mellow fruits because of which we could survive one day.' Kabeer looked around, searching for a source to satisfy his hunger.

They have entered the jungle.

'We're also quite peckish, don't we, Kanak?' smiled Prithvi tenderly.

Kanak said, disgruntled, 'Stop talking to me, Mr Malhotra.'

'This is one of the things Prithvi cannot do,' said Aavishkar, going after Kabeer.

Samrat and Kabeer burst out laughing. Kanak averted her eyes in embarrassment to find Prithvi grinning playfully.

***

Shaurya, Urvashi, Pravesh and Alexander were sitting in a nearly vacant grandstand at the race course in Eklavya Sports Club. Some students of Vasundhara and Mangal group sat at the back, resting and disporting themselves.

'You're now peerless in sports car racing,' carolled Alexander. 'You've been practising so hard.'

'I want to be ready next time.' Shaurya's eyes firmed his intention.

'Shaurya, I like your *lucky coin*. You always wear it, don't you?' asked Urvashi.

'It's a gift from my mother.' Shaurya wore a silver chain having a golden pendant shaped like a coin. 'She thinks it's been protecting me since I was a baby, keeping me safe and sound.'

'Will they be safe and sound? Why have they not come back yet?'

'You're worried about them, Alex?' Pravesh, right behind him, was mixed up.

'Of course, and we all should. We did never want to throw them into this trouble. Did we?' Urvashi looked at Shaurya with hope.

Shaurya said, rotating the golden coin by his fingers, 'Kanak challenged me in the sport I don't like. Was it a fair game?'

'And what Saif and Lara did to Abhyuday and Kabeer, was that fair?'

Shaurya sharply turned to Urvashi, his solemn gaze roved over her face, and then he looked away.

Urvashi saw a conflict of emotions in his eyes. 'You always knew this, even then you sided with Saif and Lara. I understand they're our friends, but it doesn't mean that we hate…'

Shaurya stood up, speaking impulsively, 'Hate is a big and heavy word, Urvashi. I just wanted a payback as already said.'

***

'You have inkling on it?' asked Zaheer, brooding.

'Something is there constraining me to think about it. Damini's very angry as well as upset,' said Jaywardhan. 'Zaheer, scan that photograph through supercomputers for the duration of twenty years. If it's related to Vikrant, we must not be late.'

'Your doubt never went wrong, Jay.'

'I wish this time it'd go wrong. In my point of view, it'd be Vyom's great loss.' Jaywardhan seemed thoughtful.

***

'What are you doing?' Kanak saw Aavishkar looking up, standing on his tip-toe under a tree, a dagger in his hand.

Aavishkar gestured her towards a bunch of lychees. 'Trying to get them. The branches are high so I thought I should use the dagger king Karnaveer had given us. Samrat's plucked some of them using his bow-arrow.'

Samrat said, approaching her, 'Let him try, Kanak. He should learn how to use a dagger.'

'Anyway, how will we go back?' asked Kanak. 'DTM is not here.'

'We cannot go back now,' said Samrat thoughtfully.

Aavishkar discontinued his task. 'Then when?'

'After getting the Royal Weapon.' Samrat spelt out Damini's conversation with Zaheer.

'*Painting?* Was ma'am telling about the same painting which is in Mr Chancellor's cabin?' asked Aavishkar.

'What are you all discussing? We hadn't come here to find any Royal Weapon or Ananyaakashganga. We came here for Samrat and Kabeer, and now we have to return,' said Kanak.

Prithvi didn't see eye to eye with her. 'Don't you get it? If Vikrant finds the Royal Weapon, everything will be in danger.'

'I too want to protect Vyom, but searching the Royal Weapon is S.T.F.'s job, not ours. If it's so important, it can't be reached easily. Anyone may get hurt. Mr Chancellor will be waiting for us. We should worry about *him*.' Kanak tried to reason with Prithvi.

Kabeer asserted, 'If you're in Vyom, nothing is easy. And our first duty is to protect *it*.'

'As far as the difficulties are concerned, we together can face any problem, I firmly believe.' Samrat looked at her expectantly.

'I understand, but...'

Prithvi snapped, 'No another *but,* Kanak. If you don't want to come with us, fine. We can move without you.'

'Prithvi, what...'

'I'm talking to *her*,' an exasperated Prithvi interrupted Samrat. 'You want to go back, I won't stop you, but right now we don't have any way to send you back. So until we return, you and Avi go to Sitara,' he talked breathlessly, and Kanak listened, unblinking.

Prithvi continued, looking away, 'Let's go. We can't await anyone.'

Kabeer whispered to him, 'Think again. She's brilliant. We cannot...'

Prithvi gave him a look. 'You're coming with me or what?' After a few steps, he stopped and turned around. 'I know you don't like to work with me, but I always felt one thing, Kanak that for our country, our Vyom, we together could face any problem. *You proved me wrong.*' Then he walked away.

'Take care of her,' Samrat said to Aavishkar and went after Prithvi and Kabeer.

Kanak looked up at them, leaving. She couldn't fathom why she held off her decision.

Aavishkar spoke, 'I always agree with you, Kanak, but today something is going wrong, and you know it in your heart.'

Kanak was in a fix. '*I couldn't do anything for my country, but you all can.*' '*I'm happy to know that you care of your institute and friends.*' '*Vikrant is our enemy, and evidently if he gets it, most of the things we know may be ceased.*' '*I know you don't like to work with me, but I always felt one thing, Kanak that for our country, our Vyom, we together could face any problem. You proved me wrong.'* Samarth, Jaywardhan and Prithvi's words ran through her mind.

***

In Kshitij hall, Jaywardhan held a meeting to order. Zaheer, Damini, Sagar, Prayas, Samriddhi, Arunima, Siddhant and Devraj were called.

Samriddhi initiated, 'The person who planned the ambush on Mandakini and stole Manasvi-55 is someone we did never expect.' She communicated through his wrist belt, 'Bring him in.'

After a second, two commandos brought a handcuffed Tushar with bruised face in.

Prayas said, 'Shall we begin, Lieutenant Kesarwani?'

'I helped one of the scientists of the technical department to ambush Mandakini,' told Tushar in a feeble voice, looking down.

'Ali had taken a photograph of the exit of the research centre Vikrant is working a day before he was killed,' told Siddhant, gesturing to an LED screen on the right wall. As he turned it on, a picture flashed showing a woman leaving a multi-storey building. 'Do you recognize yourself, Arunima? Pardon me, *Anushka Kapoor*? This is your real name, isn't it?'

Arunima erupted, 'What are you talking, Siddhant? Have you…'

'He's telling how you broke our faith, murdered our love,' Damini's words boomed across the hall.

Arunima tried to stand, but Prayas and Samriddhi pointed their gun at her.

'Sit tight,' said Sagar in a strop.

Arunima put her side, 'What's wrong with you all? You're accusing *me*?'

'Yes, we're accusing Vikrant Kapoor's daughter.' Devraj didn't give Arunima a single chance to find any excuse. 'You did your job skillfully but couldn't whitewash your every mistake. You trusted a weak man like your stalwart companion, Lieutenant Tushar Kesarwani. I hope you didn't forget him.'

Arunima looked up at Tushar with an odd mixture of fear and anger.

Damini picked holes in her plan. 'You asked me to go to Delhi but you went to Mumbai. What did you think we'd never get it?' She pointed to the LED screen. 'This picture was taken when you'd gone to Delhi, I meant *Mumbai,* to meet your father.'

Arunima's face turned pale.

'Vyom's spies are all around the globe, Anushka.' Siddhant seemed to be on the warpath. 'Vikrant did not kill Ali, *you* did. *You* told Vikrant about him, didn't you?'

'What happened? You really can't recognize yourself in this picture?' Zaheer rose from his chair. 'Then how could you do the same when you were a small girl?' He swiped the LED screen to display the next image.

Arunima was too thunderstruck to reply as she saw an eight-year old girl cuddled by Vikrant.

'This is a scanned copy of a photograph I have,' said Jaywardhan finally. 'We've come to know through supercomputers how this girl looks like after twenty years.' He turned to Arunima. 'I won't ask why you did it. I just want to know what next. If you don't want to suffer, just call a spade a spade or you'll be treated as Vyom's every culprit is.'

***

Chapter 12
The Sun amid a River

'Where are we going? Prithvi asked us to go to Shivnagar,' said Aavishkar, running behind Kanak.

'Keep your legs moving.' Kanak continued to bustle, Aavriti in her hand. 'You were right. Something's going wrong, and I won't go with *Prithvi's* decision,' she said, up in arms, 'rather I'd like to deliver a punch on his *charming* face and ask how he could leave us.'

The night had set upon the jungle. It'd been twenty minutes, and Prithvi walked continuously without uttering a word. Kabeer and Samrat followed him with a heavy heart.

'You have any plan what to do next?' Samrat took a morose Prithvi out of his thoughts.

Prithvi exhaled deep. 'We should think about the painting. Damini ma'am had said it's the first step to reach the Royal Weapon, hadn't she?'

'Then we...' Samrat was barged in as Prithvi spun around. 'Kanak is really insane, Samrat. What was the need to argue with me? She's always been so stubborn.'

Kabeer seemed to study him. 'Are you upset not bringing her and Avi with us?'

Prithvi bent his eyes. 'I couldn't have done anything. It was her decision.'

'Did you really try to know what her decision was? You just fired up.' Samrat said grimly, 'I hope they've met Sitara.'

Kabeer said, turning about, 'Some people are coming here.'

He, Prithvi and Samrat expeditiously hid behind a huge rock stood to the left.

Vikrant leading a bevy of people was passing. 'What have you been doing for last two days? You haven't got DTM's location yet.'

'Vikrant sir, we've been trying our best.'

Vikrant berated, 'Listen, Prateek. I want results. My mission will never be accomplished without it.'

Samrat peered at them. 'Vikrant! He's here in the past!'

'And I believe they're the same who'd attacked us,' said Prithvi, spying them.

'Sir, according to Manasvi-55 catch-machine, DTM is still here in 1180,' told Aashutosh, right behind Vikrant.

A wide-eyed Kabeer said, 'Manasvi-55! How can *they* have it? It was in the museum.'

Samrat saw Prateek whisper in Vikrant's ear, gesturing towards the rock.

'They've seen us. RUN.' As Samrat said, three of them skedaddled.

Vikrant shouted, 'Who were they? Catch them.'

Three men led by Prateek ran after them bereft of any delay. Prithvi, Samrat and Kabeer without looking back sped away and soon found a way to exit the jungle, but Vikrant's men continued to chase them.

'Keep running…' said Prithvi.

'Where to go *now*? Inside water?' asked Kabeer frantically.

Samrat and Prithvi were bewildered to see a lake almost fifty metres from them which reined back their running feet.

'We're in a mess,' said Samrat, stumped.

'I've seen this lake before.' Prithvi suggested, seeing Vikrant's men nearing them, 'Run along its perimeter.'

Before they could begin their escape plan again, DTM appeared to the right, ridden by Aavishkar and Kanak. No sooner did Aavishkar open its door than Kanak cried, 'GET IN.'

As Prateek, almost forty feet away, flashed his torch on them looked stunned. '*DTM*!'

Aavishkar shouted as saw Prithvi, Samrat and Kabeer standing baffled, 'You want to be caught?'

Three of them managed to control the look of shock on their face and entered DTM in a word. If Aavishkar were two seconds late, Prateek could shoot one of them. Those three bullets from his gun couldn't touch any piece of flesh. They could only cleave the silent air. DTM had vanished.

Prateek and his men were so close. He still seemed to be in a daze. 'It's gone?!'

***

DTM appeared on the other side of the same lake, out of Prateek's approach.

'God! We had a narrow escape!' A horrified Kabeer got his breath back.

'How did you reach there, Avi?' asked Samrat, coming out. 'You were supposed to go to Sitara.'

'Samarth sir had hidden DTM near this lake. Kanak took me here, hoping to find it. We tried thinking Mr Chancellor might've sent it for us and took it out by means of Aavriti.' Aavishkar gestured to the watch on his wrist. 'Before we could do anything, we saw you all running to the lake. We thought you needed our help so...'

'Kanak, Prithvi had...'

'He's not my boss, Samrat, so lays down the law.' Kanak cast an indignant glance at Prithvi.

Aavishkar asked, 'Anyway, who were they?'

'Vikrant's men. They've still searching DTM,' told Kabeer, 'and been acquiring updates on its time through Manasvi-55.'

Kanak's eyes widened in surprise. 'What!'

Kabeer said, 'Since Manasvi can assure the presence of a time machine in a particular year but cannot track its location that's why they couldn't find DTM yet, I think.'

'They've seen DTM,' said Aavishkar. 'We must hide it cautiously as Samarth sir did.'

Kanak asked, 'Aavishkar, may I borrow Aavriti?'

Aavishkar gave the watch to her. 'What are you doing now?'

Kanak, without answering, pressed Aavriti's yellow crown. The titanium shield cloaked DTM all around. As she pressed the green crown, its rotary excavator began digging the earth with DTM landing down.

'Let's hide its top,' she said, having pressed the blue crown. 'Give me your hand.' She found four of them staring at her.

'Are you sure?' asked Prithvi quizzically. 'I mean you can go back to…'

'Samrat, you too want to abandon me as someone else did,' put in Kanak. 'Will I have to do this work *alone*?'

'No. We'll help,' replied Samrat, raising the sleeves of his kurta. He signalled to Prithvi. Prithvi hesitated at first, but joined four of them in throwing soil over DTM.

No one uttered a single word for one minute.

'Why is Vikrant after DTM?' questioned Samrat to break that awkward silence. 'He wants the Royal Weapon, doesn't he? He must have his own time machine he came here through.'

Prithvi said, 'He was talking about a mission. It must be related to the Royal Weapon. He needs DTM for that, I guess.'

'Do you all remember what ma'am Barua had told about DTM?' said Kabeer, rubbing hands against his kurta to remove soil. DTM had been hidden perfectly. 'MTM's system was going to be transferred in it. Vikrant might know that DTM contains MTM's system.'

Aavishkar deduced, 'So he needs Professor Dhanraj's time machine's system means MTM's system to get the Royal Weapon.'

A linkage flourished in Kanak's head. 'Professor Dhanraj's painting and Professor Dhanraj's time machine, both of them are connected to the Royal Weapon. We need to mull over the relation among them.'

***

Kanak, standing quietly, was watching the reflection of the rising sun in the lake. Five of them had spent the remaining night near it. Samrat, Aavishkar and Kabeer sat a distance away while Prithvi came and stood alongside her.

'It's looking beautiful, isn't it?'

Kanak didn't respond.

Hearing no words from her, Prithvi mumbled, 'It's not a good sign.' He cleared his throat, 'Are you okay?'

Kanak turned sharply. 'Do you care?'

Prithvi continued, glimpsing the anger in her eyes, 'Kanak, I just wanted to say that *I did not abandon you*. I was just…'

Kanak turned before he could finish, 'Samrat, I think we should start from the painting. That's the first step to reach the Royal Weapon.'

Rising quickly to his feet, Samrat came to Prithvi. 'You think just like *him*,' he said, giving a soft smile. 'Don't feel bad,' he whispered to Prithvi, 'she'll be back to *the original Kanak* very soon.'

Kabeer said, 'I guess the Royal Weapon would've also been the reason why Mr Chancellor sent the S.T.F. here.'

Samrat asked, 'What about the painting? None of us has seen it.'

'If we're talking about the same painting in Mr Chancellor's cabin, one of us has done it mindfully,' told Kanak.

Samrat asked, pleasantly surprised, 'Who?!'

'Why is it here?' Aavishkar took a map out of the haversack Samarth had given to Kanak. 'I just wanted to know what was inside the bag and found *this*. Why is a map showing Professor Dhanraj's painting in Samarth sir's bag?'

'What?!' Kabeer took the map from him. 'This is Professor Dhanraj's painting?'

The map diagrammed an area showing a narrow dale with vertiginous, rocky walls located between red mountains, a river running through it.

Samrat spoke, 'Maybe Kabeer is right. Samarth sir *had* come here

to search the Royal Weapon with the help of this map or facsimile…
whatever.'

'Though I'd not seen that painting noticeably, these mountains, this
river…' Kanak scanned the map, trying to recall at her best. 'I've
seen them somewhere.'

Prithvi asked, 'On Niketan?'

'Not there.' Kanak exclaimed, raising her index finger, 'GOT IT.'
Her face lit up.

***

'How did children of this age get to know about the time machine?'
Vikrant's acrimonious words echoed through the tent. Aashutosh
and Prateek were standing behind him.

'Don't worry, sir,' said Aashutosh. 'DTM is still here.'

'And what about those kids?'

'We've got no information about them since last night,' informed
Prateek. 'But we're on the scent of them.'

Aashutosh said, 'I think they would've happened on DTM but
didn't know…'

'How could they run a time machine without knowing about it?'
Vikrant's forehead crinkled into an apologetic frown. 'And if they'd
stumbled across it and could've operated it fortuitously, then and
only then it'd be relieving for us.'

Prateek asked, 'What's your order?'

'We must concentrate on DTM. Find it as fast as possible not to
exacerbate the situation,' said Vikrant with a sense of foreboding.

***

After an hour quest, Prithvi, Kanak, Samrat, Kabeer and Aavishkar
reached a pond.

'Thanks Aavishkar for remembering your mango tree otherwise a
whole day would've been wasted searching for it,' Kanak's voice
was warm and gentle.

'I don't say pointlessly. *This passenger train* does have an inconceivable memory,' grinned Samrat.

Kanak showed them a gorge a long way off. 'Look, this map has the same red mountains and the same river.'

'Why does the map have a valley? How could it be pertained to the Royal Weapon and Ananyaakashganga?' asked Aavishkar, catching nothing.

Prithvi said, 'What if the Royal Weapon was hidden near it?'

'Then what about Ananyaakashganga?' asked Aavishkar.

Kabeer said, 'Those mountains may be called Ananyaakashganga.'

'What's this?' Samrat took the map from Kabeer. '*Why is the sun amid a river?*'

A shining yellow sun was drawn in the middle of the river on the map.

'I'd asked Kanak the same question, but she said we'd talk about it after sometime, and that time never came,' complained Aavishkar.

Kanak said regretfully, 'I'm sorry, Aavishkar.'

'You should've listened to him, Kanak.' An engaging smile floated on Prithvi's lips. 'He always listens to you.'

'You're right. I should have as he never abandoned me.'

Prithvi came closer to Kanak, sensing irony in her words. 'You're running after the same topic. I said I didn't abandon you.'

'How's that, Mr Malhotra? Leaving me behind is not called *abandonment* in your dictionary?'

'Friends, we have more pressing issues right now,' Samrat stepped in. 'We've to reach the river.' He grabbed an angry Kanak by the wrist and walked ahead.

Kabeer, Prithvi and Aavishkar followed them, maintaining a distance.

'Samrat saved you, Prithvi,' said Kabeer in a low voice, 'otherwise this time you'd definitely have got *a super punch* from her.'

Aavishkar spoke, '*Definitely*. Kanak said that she'd ask you how you could leave us *after* delivering a punch on your charming face.'

'What did she say?' asked Prithvi, turning his attention to Aavishkar.

'That how could you...'

Prithvi interrupted Aavishkar's words with a playful smile, 'No. About my face? She said it *charming*?'

'She also mentioned that she wanted to damage it with a blow,' Aavishkar sounded grave.

'It doesn't matter to me,' said Prithvi, his smile growing more ecstatic. 'I loved the fact that she liked it.'

Kabeer appeared to have difficulty in controlling his laughter while Aavishkar continued giving him a serious look.

***

Chapter 13

A Silver Tablet in a Silver Box

'What did she tell?' asked Jaywardhan. He and Devraj were heading for the fifth floor of Vyom Intelligence Bureau, a department of Home Affairs in Vyom Mandal.

'We were right. She gave Manasvi-55 to Vikrant, and the ambush on Mandakini was just to distract us. Our interrogators had to pin her down to make her spell out everything.'

'Vikrant's gone to the past with Manasvi *definitely*.'

'DTM may be in pitfalls then.'

'No, Dev. Samarth is there. He will never let Vikrant succeed,' said Jaywardhan, entering the interrogation room. 'What about the code?'

'She said she didn't know anything about it.'

Jaywardhan came to a phlegmatic Anushka sitting on a chair, looking down. 'You'd already been warned so why didn't you tell about the code?'

Anushka remained cagey.

Devraj said loudly, 'He's asking *you*.'

Anushka broke her silence without looking up, 'How did you get that photograph?'

'You have no right to ask,' said Devraj, infuriated.

'Dev, let me handle this.' Jaywardhan shifted his attention to Anushka. 'You want to know about your picture?'

Anushka looked up at him, her eyes flashing rage and hatred.

'Vikrant gave it to me when he was in Vyom with us. Three years ago when you came here, I could've never imagined you as his daughter, though your face was somewhat familiar.' Jaywardhan turned around. 'When I started investigation against you, that photo was the only way to know the complete truth as I never met you before you joined Vyom. Vikrant had told me about you and Kadambari. Her death came as a terrible blow to us.'

'YOU'RE LYING...' cried a furious Anushka. 'You never grieved. Neither for my mother's death nor for destroying my father's dreams. Because of you, he couldn't become Chancellor, he had to leave Vyom. Because of you, Professor Dhanraj never told him about the Royal Weapon.'

'These are not your father's dreams but his boundless ambitions which can annihilate everything. Our country, our people, our Vyom.'

'You think Vyom can always survive?' Anushka's question took Jaywardhan and Devraj by surprise.

Jaywardhan appeared perplexed. 'What do you mean?'

'Very soon, something is going to be cropped up that will create only ravages in Vyom. Mr Chancellor, save your Vyom. Save your dream *if you can.*'

***

Prithvi, Kanak, Samrat, Kabeer and Aavishkar had reached an open area outside the jungle, at a distance of four-five kilometres before the gorge started, following the course of the winsome river flowing smoothly farthest to the south. The land was covered by a green canvas of grass.

'*How celestial!*' Kanak was rapt watching the panorama around, feeling chilly and soothing breeze across her face.

Prithvi said, looking around, 'We should be forearmed. Vikrant can attack us again.'

'You're being a foreteller,' smiled Kabeer.

'I wish I too could foresee the future, Kabeer,' said Kanak, walking ahead of Prithvi. 'I would never have come here with Mr Malhotra then.'

Prithvi opened his mouth to say something, but Samrat signalled to him to be quiet. 'You should be glad, pal. She's becoming *normal*,' he whispered.

Aavishkar asked, stuck with the same question, 'Why is the sun amid this river?'

Kabeer guessed, 'The sun may be the Royal Weapon.'

Prithvi put his finger over the sun on the map. 'First, we've to find out whether we're at the exact location.'

'This river comes here after passing the gorge,' said Samrat, pointing towards the mountains to his left, 'and the same thing is on the map. It glides on and vanishes into the forest.'

'Exactly,' said Kanak. 'The place where the sun is present over the river is closer to the mountains than the forest. It means we need to move towards the gorge.'

Aavishkar's focus went to a symbol drawn on the map near the river. 'What is this *I* doing here?'

'It tells about either any particular tree or rock,' surmised Samrat.

'Whatever it is, it locates the sun,' said Kanak. The map showed many rays emerging from the sun. Out of them, one was stretched towards a symbol looked like the English letter *I*. 'This ray connecting the sun and the *I* gives us its exact location.'

Aavishkar fell in with her. 'Yes. This *I* is here to get the sun. How will we find it?' he asked, looking here and there. 'Not a few rocks and trees are here.'

Kabeer contemplated the symbol. 'It's not a tree but a megalith in the shape of the letter *I*. It's found once in a blue moon.'

'This place is prehistoric?' said Samrat. 'Quite a cool location to hide the Royal Weapon.'

Five of them scattered in the glade stretched around one square kilometer, searching for the megalith.

After a fifteen-minute quest, Kabeer stopped in front of a large single dun stone looked like the *I*. 'Friends, I got it.'

Four of them immediately reached him.

'If we follow the map, the sun must be here somewhere,' said Prithvi, going towards the river.

'It's been shown on the surface of the river, but I can't see anything,' said Samrat, peering into the water. 'Where is it?'

Kanak said instantly, 'Inside the river.'

A bemused Samrat asked, 'How can you say that?'

'If this sun is the Royal Weapon, it must be kept hidden,' said Kanak. 'We can at least try.'

'Alright,' Prithvi gave into her wish. 'We go one by one and will search the Royal Weapon so that no one has to stay inside the water for long.'

First of all, Kanak dived into the river. She swam deep, looking around gingerly. After some time, she came out. 'Aavishkar, you try there,' she said, indicating to the right.

Aavishkar nodded and dived.

'If he doesn't get the sun, I'll have to go. Unfortunately, I have aquaphobia,' murmured a keyed-up Kabeer.

'What happened?' asked Kanak as Aavishkar came out of the river.

Aavishkar told, huffing and puffing, 'I saw something shiny, appearing like the sun near the river bed about thirty metres away, opposite to the flow. I felt difficulty in breathing so had to come out.'

Prithvi said, 'Okay. Now I, Samrat and Kabeer will go together.'

'May... I...I stay with Avi?' faltered Kabeer.

'You're coming or not?' Samrat gave him a look.

Kabeer couldn't dare to speak more.

Having plunged into the river, three of them swam to the same location Aavishkar had told. As they passed a big cluster of green-aquatic plants, Samrat got a glimpse of an oblong silver box with a sculpted silver sun on its lid, stuck amongst them.

'Why have they not come up yet?' An apprehensive Aavishkar turned to the river. 'What's that?' His eyes strained to notice something swimming in the water.

The colour drained completely from Kanak's face. '*Alligator?*'

Samrat tried to pull the adhered silver box out. Prithvi and Kabeer removed the aquatic shrubs surrounding it.

'What to do? They're inside.' Murmurs of dismay filled Aavishkar's mind.

Kanak said, drawing her sword, 'Whatsoever happens, you will stay here only.' She without wasting a moment dived into the river.

'What are you doing?' asked Aavishkar, trepidatious.

The alligator was attracted towards the rumpus in the river and dived underwater. Kanak swam with powerful strokes and then took a plunge in the nick of time, going deep. The alligator followed her. Now she emerged onto the surface, wanted to distract it. The advancing alligator closed in on her, trying to make an onslaught. She quickly maintained a distance but not a safe one. She wanted to assault its back, but it was quicker. It pounced and grasped her arm.

Aavishkar filled with consternation apace took out his dagger and aimed its back. The dagger went wide of the mark and slugged its tail. He was crestfallen, his face contorted.

The dagger had gashed the alligator's tail. It had to leave Kanak's arm. She instantly held herself up.

Prithvi, Samrat and Kabeer came out of the water from the other side, the box in Kabeer's hands. Their beaming face lost their smile as they saw the terrifying scene.

Kabeer shook with horror. 'What's going on?'

Before they could do anything, Kanak got a way for her. She raised her sword high and rapidly stabbed the alligator's back. Her rap made it motionless.

'I hate sanguinary incidents.' She took her sword out.

The alligator sank down spilling blood, making water around her bright red.

Samrat and Prithvi lent their hands to bring her out. They sat her near the bank.

'How did it catch you?!' asked Samrat, supporting her back.

Aavishkar spelt out everything.

'Thank you,' said Kanak, returning Aavishkar his dagger. 'Hadn't you slogged the alligator with it, I would've been...' she masked her pain with a smile.

Concerned, Kabeer said, 'Kanak's hand's bleeding.'

Aavishkar suggested, 'We need something to cover her arm.'

Prithvi said, 'Kabeer, give me your belt. It'll help stemming the flow of the blood.'

Kabeer gave his cotton-girdle to Prithvi. After ripping it in two, Prithvi returned one half to him. 'I don't want to spoil your getup.' He said, looking into Kanak's eyes, 'Do tell me if it hurts. *Please.*'

Kanak nodded, her face had a serene smile.

***

Anushka's words had created a huge disruption on Niketan. Everyone had been warned. Siddhant had given himself to decipher the code hell for leather. They'd knuckled down to face an unknown jeopardy. Jaywardhan had called Zaheer to Vyom Mandal.

'What if this happens to be her conspiracy?' said Zaheer, sitting on a sofa in VIB's office. 'What if it's disinformation?'

'We cannot ignore her words,' said a watchful Jaywardhan. 'We have to keep our eyes open.'

Zaheer said, 'You think she's telling truth?'

'Yes sir, she is,' an alert voice spoke.

Both of them turned their eyes to see Siddhant at the door.

Jaywardhan asked impatiently, 'What did you get?'

Siddhant told, coming to him, 'I've cracked the code, Mr Chancellor. It shows six numbers 18, 15, 2, 15, 20, 19 equal to 26, and the English alphabets have 26 letters.'

Zaheer rose from the sofa. 'Code is pertained to the English alphabets?'

'Yes, sir. Each number directs its corresponding letter like 18 represents R because R is the eighteenth letter of the English alphabets. Likewise, 15 represents O, 2 represents B, and when we decode the numbers into their corresponding letters as 18 in R, 15 in O, 2 in B, 15 in O again, 20 in T and 19 in S, we get an English word, R O B O T S, *Robots*,' interpreted Siddhant.

'And the complete code refers to *ROBOTS UNCONTROLLED*.' Jaywardhan looked stunned as truth dawned upon him.

'She's her eyes on our robots?' said Zaheer, highly disturbed. 'But which ones?'

***

Prithvi, Kanak, Samrat, Kabeer and Aavishkar were conferring about the silver box on the riverside.

Aavishkar asked, 'Were we supposed to find this?

'Yes, because this carved sun appears the same as shown on the map,' replied Samrat.

'We pulled it out with great difficulty. I was going to suffocate.' Kabeer took a deep breath. 'As well as, poisonous plants were there. *I* warned Prithvi and Samrat.'

'I'm impressed, *charlatan*. You've done a great job,' said Samrat with a forced smile, taking the box from him. 'So, this is the Royal Weapon? I imagine it a coffer filled with gold bullions.'

'Mosses…' Aavishkar's face expressed disgust. 'It'd been inside the water for a long time. But why a silver box?'

Kabeer explained, 'Silver remains stable in oxygen and water and reflects light very well. I guess it's easier to search a silver box then, *inside a river*.'

The rest looked content with his theory.

Samrat unlatched the box to find a silver ingot inside. 'See, what I'd said.' He took it out.

'Samarth sir had come here for *this*!' said Kanak, confounded.

'There is something inscribed on it. Some sort of verse or…' said

Prithvi, noticing the plate. 'And a structure like a fort is carved on its back.'

Samrat said, his face bore a comic smile, 'A poem! On a silver plate! Who's this rich bard?'

'It's not *just a verse*, I guess. It would've been inscribed on a silver plate to preserve it inside the water,' rationalized Kabeer.

Kanak said, 'It means it isn't an ordinary plate. It is a tablet.'

Kabeer began to read the verse, '*125 years ahead into the shadow of the past, search the treasure and the pearls everlast.*'

Samrat spoke, 'Treasure and pearls? But we've to find the Royal Weapon.'

'It might've another meaning.' Kanak's words seemed considerable to everyone.

Kabeer continued, '*In one part of the treasure the world of yours, characterise a desert's mound by your source. Proceed towards the Heaven on Earth at any cost, prove yourself that you will never be lost. Whatever is, will still be there unaffected by air, this story depends on wisdom and overcoming fear.*'

Samrat let out a long breath. 'What a crass poetry is it?'

'I guess this is not a verse but a riddle,' told Kanak, rising to her feet, 'and this tablet cannot be the Royal Weapon, but this riddle has got something to do with it.'

Samrat asked, 'We need to work on this *cryptic verse cum riddle?*'

'And we have to get out of here with DTM as well,' advised a vigilant Prithvi. 'If Vikrant can figure its time out, he can get its location too.'

Aavishkar said, discombobulated, 'Where'd we go now? If we want to make a start, we have to solve the riddle.'

Kabeer looked buoyant. 'Its first line has been solved. It tells us where we need to go.'

'What! *You* have solved the first line?' Samrat was all in a shock. 'How's this possible? You cannot do it.'

Kabeer bordered on him. 'What do you mean by *I cannot do it*? I have done it. It's very lucid. *125 years ahead into the shadow of the past.* We're presently in the past and need to move 125 years ahead.'

'*In 1305*,' computed Aavishkar.

'Well done,' said Kanak, deeply impressed by Kabeer's intellect.

***

Chapter 14

125 Years Ahead

In Vyom Institute, the attempts to deal with the coming threat were on their high, everyone ready to drown themselves to save their home, Niketan.

'Maitreyi, have you vetted the systems of the Plasma robots?' enquired Jaywardhan, ready to tackle the worst possibility of the events. Accompanying him in Saptarishi lab were Damini and Dr Maitreyi Sharma, a robotic scientist.

'Yes, Mr Chancellor. Twenty-five P-Robots have been checked. They are functioning properly, completely viable.'

As Maitreyi finished, Damini asked, 'And what about the Supernova robots of Revati lab?'

'They'll be examined right now,' replied Maitreyi.

Five feet tall silver-black Plasmas and six feet high brown-black Supernovae were the autonomous humanoid robots, one of the best machines Vyom Institute had. They had torso, two arms, two legs and a head designed to replicate human facial features such as eyes, nose, mouth and ears. They were equipped with advanced built-in sensors, actuators, weapons and many more.

***

Prithvi and his companions were moving across the jungle. Aavishkar was leading the group as he remembered paths better.

'Kanak, I...I want to...to...' Prithvi seemed to hesitate for a moment. Everyone drew up.

Kanak looked at him with a befuddled frown.

Prithvi exhaled sharply and came closer to her. *'I'm sorry.* I should not have left you,' he said, overcoming his hesitation. His unanticipated confession made Kanak speechless. He continued, 'I should've convinced you. I agree it wouldn't have been easy, but I should have tried.' His eyes reflected repentance. 'That's all I wanted to say.' He stepped ahead.

'*I am sorry, too.*' Kanak's voice caught his moving legs. 'I should have listened to you.' She turned to gaze at him with regret. 'I'd forgotten my aim, Prithvi, but you reminded me that *our country is above everything, above us, above all,*' she accented. 'Thank you.'

'You…' Prithvi's tongue was not cooperating.

'No need to thank us, Kanak,' interceded Samrat. 'We're glad that you came back, not for Prithvi *of course* but for us.' His face lit up with impish glee.

'Yes. If I forget something, you'll remind me for sure,' said Kabeer with a broad smile.

'But you can continue thanking me because we're not friends.' Prithvi's words made Kanak's grin vanish.

'*Absolutely.* Because I don't befriend people *I hate,* Mr Malhotra.' Kanak walked ahead, pushing him aside with her shoulder.

Prithvi barely stopped himself from falling. 'Are you an android?' he grimaced, raising his eyebrow. '*Metallic girl.*' His eyes went to a frowned Samrat. 'What?'

Samrat looked a little bent out of shape. 'Thank you so much for spoiling the moment.'

***

Aashutosh, sitting inside a tent, was working on a calculator-sized jade device having a keyboard for digits and alphabets and a liquid-crystal display.

Vikrant, lifting the tent curtain, walked in. 'Have you got anything from your catch-machine?'

'It cannot hack DTM's system. It's inaccessible,' said Aashutosh despondently.

'Jay is behind this. He knew DTM would be in danger, hence he appointed Kushal for its security,' said Vikrant, nettled. 'Anushka couldn't learn much about it.'

'But she's given us Manasvi,' Aashutosh gestured to the catch-machine, 'which is connecting us to a system detecting DTM's time.'

'What?!' Aashutosh's words startled Vikrant. 'If it's telling about its time, it should find its location.'

Aashutosh's dispirited face showed a faint hope. 'It's feasible, sir. I'm trying.'

'Where is this system? Wait a minute...' A thought hit Vikrant. 'We can't get details of another time. It meant...'

Aashutosh told, 'Yes. The source-system is in 1180.'

'Who could have such a machine *here*?' pondered Vikrant. Just then, a sound of beep distracted him.

Aashutosh jumped, the catch-machine in his hand. 'Sir... sir... it's traced DTM.'

'What did you say? Where is it?' Vikrant was on cloud nine.

Aashutosh told, looking at the catch-machine, '23.8 degree east, 80.9 degree south, 7.6 kilometres away.'

***

Having taken out DTM from the ground, Prithvi, Kanak, Samrat, Kabeer and Aavishkar entered it with no delay.

As Aavishkar touched some symbols on one of the screens, two bullets struck DTM's front glass window. Five of them jumped back, at a loss by this sudden event. They saw Vikrant, standing at a distance, his men aiming their weapons at DTM.

'Glass is bulletproof, Prateek,' said Aashutosh, lowering his gun. 'Fire what we've got.'

Prateek nodded and put a rocket-propelled grenade on his shoulder.

'NO...' cried Vikrant, coming in front of Prateek. 'No one will harm DTM. I cannot repeat the same mistake.'

'HURRY UP, Avi,' said a frightened Kabeer, 'if you don't want us to be charred.'

Wasting no time, Aavishkar pressed four buttons 1, 3, 0 and 5, followed by a white button on a keyboard. As he pushed the thrust lever, DTM disappeared at the double.

A staggered Vikrant thundered, 'Who were they?'

Prateek told, 'The same children who'd activated DTM last time.'

A message displayed on the LCD of the catch-machine with continuous beeps.

Aashutosh's heart skipped a beat. 'What!'

'What happened now?'

'Sir, DTM...' Aashutosh was in no state to utter.

Vikrant's anger rose higher. 'Why don't you tell me?'

Aashutosh replied, 'It's not in 1180 anymore.'

'*What!*' Vikrant shouted, seized with an impotent wrath, 'Where is it now?'

Aashutosh pressed many buttons on the keyboard of the catch-machine. 'It's stopped receiving signals.'

'How's it possible? You try to access that source-system,' said Vikrant, still hoping for something positive.

'I can't do it.' Aashutosh felt shaken up. 'It's gone, too.'

Vikrant wasn't able to digest what Aashutosh told. 'What does it mean?'

Prateek said, 'The source-system might be with those children.'

Vikrant was completely mystified. 'They'll be very dangerous for us then. I must not underestimate them, not this time.'

***

DTM landed near a farm with Prithvi, Kanak, Samrat, Kabeer and Aavishkar, the bearer of the source-system, Aavriti, who'd just faced a hair-raising moment. They uttered not a single word for a while, standing still.

Kanak broke the silence. 'That was Vikrant, I guess.'

Prithvi, Kabeer and Samrat could only nod.

Aavishkar pressed a button on DTM's door to open it. 'Let's move out, friends.'

As everyone exited from DTM, a voice spoke from behind them, 'Who are you all?'

Five of them turned to see a group of people, seemed to be locals. They were led by a tall and sturdy boy, hardly older than twenty, dressed in a mid-length, tight-fitting dandelion tunic, a kind of hunter-green baggy trousers tucked into calf length brown boots and a leather belt over the tunic. He looked intense, had powerful shoulders with light curly hair short to his nape. He was the one who'd asked the question, but they couldn't find a good answer of it. His widened black eyes glanced up and down DTM. He relaxed his gaze and moved his eyes to them. 'From any royal family?'

A confident Prithvi said, 'Yes... we...we are princes.' He gestured to Kanak. 'And she's a princess.'

The boy's eyes moved from Kanak's toes to her head. 'Her outfit is not telling it. '

'She's a bit complicated,' replied Prithvi playfully.

Kanak gave him an annoyed sideways glance.

The boy gestured his eyes towards DTM. 'And what's that?'

Kabeer managed to say, 'That's nothing... I meant it's our...our... chariot. Yes... it's our chariot...'

The boy raised one eyebrow. 'Where are the horses then?'

Kanak played along. 'It doesn't need horses... I meant... it's Vyomnagar's chariot.'

The boy asked, his gaze musing on DTM, 'Really? So does it fly? '

Samrat whispered to Kanak, 'Are we having a quiz?'

'Let's go, Arjun. Sun's set. We must leave,' said a rangy girl next to the boy.

The boy, Arjun, looked briefly at DTM and then left with her, followed by rest of the locals.

Samrat stared at Arjun, leaving. 'This boy *ruminates*. He must be in Vyom.'

'We already have a person who thinks *a lot*. Do you want yourself in trouble by having another one?' smiled Prithvi stealthily.

Irritated, Kanak pushed him. 'What's your loss if I think *a lot?*'

Prithvi raised his eyes in disapproval. 'It *was* my loss. If you hadn't thought *a lot*, you would've come with me, but you racked you brilliant brain, and I had to leave you, *fighter plane.*'

'Welcome to our world, *again.*' Aavishkar turned to DTM. 'I do my work till this flux-reflux gets over.'

'You always try to rule the roost, try to be brainy because you think you're unequalled, *sophist.*' Kanak seemed clearly miffed.

Prithvi's ire intensified. 'I know *I'm the best*. Are you jealous? And that's why I call you *fighter plane*. You just want a chance to fight, *rumbustious.*'

'Mute your sound, please. You both are excellent.' Kabeer was frazzled being an intermediary. 'Why do you both always comport yourselves like radioactive substances? Ready to beam gamma rays to vandalize each other?'

'A radioactive substance emits gamma rays?' asked Samrat, confused.

Kabeer folded his arms. 'How did you qualify your intermediate examinations, Samrat? Every radioactive substance emits alpha or beta particles along with gamma rays.'

'Yes. I got a question related to radioactivity in my board exam. I left it, but I passed with *first division* instead,' bragged Samrat.

Kabeer said, his hands on his hips, 'Good job, *adroit Samrat*. You're an ideal.'

'Let's cover it, mates,' said Aavishkar, tying Aavriti. He had landed DTM down perfectly.

***

Jaywardhan, Damini and Maitreyi were heading for Revati lab, but they met an edgy Venugopal on the first floor of Gagan Bhavan.

'We're in trouble,' said Venugopal, trying to control his breathing. 'The Supernova robots have been out of our hand.'

Three of them palpitated in disbelief. They rushed towards the basement.

'It's been almost impossible to regulate them,' told Venugopal, 'they've walked out, running riot, ruining Revati. I had to leave it. They were after my life. I somehow saved myself.'

When they reached the lab, they could see only sabotage all around. No any Supernova was there.

'Jay,' said Damini, indicating to the left to four Supernova robots going upstairs by a staircase.

'*Get ready*. We have to fight against *our own machines*,' said Jaywardhan decisively.

***

The sun sank beneath the horizon. The navy blue sky began to darken. The light of the radiant waxing-gibbous moon started creeping into every corner of a beautiful village near the farm Prithvi and his team had landed. The high hills to its north seemed to be rising and falling in soft waves.

Five of them were passing through the village. Some villagers were sitting on a platform around a huge Banyan tree, some children playing near them. Mud houses built around courtyards were lit with lamps.

Samrat saw a constant stream of smoke coming out of one of the houses indicating the kitchen area. 'I am ravenous, friends. But I don't want to have fruit salad anymore.'

Kabeer said, fed up, 'I'm not interested, too.'

'Follow the same street for one kilometre,' a familiar voice spoke. Five of them turned to see Arjun, the boy they met near the farm, at a distance. 'There is a public eatery. You'll get a lot of things.'

Aavishkar asked, 'Are you following us?

Arjun's face bore a stellar smile. 'I'm only helping.'

'Then why don't you tell us where we are? I meant which village or town is this?' asked Kabeer.

Arjun's eyebrows arched in disbelief. 'You came to this village and don't know its name?'

'We…we were on a hunting trip…, but got lost… and… reached here,' Prithvi concocted a story again, even getting uncomfortable.

Arjun asked with a sarcastic smile, 'A hunting trip? With a queer chariot?'

Kanak said in a firm voice, glowering at Arjun, 'Let's go. We're wasting our time.' She turned to leave, followed by four of them.

They walked for around one kilometre and found an eatery to the right of the street.

Prithvi said, 'So *actually* he was helping.'

Kanak spoke, ignoring his words, 'It's a kind of dhaba. We'll have to pay here.'

'We can use Avi's bracelet.' Kabeer gestured to Aavishkar's left hand. 'Gold has always been very expensive.'

'Good idea,' agreed Prithvi. 'And it's not *his* bracelet. It's in lost and found list.'

Aavishkar demurred, putting his hand on the left wrist, 'I don't care. It's my *favourite*. I won't give it.'

Samrat put his hands around Aavishkar's shoulders. 'Don't be impassioned. We're hungry. Your charity has no parallel, pal.'

'I know you won't let your friends starve, will you?' Kanak tried to convince Aavishkar.

Aavishkar looked gloomily at the bracelet. A pained look crossed his face.

***

'Aashutosh, I want that machine, *anyhow*,' said an exasperated Vikrant, tired of being troubled, yearning for DTM.

I'm trying, sir,' said Aashutosh, looking up at Vikrant standing next to him. He hadn't been left his tent for almost four hours, had been working on the catch-machine to get DTM's location. 'Sir, did Professor Dhanraj come to the past through MTM whose system is fitted in DTM?' he asked.

'*That eyesore Dhanraj* is the root of all problems,' said Vikrant, his voice infused with vengeance, his blood boiling. 'He thought he was doing Vyom a good turn by storing the information of his past journey in MTM, but he didn't know that I wouldn't let it happen.'

'If MTM was so important, why did you try to destroy it?'

'That was my single mistake. But when Anushka told me that I could know the time of the Royal Weapon through MTM, I realised how important it is for me. And then, I left everything on her, and she without questioning, being a good soldier, kept on working for me.' A tormented look on Vikrant's face was replaced by an exulted expression.

Aashutosh said, 'Sir, we'd mowed down Samarth. What if Jaywardhan comes here for him?'

Vikrant gave an artful laughter. 'It will never happen. It cannot be. I do have an ace up my sleeve. Jay will come here, if he gets the chance, if he saves his Vyom,' he said, turpitude glinted in his eyes. 'He loves his Vyom and his companions *greatly*. But when his machines trash his Vyom and crush his companions, he'll realise how I feel when I want to do something but cannot do it. He will feel helpless what *I* always do.' He looked upset, his voice seethed in anger.

***

Prithvi and his friends received sufficient food in exchange of the gold bracelet. Since it was expensive, they got twenty gold coins too.

The eatery was a clean, cozy and well ventilated place, contained seven-eight wooden tables with six stools each. It was filled properly with yellowish light of oil lamps, the smell of food hanging in the air.

Samrat sat on one of the wooden stools with a plate full of rice, dal and cooked vegetables. 'Avi, where did you find the bracelet?'

'From the same wardrobe we got our costumes. *Goldie* was kept there on one of the shelves. When I saw it, at once fell for it, but you all snatched *my Goldie*.' Aavishkar glared at Kabeer and Samrat with a strange mixture of anger, pain and disappointment.

'We're sorry. Your favourite things always go away because of us.' Kanak's words seemed to compose Aavishkar.

'It's okay, Kanak. I never care about things. *Materials are immaterial*. We find and lose them, but my friends are always with me, and no bracelet is more valuable than them,' said Aavishkar in a soft and calm voice.

With wondering eyes, four of them watched Aavishkar, their face filled with pride.

'I'm not in the mood of hearing prolix speech, but I must say, Avi, *you're great*,' said Prithvi, overwhelmed.

***

Vyom Institute was under threat by its own machines. The forces had been warned about the red alert. An immediate action was imperative. Damini and Maitreyi were taken up with their jobs and trying to know about the S-robots' malfunctioned systems. The students were asked not to leave Parikrama-1, *whatsoever*.

'Supernovae are heading towards Vyom Mandal,' Devraj informed Jaywardhan through his wireless. 'The officers have been peppering them with gunshots, even strafing them, but they aren't being affected. They're utilising their powers perfectly.'

He was in Operations Control Room of Vyom Mandal and Jaywardhan and Zaheer in Kshitij Hall, keeping their eyes on Supernovae while a group of Air Force officers were following them through their gunships.

'They've been laying waste to each and every hindrance of their way. Should we tear them up by bombardment?'

'No Dev,' said Jaywardhan. 'They won't be impaired to the hilt by those bombs. You just try to damp down the situation. They must not reach Vyom Mandal.' He disconnected, a distraught look on his face.

'They have plasma guns, rifles, bombs, metallic shields. And so far as their capability is concerned, it's many more times than a human,' said a perturbed Zaheer. 'When we attack, they stop for a while, but we're not able to do it for long, Jay. I wondered that they destroyed only Revati.'

'Our institute wasn't their target. Their target is *Sangrah*,' said Jaywardhan, preparing for the worst.

The ambience of Vyom Institue and Vyom Mandal was of disturbance and agitation. Vyom had faced many challenges before, but every time they were raised by the external factors. It never stood against its own inventions.

***

Chapter 15

The Golden Armour

'It was good that dhabaman understood our problem,' said Kabeer, washing his hands after having dinner. 'We should've some benefits. We're *royals*.'

'You aren't. I, Kanak and Avi are. You both are our bodyguards. This was the title the dhabaman honoured you with,' giggled Prithvi.

Kanak meddled, 'You again started, *imperious Prithvi?*'

Prithvi's countenance changed. 'Why do you dislike everything about me, critic *Kanak?*'

'Who said I dislike you?' said Kanak, straight-faced.

'What!' Prithvi straightened up in surprise. 'Don't say you like me!'

'I hate you. *Remember?*' Kanak grinned broadly.

'Friends, please,' interposed Aavishkar. 'If you both want a dose of skirmish to digest your dinner, fine. We do not. I'm begging.'

Kabeer said, taking the tablet out of the haversack, 'We must rather work on the riddle. I'm beginning with the second line.' He placed it on the table. '*Search the treasure and the pearls ever last. In one part of the treasure the world of yours, characterise a desert's mound by your source.*'

'Our world refers to the Royal Weapon, doesn't it?' speculated Samrat. 'And a desert's mound means a sand dune. But where is this desert?'

'Give my arrears back, Arjun, if you want to live in Khazanapur,' a firm but harsh voice spoke from outside the eatery.

'Khazanapur?' mumbled Kanak, pensive.

'What's going on?' Samrat exited from the eatery, followed by four of them to find Arjun imploring in front of a man.

'I'll return your money soon, but don't take my Moksha.'

Half a dozen acolytes were standing behind the man.

'Who's he? Have I met him before?' thought Prithvi, seeing the man.

'Three months have been passed since you located your stable,' said the man furiously, edging to a dapple grey horse next to Arjun, 'so I'll have to cage your *lovable Moksha.*'

He was burly and muscular, in his early forties, stark eyed, had huge shoulders, a sharp moustache and a coarse-black beard. He wore a knee-length tunic, a pair of baggy-pleated trousers and a leather belt like most men of Khajanapur.

Arjun's heart sank. 'Please, NO.'

Prithvi stepped ahead. 'Don't dare to touch his horse.'

The strapping man turned, his eyes narrowed. 'Who are you? His well-wisher?'

'Does it bother you if *a prince* is his friend?' asked Prithvi in an orotund voice.

The man said with a mocking look in his eyes, 'Well, I didn't know he had a *prince friend.*'

'Do you envy him now?' Prithvi motioned towards Arjun. 'Anyway, how much does he have to pay you?'

The man answered, 'It's my bailiwick, boy. Keep yourself...'

'I don't care,' Prithvi cut in rudely. 'Just tell me the amount.'

The man shot him a black look. 'Fine. He'd bought the stable in ten gold coins. He's to give me fifteen, *interest included.*'

Prithvi asked Kanak, 'Give me the pouch.'

'Prithvi...' Kanak seemed to deliver a message through her eyes.

'I know you believe me.' Prithvi flashed a wide smile.

Kanak looked at Arjun for a brief instant, reached out into the haversack, pulled out a pouch and handed it over to Prithvi.

'Twenty coins,' said Prithvi, extending the pouch to the man. 'I'm giving you five more not to give him any trouble. *For your business.*' He gave him a smug look.

Arjun looked to be at sea.

The man frowned, clearly surprised. He took the pouch. 'Welcome to Khazanapur, *prince.*' He now made off, followed by his acolytes.

A marvelled Samrat asked, 'Why did you do it, Prithvi?'

Arjun's voice spoke, 'I should've asked this.'

Prithvi turned to him and extended his hand. 'Prithviraj Malhotra. A pleasure to meet you, *Arjun.*'

'Prithviraj and what?' asked Arjun, confused, staring at his hand.

'You can call him *Prince* Prithviraj,' intervened Kabeer, now lowering his voice to a whisper, 'Prithvi, I don't think he knows how to shake hands.'

Realizing his mistake, Prithvi withdrew his hand. '*I was only helping.*' He had an enigmatic grin on his face.

***

Vyom's conundrums had swelled because of the Supernova robots, total bedlam in the institute, lives at stake. Though Vyom never ran out of road, this situation came as a bolt out of the blue.

'Institute is in big trouble. We must do something,' said Aaryaman Upadhyay, a student of Mangal group, fourth year, shuffling back and forth in the common room for students.

Accompanying him were around twenty five students of Buddha, Vasundhara and Mangal group, distressed, fraught, overwrought.

'What do we do? Supernovae are very powerful. It's not easy to overcome them,' said Prarthana Malhotra, a Mangal group student and Prithvi's elder sister.

'We can't stop forty *unstoppable* Supernovae,' said Swastik Rao, one of her classmates.

Aaryaman spoke, 'We can control over one, at least.'

'*Only one?* Will our problem be ironed out then?' asked Jannat Zehra, a student of Vasundhara group, third year.

'I hope so,' said Aaryaman. 'The question is why Mr Chancellor can't control his own robots? It means their original programs are dysfunctional. They're not controlling them now.'

Prarthana said, 'You're saying that a foreign operator was loaded into them, deranging their own system?'

'Exactly,' confirmed Aaryaman. 'That's why they're not following their original commands.'

'So, if we capture one of them and can learn about the operator, it'd be easy to stop the rest of them.' Swastik got hold of Aaryaman's plan.

'It'll be a tall order to stop even a single robot, won't it be?' asked Paridhi.

A determined Jannat said, 'If we team up, nothing will be impossible.'

'We want about twenty students out of you. The rest will stay here to cover us,' said Prarthana, looked painstaking.

'How will we leave the campus?' asked Swastik.

Abhyuday informed, 'Supernovae have left so here security is not tight.'

'And most of the security guards have taken charge near Vyom Mandal,' added Kavya.

Prarthana asked, 'Shaurya, what about you and your friends?'

A recalcitrant Saif instantly replied, 'We're not in your...'

Shaurya said without a moment's hesitation, 'We'll help.'

Saif darted at him, raring to know his intention, but he acquiesced in his decision.

'Swastik, take five smoke bombs with us,' said Aaryaman.

'Those are for...'

'Trust me. Just bring them.' Aaryaman turned. 'Jannat, I've heard that you prepared a chemical which can produce excessive electricity when mixed with water?'

'They're Vyom's robots. Easy shock will not affect their external parts.' Jannat looked uncertain.

'Its full name is *Prarthana Easy Shock* aka *P.E.S.,*' chimed in Prarthana. 'Jannat said it'd be on my name, *in my honour*. Well, she's tried it only once.' She grinned heartily.

Jannat joined in.

'In chemical sciences, Jannat is the best we've got. We can reckon on her easy shock, I meant, on *P.E.S.*' Aaryaman looked at Prarthana, beaming ear to ear.

***

Arjun had taken five of them to a paddock around four hundred metres away from the eatery.

'I will always be indebted to you, prince Prithviraj. You saved my friend,' he said, fondling his horse.

'Its name is Moksha?' asked Kabeer.

Arjun shook his head.

Kanak whispered to Prithvi, 'So you want to ask him about the riddle.'

Prithvi's eyes showed mild surprise. 'How do you know?'

Aavishkar overheard them. 'She only pretends that she doesn't know you, Prithvi.

Kanak, clearly vexed, punched Aavishkar on the arm.

Prithvi stepped with a controlled smile. 'Arjun, we want your help to know something. But why we're doing it, what's our motive, please never ask about it.' His smile was replaced by the most sincere of expressions.

Arjun stared at him with a questioning face.

'Your help may save our world. We can do something for our people,' continued Prithvi, looking at Arjun, waiting for his decision.

Arjun was standing puzzled, unable to decide anything.

A disappointed Kanak said, hearing no reaction from him, 'And if you don't want to help, it's okay. We...'

'I'll help,' acceded Arjun.

Kanak's distress turned into hope.

Aavishkar took the tablet out of the haversack and showed it to Arjun. 'We have to solve this riddle. According to Kanak, the word *treasure* signifies this village *Khazanapur*, but we don't know where this desert is.'

'The desert having our destination is in one of the parts or regions of Khazanapur,' Prithvi clarified the third line of the riddle.

'If you're talking about *the desert of Khazanapur*, I know where it is,' told Arjun, running his eyes across the tablet.

Happiness slid over their face.

'It's very far. If we walk, a whole day will be spent, but I have one more option.' Arjun looked up at them. 'What about riding a horse? I have three of them.'

'Fine,' said Prithvi. 'When are we leaving?'

'It's not safe to journey to an unknown place at night,' said a vigilant Kanak. 'We must take each step watchfully.'

Arjun saw eye to eye with her. 'Then we'll leave in the morning.'

Aavishkar aksed, 'Where will we stay, by the way?'

'I have a small room alongside the stable.' Arjun showed them a structure near the field. 'If you manage…'

Kabeer said with an appreciative smile, 'Thank you so much.'

'I live near that eatery,' said Arjun. 'You all relax. I'll come tomorrow.'

Kanak's eyes caught Arjun's right hand. 'What's on your palm?'

Arjun wore a piece of golden armour on his right palm, looked to be a fingerless glove. It, on both the sides, had a carved jewelled sun in the middle with rays streaming outwards.

'My mother gave it to me before she died,' said Arjun, masking his pain with a gracious smile.

Prithvi gently touched his shoulder. 'I can say she's still with you.'

'Yes. I wish I could see her again, prince Prithviraj. But no matter how bad I wish, it's never going to happen.' Arjun turned his face, tears flashing in his eyes.

***

The attacks on the S-robots had been stopped as they weren't fruitful, but the forces could divert them to an almost no populated hilly area. The commandos and officers knew they wouldn't stop heading towards Vyom Mandal so they'd been recording their locations and activities through CCTVs, drone cameras, etc.

Aaryaman, Prarthana and their teammates were rushing to an appropriate site, they'd already chosen, with bags full of requisites on their back and torches in their hands.

'What's this, Shaurya? You're helping *Prithvi's sister?*' said Saif, reluctant to move his feet.

Shaurya replied passionately, 'I'm protecting our home. We all should. That's what we're taught.'

'Those machines are butchering our people, Saif. Give up your surly nature for a while,' said Urvashi, a hint of disapproval in her voice.

Saif couldn't question Shaurya's decision. He had to speed up with them.

Having reached a spot three kilometres before the hilly area ended, Aaryaman stopped, an enlarged map of Niketan in his hands. 'We set to our work here.'

'How did you know, Swastik, they'll pass this area?' asked Prarthana.

Swastik replied, getting uncomfortable, 'Our…our people are using some devices… to track… them and…'

'Did you hack…?' said Prathana. 'It's illegal.'

'What we're doing right now is legal?' said Swastik, smiling.

Mayur stood on a higher ground in the rear to keep an eye on the surroundings. Aaryaman, Ujjawal, Ibrahim, Lara and Saif pitted the single unmetalled road in the area connecting it to Vyom Mandal. One side of the road was a land full of huge rocks and trees scattered randomly where Swastik, Paridhi, Pravesh and Abhyuday dug a second cuboidal pit near a bunch of trees. Jannat, Narayani and

Shikhar filled it with water they carried with them. On the other side was a series of small, sloping hills. Shaurya, Urvashi, Alexander and Jessica led by Prarthana climbed up one of the flat-topped hills.

Kavya asked, 'For how long will that robot go into sleep mode after bearing an electric shock of 440 V?'

'Only for one minute,' told Aaryaman. 'It tends to protect its motherboard from a sudden shock.'

Paridhi seemed unsure. 'One minute is not enough, isn't it?'

'We have to take risk.' Aaryaman sighed deeply.

A peremptory challenge was before them, and they together could face it. Unity had altered the world's map. Why wouldn't it change Vyom's destiny?

***

Kanak, Samrat, Kabeer and Aavishkar went into the room Arjun had shown while Prithvi liked to be with him a little longer.

'Prince Prithviraj, what you...'

Prithvi discontinued Arjun, '*Just Prithvi* will do.'

'Okay. *Just Prithvi*,' Arjun smiled genially. 'What you did for me, I'm doing nothing in return. You went against princess Kanak.'

'Friendship is not a trade, Arjun. I want you to help me because you want to do it, not because I did something for you.' Prithvi looked towards the room. 'And as far as, Kanak is concerned, she's little fastidious, not credulous.' He smiled and turned to Arjun. 'She likes to help others. But many a time, her brain faster than a computer doesn't allow her.'

Kanak came out, calling, 'Prithvi, you're coming?'

'You too take rest, Arjun. After all, you'll show us the right path.' Prithvi walked ahead, then turned. He said, lowering his voice, 'And yes, never call her princess otherwise what she'll do with you, I don't know. She's made me fall down already *seven times*. So, all the best in advance.'

Arjun thought, 'All the best to *you*, Prithvi. You need it more than I do.'

***

Chapter 16
Vyom versus Vyom

Jaywardhan and his companions had been putting their head together to stop Supernovae.

'Why did you ask Sagar to call the army back?' questioned Zaheer.

'I had to abort our plans for Supernovae. We've already lost fifteen people,' said Jaywardhan without any hint of hope.

Sagar told, 'They're becoming more dangerous to defend themselves. They're killing our commandos and officers as well as ruining the regions around.'

'Robotic Department tried to disable their operating system through supercomputers, but it didn't affect them as though those OS weren't controlling them,' spoke Devraj.

'Because they're controlled by a foreign operator now,' said Damini, looking disappointed, 'I wish we could figure out how it works.'

Jaywardhan decided, 'As soon as Supernovae arrive at Vyom Mandal, we'll attack.'

Sagar filled Jaywardhan in on the latest, '*Aakash* missiles have been deployed outside it.'

Zaheer's eyes darted at Jaywardhan in surprise. 'We're exterminating them?'

Downhearted, Jaywardhan said, a worried look on his face, 'Anushka knew our weakness that we would never annihilate our robots. I wanted to terminate only their operator, but now we're left with no option.'

***

Mayur came running and said breathlessly, 'Are all of you ready? They…they…, I forgot whose name, are coming.'

Everyone took their position instantly, the murk of night helping them to hide. Aaryaman, Swastik, Paridhi, Pravesh, Mayur, Narayani and Ujjawal hid themselves behind a group of trees. Prarthana, Shaurya, Urvashi, Alexander and Jessica lay face down on the flat top of the hill, their eyes scanning the road. To Aaryaman's right, ten metres away was a cluster of rocks Jannat, Saif, Lara, Kavya, Abhyuday and Shikhar were sitting behind.

The students were waiting for the robots, holding their breaths. As Supernovae were making their way towards the plate in a single line one after the other, so was increasing their dread. Had they made any mistake? The answer was *yes*, they had. Would they have to defray a huge cost for it?

A deep excavation, three-foot in diameter, had been made on the road, a circular wooden plate over it. The plate was roped from its two opposite edges along the diameter. Aaryaman was holding an end of a length of rope whose other side was tied to one edge of the plate. The rope tied to its other edge was to be held by Prarthana, but it wasn't so. Thus the plate didn't cover the excavation completely, revealing the presence of the pit.

'We have to distract them,' propounded Shaurya, lying next to Prarthana.

Prarthana immediately shared her plan to him and Urvashi. Both of them quickly collected some stones and threw them behind the robots. The long silence was broken by their crackle. As soon as Supernovae about thirty metres away from the plate turned back, Prarthana descended the hillock.

'What's she doing?' Aaryaman's breaths were running fast.

Supernovae fired on the stones. Prarthana rapidly adjusted the plate, took the other end of the rope and tried to climb the hillock. She was getting decelerated because of the slope. Her teammates were on tenterhooks for Supernovae were about to turn.

Swastik without delaying flung two smoke bombs towards Supernovae. They hit against the ground and their smoke surrounded them. Supernovae stopped firing because of their disability to see anything. Prarthana took gain of this opportunity and got back to her position before the smoke vanished.

Supernovae raked the road and then moved ahead, finding no risk. The students geared up completely, this time ensuring no any blunder. The robots began crossing the plate. As soon as the last one was about to step on it, Aaryaman immediately pulled the rope, shifting the plate to his side. The robot fell down into the fifteen-foot deep pit. Now, Prarthana pulled the rope, covering it with the wooden plate.

An iron circular sheet was spread over the bottom of the pit which was connected through a copper wire, running along the wall and the road then towards the land area, to a brown metallic box looked like a fan regulator Kavya was holding. No sooner did the robot fall than she rotated a rotary switch knob on the box clockwise by two steps. As Supernova landed on the iron sheet, its body shook, suffering an electric shock of 440 V that threw it into sleep mode.

The robot just before the fallen one turned around. It saw all sides and having satisfied, walked ahead. When all the S-robots reached the far corner of the road, Aaryaman shifted the plate.

'Be ready. One minute is over,' as Kavya told, looking at her watch, every eye turned to the pit to find Supernova jump out of it, almost flying.

Jessica looked stirred. 'That was an incredible jump,' she whispered.

Supernova took a few steps to the land area carefully; fingers of its right hand turned into gun barrels and discharged in all directions.

'It'll kill someone. Make it stop,' said Aaryaman to Swastik.

Swastik flung three smoke bombs towards it. It stopped firing surrounded by smoke but made an arrangement to expunge it. It began exhaling a stream of air from its mouth.

'It's not what we mapped out,' mumbled Swastik.

Prarthana and her companions slid four large rocks one after the other towards the robot before the smoke vanished completely. It heard them rolling and turned abruptly. Its left hand acted as a missile launcher and fired three lightweight pen-sized missiles on them which exploded three of the boulders, but the fourth one succeeded. It smashed into Supernova speedily. Its body was broken, but its brain and sensors were still active.

The machine got up, actuated the plasma guns fitted into its eyes and targeted all directions, burning down four trees. Unfortunately, it saw Paridhi, sitting behind a tree. Its eyes scanned her and indicated the presence of a human. It focussed its iris at her. Before it could shoot, it was pushed from the back and rammed into a seven-foot deep cuboidal dig, one metre away, full of water.

Abhyuday appeared, hanging through a rope bound around a limb of a tree. He got his feet back on the ground, a triumphant smile on his face.

The robot sank into water, but immediately its feet converted into swim fins which helped it to be partially submerged, saving it from drowning. Jannat had mixed P.E.S. in water which started affecting it. P.E.S. mixed in water found ways to enter its internal parts through its broken body. It produced excessive electric current what led to excessive generation of heat and the risk of damage to Supernova's motherboard, vitiating its electronic circuitry. Its temperature sensors indicated the extreme limit, but it couldn't stop the current flow through the circuits as its current limiters were damaged.

Its operating system was gradually falling through. Its movements were pared down. It couldn't do anything against P.E.S. It had left with two options. Either it let its motherboard burn or incapacitated itself. Being an intelligent machine, it opted for the second one. It shut down its operating system, accepting the defeat. It sank down, immobile and inactive.

The students collected around the pit, their face lit with victory, their eyes glimmered pride, their lips broke into a very big smile. They had trounced an S-robot by their teamwork. The place was filled with the sound of revelry.

'Your easy shock works perfectly, Jannat,' said Swastik, flashing her an admiring grin.

Aaryaman corrected him, 'Its complete name is *Prarthana Easy Shock*.'

Everyone laughed along with him.

***

All the preparations had been done to destroy the S-robots. The task force was settled, awaiting their advent at Vyom Mandal.

'*What!*' Operations Control Room echoed with Devraj's voice.

'Yes sir. One S-robot is missing,' an officer told.

She touched one of the digital panels placed on her table thrice. A wall-sized electronic display in front of them showed satellite pictures of an area.

'Sir, two minutes ago, Supernovae passed through Highway N5. They were thirty nine, not forty.'

Devraj stared at the screen quizzically.

'As well as we've recorded the presence of humans near route-69,' she added. 'They aren't our commandos, sir. They are someone else.'

Devraj's eyes went wide, an audible gasp escaped him.

***

As Aaryaman, Prarthana and their team got the inoperative S-robot out of the pit, they heard a chopping noise, echoing across the hills, growing louder with time. Three helicopter-searchlights flashed over them before they could comprehend its reason.

After fifteen minutes, Aaryaman and Prarthana were standing before Jaywardhan, Zaheer, Damini and Maitreyi in Kshitij Hall; Supernova lying on the table, kaput. The rest of the students were sent to the hostels. Four of them, even nonplussed and bewildered, patiently listened to what their students wanted to explain.

'We know we've broken Vyom's rules, but we couldn't see our people in trouble,' said Aaryaman in a low, steady voice, looking into Jaywardhan's eyes.

Prarthana said, gauging the gravity of the situation, 'This robot may be our *panacea*, Mr Chancellor.'

Jaywardhan exhaled sharply. 'Go back to the hostels and *stay* there. We talk about it later.'

Aaryaman and Prarthana nodded and exited from Kshitij.

Damini and Maitreyi scanned Supernova to detect the presence of the foreign operator.

'A very powerful Robot Operating System, ROS-6, with a specific set of commands has been installed,' told Damini, having examined the S-robot from top to toe. 'We have to disable it, turning off its motherboard.'

'They're uncontrollable. How will we do it?' asked Zaheer.

Maitreyi told, '*Agni gun* is the only weapon which can pierce Supernovae's body. We can use it to destroy the main connection to their power supply that will result in turning off the motherboard.'

Agni gun was the world's best Robots Utility Gun, had 7.95 mm cartridge, proffered target's perfect penetration, controllability and destruction.

'*Our robots* carry Agni gun, Maitreyi. Why will they use their own gun against their own motherboard?' asked Jaywardhan.

Kushal and Siddhant appeared at the door before anyone could find its answer.

'Why don't we utilize the Plasma robots, dad? They are under our thumb,' said Kushal.

Zaheer liked his plan. 'He's right. Plasmas with their own Agni gun can successfully assault Supernovae.'

'That's why a line was written in the code, *diamond cuts diamond*.' Jaywardhan's eyes flashed hope.

'Supernovae are about two kilometres away from Vyom Mandal. In such a short time, how can the Plasma robots reach there?' asked Damini.

Siddhant said, 'It's an appropriate time to use *Black Hole*, ma'am. It can take Plasmas to the location we want before Supernovae.'

Black Hole was a network of underground tunnels, containing supersonic jets, extended beneath Niketan's entire surface. It'd bolstered Vyom to accomplish many of its missions.

***

The unbridled Supernova robots blasted Vyom Mandal's glass doors and strode to the lobby. Vyom Mandal was vacated. *Aakash* missiles were deactivated.

Having boarded on the escalator, the S-robots reached *the Aquarium Hall.* They lifted their left hand to use it as a missile launcher and vandalize the aquarium-cum-gateway, but it opened itself, revealing twenty-five protector Plasma robots; a brown-grey, 6.5 inches long, 9 mm gun in their hand.

As soon as Supernovae saw Plasmas, they quit the idea of using the missile launcher, knowing they wouldn't affect the P-robots at all. Their right thigh split open as a case, and they took out what affected Plasmas the most. *The Agni gun.*

Supernovae fired Agni. Bullets flew in a deadly shower over Plasmas. Plasmas took sudden movements, avoiding most of them. They immediately counterattacked Supernovae. Their target was Supernovae's left shoulder where the power supply to their heart, their motherboard, was located.

The Aquarium Hall and the port witnessed a fight between Vyom's two advanced machines to save it. Those machines suffered detriments, far less than what Vyom would've endured if the S-robots had been exterminated. The Plasma robots were doing their job perfectly, switching the uncontrolled robots' power supply off, deactivating their motherboard.

Supernovae shot seven Plasmas at their left shoulder, but number of disabled S-robots was much more as Plasmas had been given definite and clear commands what to target and how.

Jaywardhan and his team in Kshitij Hall had been watching this battle through Vyom Mandal's CCTVs. Twelve Plasmas and thirty-five Supernovae were down. It took two P-robots to make the remaining five S-robots non-functional. Ultimately, the protector Plasma robots won the fight, repressing the uncontrolled Supernovae.

Jaywardhan and his companions got their breaths back. Their heart and brain felt massive relief, a smile of contentment on their face.

***

Chapter 17
The Traitor

Prithvi and his friends had a hearty breakfast with Arjun in the eatery and then gathered near the stable.

Arjun suggested, mounting Moksha, 'I have three horses, and we're six. So go for your partners.'

'Kanak, you pair up with Prithvi. I'm going with Arjun,' said Aavishkar.

Kanak reacted, 'Aavishkar, two lions never share the same forest.' She sat behind Samrat on a chestnut horse, staring at Prithvi.

Holding reins of the last horse, a red dun, Prithvi murmured, 'When will her poisonous tongue shower nectar?'

Kanak retorted, 'It's never going to happen for you, Mr Malhotra.'

'How does she do it?' Kabeer on horseback behind Prithvi whispered in his ear, 'if you speak in vacuum, I'm sure she'll hear you there too.'

Prithvi galloped ahead, followed by the rest of two horses. 'What can I say? She's my biggest fan,' he whispered back, grinning.

Samrat said, 'Have you ever sat on a horse before, Kabeer? Why didn't you attend your equitation classes? Sorry, I forgot. *Graphology* is your optional subject.' He giggled softly.

A nervous Kabeer frowned, but didn't say anything.

***

'Mr Chancellor, the S-robots are under our control now,' informed Maitreyi. She and Jaywardhan were heading for the interrogation room in Vyom Mandal. 'They've been transferred to Revati lab.'

'What about the damages they and Plasmas have suffered?'

'Don't worry. I, Venugopal and Kushal with our team will repair them as soon as possible.'

'You've to carry through it without Kushal, Maitreyi. He's to finish his unfinished work.' Jaywardhan stopped and laid his hand on her shoulder. 'I believe in you and Venugopal. You're capable of accomplishing your job.'

Maitreyi's face bore a grateful smile.

***

The sun was straight up the head. Prithvi, his friends and Arjun could see many rectangular, square arable lands stuffed with fully grown crops on the outskirts of Khazanapur.

Prithvi asked Arjun riding Moksha to his left, 'How far is the desert now?'

'We're about to reach,' said Arjun, pulling over.

'Then why are we stopping?' asked Aavishkar.

'Our horses need some rest.' Arjun tied Moksha to a tree of a wooded area to the right of the passage.

Prithvi dismounted, followed by the rest of them. 'Arjun, we'll certainly carry off with your help. I'm glad you're with us,' he said, hoping a positive upshot of his efforts.

Kanak looked skeptical. 'So much trust in such a short time?'

Before an assured Prithvi could react, an arrow whizzed between him and her and hit a tree.

Everyone froze in shock.

Some men on horseback besieged them before they could catch anything.

'No need to worry, children. I guess you know me.'

Six of them turned to the direction a man's voice came from. They were taken aback to see him.

Aavishkar recollected, 'He's the one who was threatening Arjun outside the dhaba.'

'Good kid.' The man introduced himself, getting off his horse, 'Hello, everyone. *I'm Gajraj.*'

Prithvi asked rudely, 'What's this? Why are you here?'

Gajraj let out a peal of laughter. 'A prince should be more genteel, Prithviraj, don't you think? Anyway, I want the silver tablet.'

Prithvi couldn't react, shocked by his demand, his eyes widened in surprise.

Gajraj continued to see five blood-drained faces, 'What? Arjun told you nothing? He's the one who told me last night about the treasure you're looking for.'

Prithvi's muddled eyes darted at Arjun. 'What's he saying? *You* did this!'

'I did what I should have,' said Arjun, his face grave. 'You're going to find out a treasure and don't want to tell me anything. That's why I took *his* help.'

Prithvi and his friends' mouth hung with lips slightly parted.

'You wanted to use me,' said Arjun, coming beside Gajraj. 'Then why shouldn't I grind my own axe by getting a treasure?'

An outraged Samrat grabbed Arjun by the collar. 'YOU…'

'SAMRAT.' Prithvi made him leave Arjun. 'Fault is ours. We should've told him everything.'

'No. Our only fault is that we trusted a stranger,' said Kanak, staring at Arjun with impotent rage. 'You know Prithvi, why they've besieged us here like this?' She motioned her eyes to Gajraj. 'We were not on our guard, and now we can't escape or hide. We have to either fight or surrender.'

Gajraj clapped twice. '*Well done, girl.* You're unbelievable. You saw through my manoeuvre, but I won't let you queer my pitch. So, handover the tablet,' he said, cowing them, 'and without showing any new prowess, tell me the location of the treasure otherwise…'

Kabeer erupted. 'What treasure? Which location? We aren't going to search any *real* treasure. You know Arjun, the word *treasure* written on the tablet means *Khazanapur.*'

'I know what I should know. You just…'

Prithvi interrupted Arjun, 'No, you do not. Who didn't believe in your promise, tried to snatch your Moksha, you are with *him*?'

'They're not going to listen like this. We'll have to be abysmal.' Gajraj ordered his men, 'Grab the tablet and tie them up.'

Five of them rapidly drew their weapon, standing back to back in a circular defensive position.

Prithvi whispered to Samrat and Kabeer, 'Take a barrier, and mark your targets. *We'll* face them.'

'We aren't in Mangal group, Samrat. So we're not going to *kill* anyone until and unless the worst situation comes,' said Kanak in a firm but polite voice.

'It's a special instruction only for *me*?' aksed Samrat in exasperation.

Everyone girded up their loins. The two groups clashed.

Samrat and Kabeer immediately came behind a tree. On one side, Prithvi and Kanak with their sword and Aavishkar with his dagger were repulsing; on the other side, Kabeer with his crossbow and Samrat with his bow-arrow were aiming their targets.

A man moved to Aavishkar for a kill wound. Aavishkar stepped back to avoid the swing of his sword. Moving to his left, he brought his dagger down and dug it deep into his torso. As his opponent fell back, another attacker joined in the fight.

Prithvi and Gajraj's teams were engaged in a fierce combat. Gajraj's men were being distracted by Samrat and Kabeer's joint attacks. Both of them had been continuously blitzing them, their relentless and cruel arrows pounding down on them.

A man charged at Kanak, his sword raised. Kanak lifted her shield up for cover. Steel clashed with iron. She fought grimly, holding her enemy. She swung ferociously, pushing her sword into his shoulder. The attacker screamed in pain and fell back.

Kanak's eyes radiated shock laced with fear, catching sight of Arjun. A sword had appeared mysteriously in an unarmed Arjun's right hand.

As Prithvi's opponent fell back, another attacker charged upon him. He parried off his attack from the left and swung wildly in a smooth arc inflicting a superficial cut on his chest. Screaming in agony, he retreated. As Prithvi turned about, Gajraj punched him on the chin. He couldn't sustain this breakneck blow and fell down.

'Still want to fight, *prince*?' said Gajraj, gripping his sword.

Prithvi regained his wits and got up, raising his sword defensively. 'What can I say? I don't break easily.'

Gajraj moved unexpectedly, trying to strike Prithvi's left arm. Prithvi abruptly raised his right arm and swung his sword, inflicting a wound across Gajraj's shoulder. Gajraj's face contorted in anguish.

Arjun advanced to Prithvi and tried to stab him. Kanak, in no time, leapt forward, bringing her sword in between, foiling the attack. Prithvi turned to see two clanged swords.

'You're fond of backstabbing, aren't you?' said Kanak, strengthening her defence, forcing him to back off.

Arjun prepared his defence. 'I just know how to complete my task, and I'll do everything for it.' He deflected her swing with an adept move of his sword, stepping slightly back.

Kanak forcefully revolved her sword along with Arjun's and made his release from his hand. Without losing a moment, she threw a super-punch on his jaw. He staggered.

Amazed, Prithvi said, 'That's why you score full in martial arts!'

'One day I'll let *you* sense, how? But today's your lucky day.' Kanak made a beeline for Arjun.

Prithvi turned around not to find Gajraj. He glanced all around bewilderedly but couldn't get him.

Kanak pointed her sword threateningly close to a cornered Arjun's neck. 'First rule of the war, distract your opponent and get his neck under your blade.'

'Let him go. Something is more precious to him than loyalty and friendship,' said Prithvi, a pained expression came over his face.

Kanak took her sword back. 'I hope we will never meet again, Arjun.'

Prithvi spoke, 'Thank you for saving my life like this, Kanak. *Once again.*'

'*Once again? When?*' Kanak was in thought.

Aavishkar couldn't pay attention to the haversack, lying on the ground. One of Gajraj's men, playing his cards well, took the tablet out of it and rushed away.

'He's fleeing,' said Kabeer ardently.

'Because he has our tablet.' Samrat ran to Prithvi and Kanak, followed closely by Kabeer. 'Friends, a man has fled with the tablet.'

Aavishkar quickly picked up the haversack.

Prithvi glared at Arjun, sheathing his sword. 'Let's go. We shouldn't waste our time with *a traitor.*' He rushed off, accompanied by Kanak, Kabeer, Aavishkar and Samrat.

Arjun wiped some blood off his bruised lips and kept looking at them until they disappeared into the woods.

Gajraj's voice spoke from behind, 'Are you okay?'

Arjun turned. 'I'm fine. You're alright?' His perturbed eyes caught Gajraj's wounded shoulder. 'Where had you been, mamashree?'

'I'd to do some arrangements,' said Gajraj, unwrapping a piece of cloth covered his right palm, revealing the same kind of armour Arjun had. The only difference was its colour which was silver. 'I thought that girl...' he faltered. 'Arjun, if something happens like this, you can use your armour, son. Before anyone. Even before *them.*'

'I understand. You and babashree care about me but don't worry.' Arjun's face broke into a weak smile.

'So you took help from your horse?'

'You know Moksha very well. He'll lead them to the desert,' replied Arjun, turning in the direction five of them had gone.

***

'*NO...*' Anushka's cry echoed through the interrogation room.

'What did you think you'd be succeeded in annihilating Vyom by using our machines against us?' said a livid Damini.

'Why did you do it, Anushka? For Vikrant?' said Jaywardhan. 'You're so blind to his misdeeds, always at his beck and call that you never thought what he did to *you*.'

Anushka looked up sharply. 'My father always did best to me.'

'Then I'll dispel your doubt,' said Zaheer. He spoke through his wrist belt, 'Get our guest in.'

After a moment, Siddhant entered with a man, his hands cuffed behind his back.

'You know who he is,' said Zaheer, gesturing his head towards him, 'he's Farhan Malik and your *venerable father* Vikrant Kapoor sent this cat's paw to kill *you*.'

Anushka was shocked. 'No. My father would *never* do it.'

'You're not his daughter but a pawn. And if he's with you, why he hasn't taken a single step, made a little effort to save you yet,' said Zaheer. 'He lied to you that after killing Aaditya sir, Jay overcame Chancellor's position. The truth is, Aaditya sir was done to death by your father's man. After his murder, Vikrant disappeared. Later, he confessed everything before him.' He turned to the arrested man.

'We got this from Farhan.' Siddhant turned on an LED screen which showed a video. 'This is your father, isn't he?' he asked.

Anushka's breath caught in her throat, watching Vikrant talk about all his crimes.

'Vikrant misled you that Aaditya sir wanted to tell *him* about the Royal Weapon, but Jay killed him. Actually he wanted to tell Jay everything, but *Vikrant* was responsible for his cold-blooded murder,' told Damini, controlling her anger. 'He wanted to kill you too so that you couldn't create any obstacle in his way. He knew one day you'd be caught, so he had the arrangement for it. *Your murder*.'

'Please, stop poisoning my mind against my...'

'They're just making you aware.' Farhan's voice surprised Anushka. '*He's* a nefarious and selfish man.'

Anushka's lips sewed up.

'I'd been a factotum for him for past four years but now wanted to quit. Before he went back in time, he constrained me to kill you. When I jibbed at it, he threatened me to murder my family. *I* made this video secretly to reveal his crimes,' told Farhan, slightly belligerent.

'We could've told you all these earlier, but neither you wanted to believe us nor we had any evidence,' said Jaywardhan, looking down at her. 'You always trusted a person, Anushka, who never cared about you.'

Anushka bent her head. A veil lifted before her eyes, tears welled in them.

***

Chapter 18
Towards the Heaven on Earth

Prithvi, Kanak, Samrat, Kabeer and Aavishkar had been trying to catch up the man, around one hundred metres away from them. He'd led them into the depths of the wooded area.

'Who is he running so fast? Or should I ask *what* he is?' said Samrat, gasping.

'Let's figure it out.' Kabeer halted and released three arrows from his crossbow to him.

The man wheeled round and lifted his right hand towards them, his palm bore the same piece of armour like Arjun and Gajraj but bronze. Those arrows could not touch him. They stopped in mid-air and fell down. Five of them just goggled at him. The man smiled mischievously, seeing their ashen face.

'He is *the Unknown*,' said Aavishkar, wonderstruck.

Prithvi drew his weapon, giving silent signals to three of them to do the same. He was the first to move his feet to the man. As Kanak and Samrat stepped, followed by Kabeer and Aavishakar, a blaze of red light, appeared to be gushing out of the man, dazzled them. When they opened their eyes after the light died out, there was nothing but *an interminable desert* before them. They could see miles into the distance.

Prithvi gaped. 'What…is…!'

'How could those trees turn…?' Samrat's voice stuck in his throat. He, stupefied, was looking all around at the infinite expanse of sand.

A recoiled Aavishkar's eyes caught the tablet lying at a distance. He took it outright.

'Take care of it, Avi. It's essential for us,' said Prithvi, nonplussed.

'Why did that man lead us to here?' asked Aavishkar, keeping the tablet in the haversack.

'*What a question, Avi*!' said Prithvi, his eyes widened in realization. 'He *wanted* us to reach here but why?'

Transfixed, Kabeer said, 'And where did he go? He just… vanished.'

Prithvi spoke, 'What's happening with us? First, Gajraj suddenly disappeared and now that man.'

'Who zapped us here after flaring himself up,' added Samrat.

Kanak provided a running commentary on how a sword appeared in Arjun's hand.

Aavishkar managed to say in a trembling voice, 'Are we in *Fairyland*?'

'Where *a man* wants to help us if this is the same desert we're looking for,' said Samrat.

'We have to move then.' Kabeer took a few steps ahead. 'What else can we do?'

'Why don't you ensure, Kabeer, where the north is?' said Kanak.

Kabeer asked, 'What do you mean?'

'According to the fifth line, *proceed towards the Heaven on Earth at any cost*,' Kanak called up the riddle. 'The Heaven on Earth means Kashmir which is in the north of India.'

'*Fantastic*! First time your talent of *over thinking* helped us, Kanak,' said Prithvi in an amused tone. 'Otherwise…'

'Prithvi, it's really hard for you to appreciate Kanak?' asked Aavishkar, cheesed off. 'Then why do you do it in her absence?'

Aavishkar's question attracted Kanak's attention. 'What does he say, Aavishkar, in my absence?'

Aavishkar had to lean back to avoid a light blow from Prithvi.

Prithvi said, giving a look, 'Avi, don't do it now.'

Samrat piped up, looking briefly at Prithvi, 'How are we going to find the north, Avi? Sun's down.'

'*The cluster of stars* will point us to the north, mates,' said Kabeer, looking into the sky.

Everyone gave him a questioning look.

Prithvi registered from the corner of his eye that Kanak was still staring at him soberly.

***

Arjun and Gajraj were passing through a busy market of Khazanapur, a group of vigilant and cautious local people escorting them.

'Do they really belong to Vyom, mamashree? Are they worthy to reach us, to reach Ananyaakashganga?' asked Arjun.

'It seems to me. They reached the tablet, they had the map of Professor Dhanraj's painting, and they fought very well,' said Gajraj. 'So did we lose?'

Arjun's mouth curved into a smile. 'They're more than expected. And we were not supposed to harm them. We have to only find out how capable they are.'

'It's just an onset.' Gajraj asked, 'What about *Pradarshak*?'

'Last night when they were asleep, I sneaked into the room and kept it in their bag.'

'You know very well what to do next,' said Gajraj, coming to a stop near a crossroad.

Arjun only nodded.

Gajraj studied his serious expression. 'You want to tell something?'

Arjun took a deep breath. 'What I did to them... I meant first I won their trust and then...'

'You did what your father asked you to do. Don't think so much about it, son.'

Arjun replied, solemnity written all over his face, 'I want them to meet us again, mamashree. I wish to tell them about myself, that I am *not* a traitor.'

***

'*Well done!*' said Vikrant, patting Aashutosh on the back, his eyes emanating extreme happiness. 'You've solved half of my problem by taking us here in 1305.'

He and his team had camped near a barren valley in the east of Khazanapur, wanted to be hidden from the villagers.

'After all, the catch-machine did its job, sir.'

'How did it happen?'

'When we'd reached near DTM before its disappearance, the catch-machine was in my hand. It might've caught some signals from DTM's system. I'd to extract *the time* it travelled into from the transferred information,' told Aashutosh. 'We must thank Anushka for giving Manasvi to us.' He looked relieved and gratified. 'She's...'

'What else do you have to tell me?' cut in Vikrant.

'We still can't access DTM, but the catch-machine is obtaining the data from the source-system telling it's here.'

Vikrant said, pondering, 'I can't wait anymore. We'll hunt the source-system up. It's the only way to DTM now.'

***

'We must go back in time, Jay. DTM's not returned yet, and Vikrant is there,' said Zaheer, sitting in a front seat of a beige car.

Jaywardhan was behind the wheel. Both of them were riding back to the institute.

'Kushal is about to finish his job,' told Jaywardhan. 'He'll be back by day after tomorrow.'

'And what did you think about Anushka?'

The silence stretched on.

'*What a man Vikrant is!* He hoodwinked his own daughter,' spoke Jaywardhan in a low, steady voice. 'She didn't understand him.'

'Organization knows that Vikrant was behind all this. You haven't reported it about her. Why?' asked Zaheer, his eyes looked eager.

'I'm not saying she didn't do anything wrong, Zaheer. *Yes, she did,*'

Jaywardhan's voice was controlled. 'But should we not understand that she's what Vikrant made her?' He exhaled sharply. 'I leave this matter with you and Damini. Just let me know your decision.'

***

Prithvi, Kanak, Samrat, Kabeer and Aavishkar, plodding in the desert, had resumed their journey northwards after resting for some time. The sky was clear, a full moon shining.

'It's been a long time, pals. I'm frazzled.' Aavishkar somehow was pushing on.

'We'd rested for an hour, hadn't we, *slowcoach*?' Samrat caught his hand and started propelling him.

Aavishkar looked to be on his last legs. 'This journey has knackered me. We've been gliding on since Kabeer had found the north at the dead of night.'

Kanak said, 'Aavishkar, we're looking for a hint to get *that* dune.'

'Kabeer, you told us where the north direction is by seeing or reckoning, *whatever*, the stars, but how did you figure it out, *egghead*?' asked Samrat.

'Ma'am Zaidi had given us a topic, *We and the Stars,* for the project in the class of Astronomy,' told Kabeer. 'I studied how we could learn the geographic directions by observing the stars.'

'Since we started moving northwards, we've been seeing many sand dunes. How could we get *the one* we've to hunt down?' asked Aavishkar *ultimately.*

Samrat ribbed Kabeer. 'The location of that dune is not in any book of yours, *bibliophile*?'

'Friends, look there. Again we have five-six possibilities,' said Aavishkar, pointing towards a group of distant sand dunes. 'How can we look for *our mound*?'

'Does the riddle not say anything about it?' Prithvi's mind tried to work the problem out.

'We must have a hint. Something is escaping our notice I guess. Isn't it?'

Kanak's question hung in the air as they experienced wind taking on a sudden ferocity. Sands started diffusing, scudding and swirling with the gust, gradually formed hazy layers around them. They couldn't sink in the mystery behind these variations in the weather.

'Whether we get any hint or not, but I'm getting a portent for sure,' said Kabeer, panic overtook his face.

'And the calamity is just behind you. WATCH OUT.' Samrat drew their attention to a fierce sandstorm hastily oncoming them.

They jumped up in fright.

'We're doomed.' Prithvi walked back, baffled. 'Nerve yourselves…'

They'd left with no option but to run for their lives. As they were fast, cleaving the haziness of sand layers, so was the storm, keeping pace with them. They tried to ride out of the whirlwind, outpacing it with their whole strength.

Aavishkar turned back without reducing his pace. 'It's approaching with lightning speed.'

'Grasp one another's hands quickly,' suggested Samrat.

The boisterous vortex was so close to engulf them. It took it five more seconds to take them into its blow.

***

Anushka had to be transferred from the interrogation room to *Parishkar*, a highly secured prison perched on *Jwala*, one of the small islands of *Vyomdweep* in the south-east of Niketan. She wanted a word with Jaywardhan, Zaheer and Damini before leaving.

'I'd come here with a mission on my mind. Mission to destroy Vyom. Mission to destroy all of you. But the only thing I've done is ruin myself,' said Anushka in a feeble voice, her eyelids drooped. 'I reflected a lot about all these. Whenever papa met me, he always talked about *this* mission, not how I held up. I couldn't understand him. *His fury, his vindictiveness* wrecked me, sparked vengeance into me.' She squeezed her eyes shut.

Three of them remained quiet, gazing at her with sympathy. For a moment, there was an uncomfortable silence in the room.

'I told papa that one of Vyom's agents was with him. He definitely shot Ali, but actually *I* killed him.' Anushka looked up in apology. Tears held back in her eyes, burst forth in a gush. 'I was never worthy of trust and love you all gave me.'

Zaheer said, sensing regret in her voice, 'We're providing you an attorney...'

'I don't deserve it, sir,' Anushka's voice interrupted him. 'There's nothing left in my life I will fight for.' She wiped the tears flowing down her cheeks. *'Let's end this.'*

***

Chapter 19

The Blue Sky underneath a Desert

The storm had passed. The sun was at the horizon.

Prithvi, Kanak, Samrat, Kabeer and Aavishkar seemed to be coming to their senses. They ran their bleary eyes all around to find themselves partially covered with sand, lying scattered on the sand field in a hundred-metre radius. They stood up. Flummoxed. Agitated. Addled.

'What was that?' Prithvi brushed the sand off his clothes. 'A sandstorm!'

'Strange incidents have been supervening since we came to Khazanapur,' said Kanak, her face puckered.

'Have you noticed it?' asked Aavishkar, staring hard at a dune beyond Samrat. 'The storm altered the entire pattern of this desert. All the sand dunes have diffused erratically except *that one*.' He lifted his finger towards it. 'It's one of those five-six dunes I'd told you about before the storm came. I remember it was on the same spot.' He never once took his eyes off it.

Samrat's eyes grew large. 'Then why and how did that dune withstand the storm?'

'*We've got it*,' shouted Kanak so loudly that the rest of them jumped. She took the tablet out of the haversack. 'Seventh line of the riddle says, *whatever is, will still be there unaffected by air.* It's for this sand dune which was here before and still is, *unaffected* by the storm.'

Kabeer asked, 'So now we have to dig it?'

'First a river and now a sand dune.' Samrat looked jaded.

'We should try, Samrat,' said Aavishkar optimistically. 'According to A.P.J. Abdul Kalam, *Failure will never overtake us if our determination to succeed is strong enough.*'

Samrat concurred, beaming. 'And if we fail, never give up because FAIL means *First Attempt In Learning.*'

Aavishkar's eyes glowed in mild surprise.

***

'For last twenty minutes we've been digging out this dune in search of the Royal Weapon,' said Aavishkar desultorily, 'but forget any weapon, we didn't get even *a needle.*'

Prithvi stopped all at once. 'What's it?'

Kanak's eyes followed Prithvi's hands expectantly. '*The Royal Weapon?*'

They briskly removed the sand from the thing Prithvi had touched, revealing a removable rectangular metal plate.

'Is this a manhole cover? We're going into a sewer?' said Samrat surprisingly. 'This is a desert, friends.'

They managed to remove the metal cover though it was heavy.

'It's pitch-black,' said Samrat, peering inside. 'I guess it's time to use this.' He withdrew a mini-torch from a side pocket of his kurta.

'Where did you get it from?' questioned Aavishkar.

Kabeer told, 'We'd brought some requisites with us from the hostel.'

'Although those *insolent soldiers* snatched all our things, I kept it hidden and later put it in my kurta.' Samrat lit the torch.

Kanak asked with a complaining tone, 'Shouldn't you have told us about it *earlier?*'

'I didn't remember. How?' Samrat looked at Kabeer. 'Has somebody's company affected me?'

Kabeer's eyes rolled.

Prithvi said, 'I can see a ladder going down, but there isn't a single hint of water.'

'Our voice is echoing. It means whether it's an empty cellar or a tunnel or something like it,' informed Kabeer.

Aavishkar looked hopeful. 'The Royal Weapon may be inside. We should go in.'

'We don't know exactly what's inside,' said an irresolute Kanak.

Samrat spoke, 'According to the riddle we're going right. We have to take this risk.'

Aavishkar said, 'Please Kanak, don't do anything stupid. Prithvi really wouldn't want to leave you this time.'

Kanak punched Aavishkar's shoulder. '*Let's go then.*'

Prithvi smiled, looking at Aavishkar rubbing his shoulder, the others looked amused.

Samrat was the first to climb down, the torch in his hand. 'Be careful everyone.'

After around fifteen steps, he landed on the ground, followed by four of them.

'It appears a tunnel to me,' said Kanak, trying to adjust her eyes to the light of the torch, 'where will it let out?'

No sign of life was found in the grey-walled tunnel barely lit by the torch. The floor was littered with stones and dried leaves and twigs, crunched beneath every step and echoed.

Abruptly, Kabeer shouted, jumping back. 'NO…'

Aavishkar asked instantly, 'What happened?'

'Some…something passed, touching my ear,' told Kabeer, unnerved.

Samrat exhaled noisily. 'I thought a ghost caught you.'

Kabeer took umbrage at his remarks. 'And *that ghost* is talking to me right now.'

A riled Kanak said, 'Could you both *please* keep quiet.'

Prithvi faked surprise. 'You know the word *please*? Why don't you use it when you argue with me?'

'You don't deserve this word, Mr Malhotra,' said Kanak, annoyance clouded her features.

Samrat mumbled, 'Their epic also begins.' He stepped ahead but stumbled down.

The torch left his hand and went out, hitting the ground. Darkness swallowed the tunnel once again.

'Are you okay?' asked Kanak, scrabbling for Samrat, but she overbalanced stuck by his leg.

'Now who's gone?' Prithvi's voice conveyed a playful chuckle. Within a second, he bumped into the floor, his face forward.

Kanak said, giggling, 'You too, Prithvi.'

A vexed Prithvi smashed his fist against the ground. 'It's *eighth time*.'

'I make *Prithvi Promise*. Sooner or later, you'll say, *it's hundredth time*,' Kanak made a rude rejoinder.

Suddenly, the glow from the torch illuminated their face. Samrat, Prithvi and Kanak looked up to see Kabeer holding it. He gave a wry smile. 'I hope you two have decided to belt up. Shall we move?'

Three of them stood up, Prithvi and Kanak busy in glaring at each other.

'*Yagya...Yagya...*' a clarion but disembodied voice pealed there, a sharp echo followed. '*Yugant is awaiting you, Yagya. But before him, you will have to meet me.*'

Befuddled, Aavishkar looked all around. 'What's it?'

Kanak turned to see a perplexed and bewildered Prithvi.

A brief silence covered the tunnel, and now what they heard was a deep boom, followed by a rumbling noise.

'Thunders?' Kabeer was at sixes and sevens.

'SAVE YOURSELVES. The tunnel's falling down.' As Kanak said, they broke into a run.

The tunnel had begun to cave in. The arched walls crumbled and pieces of rocks showered, hitting them, wounding them. They, somehow, were trying to get away. Soon they saw daylight indicating the end of the tunnel. Prithvi, Kanak, Samrat and Aavishkar debouched, but Kabeer lagged. The exit of the tunnel collapsed.

'KABEER…' cried Aavishkar.

A look of terror flashed across Samrat's face. 'Kabeer, are you alright?'

'Yes. But I have claustrophobia,' Kabeer's voice quivered.

Four of them struggled to shift the unwieldy rocks post-haste, making space for Kabeer to get out. When the hole became big enough, Kabeer appeared, standing appalled. Their eyes beamed with relief, seeing him unhurt. Samrat extended his hand. Kabeer gripped it. As soon as Samrat pulled him out and they reached two metres away, the remaining tunnel shattered.

'Thank God, you didn't go into stupor,' said Samrat, leaving Kabeer's hand.

'We're beneath a desert. Is this greenery bothering anyone of you?' Kanak gaped to find herself on a piece of grassland blooming on all sides.

The land heated up. Colourful buds began to flower on the trees, casting shadows onto the fresh, long grasses.

'And what can you say about this?' Samrat looked up. '*The blue sky underneath a desert.*'

Four of them lifted their head to the morning sky; it was clear and bright. The sun was shining on their face. Prithvi and his friends were assuming themselves safe, but it was just their illusion.

'Now what happened to our Mother Earth?' A blanched Kabeer felt his feet shaking.

Prithvi looked down. 'Is it earthquake?'

Before they could catch on something, they saw debris of the tunnel go down. The ground moved up and down, screaming. The vibrations came from below with deafening noise. The grassland around them started rupturing. They turned around to race against this disaster.

'Where is it coming from?' asked Aavishkar, addled.

An iron track was laid ten feet away, seemed to be coming from the far right end of the grass field, then turning straight. A six seated sepia coaster car having two levers adjacent to its front seat, was standing over it.

Kanak said, 'It doesn't matter, Avi. You should ask *where it's leading to.*'

'Is it a roller coaster?' wondered Samrat.

'Let's have a ride.' Prithvi rushed towards the car.

'What? NO...' Kabeer seemed askance.

'We can't overcome this destruction with our speed. We need something faster.' Samrat grasped Kabeer's hand and made him move. 'Otherwise we'll die.'

'*We will die anyhow,*' deprecated a totally terrified Kabeer, pulling his hand from his. 'I'm tired of running, escaping, fighting. It's a deadlock, Samrat. We're not going to be saved.'

'Don't give up, brother,' said Prithvi, barely concealing his stress. 'It may be an inception, but we've to dare to encounter the worst possibilities, to hold out against all hopeless situations.'

Aavishkar looked beyond Samrat at the cataclysm coming to them speedily. 'Couldn't we continue this conversation later?'

'You promised that you'd be with me till the end,' said Samrat. 'And believe me, Kabeer, this is not the end.' He put his hand forward.

Kabeer pushed all negative thoughts out of his mind, seeing his friends' eyes shone with hope and encouragement. 'Then what are we waiting for?' He grabbed Samrat's hand and rushed off, followed by three of them.

As soon as they got inside the car, it sped up.

'How did you launch it?' asked Kanak, barely sitting behind Aavishkar.

'I did not touch any of two levers,' replied Aavishkar, from the front seat, dazed and flustered.

Prithvi balanced himself. 'It's running *automatically*!'

They turned about to see the disaster just a breath away, turning the land and tracks into detritus.

The car gradually accelerated, passed the twisted and steep tracks of the roller coaster, outrunning the debacle. The slides were rising in many patterns having vertical loops, turning them upside down. They could see miles into the grassland. The sun was washing it with a yellow late-morning glow. Gem-blue ponds flickered like glitter. Fluttering butterflies, singing birds, the aroma of the ambience made it a paradise. They appeared lost, their lips broke into a peaceful smile.

And the blessed moment ended.

Samrat attracted their attention to a crest of the ramp, two hundred metres away. 'We're going to cross *that*?'

'We're roaring with about fifty kilometer per hour, and its drop is approximately ninety metres,' surmised Aavishkar. 'Can we make it?'

'SIT TIGHT,' shouted Prithvi.

The car rose to the peak, stood there for a while, and after racing down the declivity, it hurtled straight. They didn't have time to get their breaths back. They had a reason to hold them. The journey through the heaven was over. The *about to finish* track was leading them to the edge of a cliff.

Kabeer took a quick peek and drew back. 'I can see nothing.'

It seemed to be their last day on earth. Death stared them in the face.

Prithvi suggested, 'Protect your head. Clasp your seat.'

The car rocketed, crossing the limit of the track, flew for ten seconds and then making a curve, swept downwards.

Five of them slammed into a bed of snow but without the car. Nobody opened their eyes for a trice. Kanak was the first to do it, followed by the rest of them. Their head whirled. Their heart pounded. Their breaths wheezed. They remained immobile, only their irises moved. It took them five minutes to come to the ground state and rise to their feet. A blanket of snow was visible as far as they could see.

'Snow… and snow… and only snow.' Samrat, bowled over, glanced upon all sides. 'It was deep-dark here.'

Prithvi for a second went blank. 'Just like only sand and sand.'

'Where are the car and those tracks?' asked Aavishkar, looking up at a dove grey sky. 'Why does everything vanish here?'

'And why does every time our fate favour us?' Kanak appeared skeptical. 'Kabeer was trapped in a nearly collapsed tunnel, and when he was rescued unscathed *only then* it fell apart. The land didn't sink until we came inside a coaster car, and then it moved *itself*. Now, a pitch-black bottom has converted into a snow bed.'

'And what about the sky we'd already noticed? Although it's changed from blue to grey,' said Samrat, pointing his index finger up. 'It's like controlling natural powers.'

Kabeer spoke, 'It's surely a snowfield, but the weather's balmy. Had such snowfall occurred in Vyom, what would've happened to us in these clothes?'

***

Tracking down Aavriti, Vikrant and his troop reached the same wooded area, Prithvi and his team had been led into by the mysterious man.

'Sir, the catch-machine can't hack the source-system now. It's stopped receiving signals,' told Aashutosh.

Vikrant fumed. 'Those children have been bedeviling me. Aashutosh, we have to hunt that system down.'

'You can reach neither those children,' a steady voice spoke from behind them, 'nor the Royal Weapon.'

Vikrant turned to see a bald man attired in a long black robe.

'They're in Ananyaakashganga.' He wore a wide grin.

Vikrant questioned, 'Who are you?'

'Saketraj.' The man, looked to be in his late forties, stepped towards Vikrant. '*From Ananyaakashganga.*'

Vikrant said, a ray of hope in his eyes, 'That's why you know about it.'

'What if I send you there?'

'*What?!* What did you say?' said Vikrant, slack-jawed.

'You're clever and intelligent as you reached *here*. But *this* is your limit,' said Saket gruffly.

Vikrant said, all agog, 'I'll do *anything* you want. Just take me to the Royal Weapon.'

'I cannot enter Ananyaakashganga. I was banished fourteen years ago from it by *my brother*.' Saket came closer to Vikrant, measuring his ambition in his eyes. 'You're left with only two options then. Either you get Ananyaakashganga's Protector Tilakraj's permission what is *impossible* or you have *this*.' He showed his right palm wearing a piece of silver armour like a fingerless glove. '*Dhruva Armour. This* is the fountainhead of powers of all the *Dhruvas*, Ananyaakashganga's inhabitants. Our world is based on these powers. *Nakshtra* and *Vidhvans*.'

Saket lifted his hand and marked his armour at a tree next to Aashutosh. As he clenched his fist, a purple light emerged from his armour and burnt the tree to ashes in a jiffy. Not a single word came out of Vikrant's mouth. An eye opener scene he and his men had faced.

Saket made an offer, 'And I can give it to you, Vikrant.'

'Why will you do it?' asked Vikrant, dubiety creeping into his brain.

'I don't help anyone gratuitously. I'll give you my armour so you can get the Royal Weapon as who are protecting it, they can be fought with it only.' Saket added, 'And in return, you'll have to bring Arjun's armour for me.'

Vikrant said, his forehead scrunched up, '*Arjun*...?'

'He's my nephew, son of my big brother, *Tilakraj*,' spoke Saket, burning with hatred.

This fact floored Vikrant. He exchanged a confused look with Aashutosh.

***

Prithvi, Kanak, Samrat, Kabeer and Aavishkar were sitting on the snowfield near a group of blue pine trees covered by snow in perfect white. The evening sun struggled through the murky clouds and succeeded in bestowing its golden brilliance on the soft, silver snow. The wind was howling, sometimes piling up snow in drifts.

Prithvi told, grabbing Aavishkar's wrist, 'Your watch's glass is open.' He pressed the black button below Aavriti's LED screen.

'It's not working.' As Aavishkar pressed the red crown, Aavriti's glass cased its face.

'I didn't know that,' said Prithvi with a look of unfeigned regret.

'We must push off now.' Kanak stood up, followed by four of them.

Kabeer said, tightening the string of his crossbow, 'I'm parched, friends.'

'And I think we've finished our water storage we brought from Arjun's place.' Samrat reached into the haversack and groped for the water bottle but he got something else. He took it out.

Kanak moved her eyes around disappointingly. 'Where will we get water here?'

Aavishkar asked to see an emerald glass sphere in Samrat's hand, 'What's it? It doesn't look like any machine.'

Prithvi took it from him. 'It...' His foot caught in the snow, and he fell down.

The sphere shed and bounced away.

'Why do you blame Kanak?' Aavishkar helped Prithvi up. 'Don't you always fall without any reason, do you?'

The sphere rolled for around ten metres and then stopped abruptly. To their surprise, it flared with a red light for a moment. They were too terrified to blink.

After two seconds, it returned to a muddled Prithvi. He picked it up.

The snow shifted from the area the sphere had halted, revealing an ice sheet.

Kabeer cautiously arrived at the place, controlling his fear and surprise. 'I guess we're standing on a frozen lake or something.' As he looked up, the ice cracked and water jetted out of it, washing him well-nigh. He receded apace. 'It's so frigid.'

An elated Samrat said, 'Great. We got water... of the *fridge*.'

'*It* did this?' asked Aavishkar, watching the sphere in rapt attention. '*What is it?*'

'I hope it's not a jinx,' said Prithvi.

'And I hope it keeps us away from death's gates.' Kanak stared at the sphere with narrowed eyes.

***

'Jay... Jay...' Zaheer rushed into Jaywardhan's cabin, gladness seemed to emanate from deep inside him. '*DTM is back.*'

'*What!*' Jaywardhan's face lit up in a beatific smile reaching his ears. 'Samarth and children have returned.' He was more than happy.

Zaheer's grin vanished. 'No, Jay. They're not back but DTM. They might be busy in their task. Samarth couldn't have sent it earlier because of some reason but now he has.'

'And now we should not be late,' said Jaywardhan. 'Four *Yatra* time machines are ready. Call Kushal, and get DTM's location in 1180.'

'Venugopal found that it's returned from 1305 instead of 1180. I'm also shocked.'

'1305!' said Jaywardhan, confounded. He whispered to himself, 'What if Samarth had discovered the gorge? What if he knew a way to reach Ananyaakashganga?' He turned to Zaheer. 'Call an emergency meeting. We're going to 1305 tomorrow.'

'Very well.' Zaheer turned to leave.

'And I'm happy from your and Damini's decision,' said Jaywardhan with a content smile. 'It wasn't an easy one.'

'You would've done the same thing, Jay.' Zaheer returned the smile. 'She deserves a second chance.'

***

Chapter 20
Mammoth in 1305!

'I don't like to crawl on the snow,' said Aavishkar. 'Where will we be heading for, by the way?'

Five of them were ready to set forth to their next destination what only God knew.

'The one thing I know from my experience is we have to move on, no matter what.' Kanak stood up. 'We'll get our ways.'

A lopsided grin flickered over Prithvi's face. 'It may be a long journey. Will you be comfortable in walking on the snow, Kanak?'

Kanak asked impassively, 'What do you want, Prithvi?'

'He just wants to hold your hand and take a walk,' said Aavishkar in a fruity voice.

Prithvi's smile disappeared as quickly as it came. 'Will you ever stop it, Avi?'

'*Not at all*. How will we get to know *Prithvi's secrets* then?' Samrat collapsed into helpless laughter.

A smiley Kabeer looked beyond an embarrassed Prithvi to find a gigantic figure loomed out of nowhere at a distance. His smile vanished. 'I pray it's not a red flag.'

The rest of them turned around. They walked back, baffled to see a tremendous quadruped brute approaching them.

'*Impossible!*' Prithvi was momentarily taken back. 'Is it a *mammoth*?'

Samrat's eyebrows arched in wide disbelief. 'Were mammoths there in 1305?'

'Its pace indicates that it can attack us,' said Kanak, staring at a huge mammoth with very long, curved tusks treading to them.

Without losing a moment, they quickly hid behind the pine trees.

Samrat whispered, 'It's too large. We have to turn its strength into its Achilles heel.'

'No need to do it, Samrat,' a heavy voice spoke from a short distance. 'I'm not here to harm any one of you.'

Their eyes stealthily followed the source of the sound.

'Why are you children taking this risk to find some *weapon*? Why don't you go back you've come from? It's easier.'

They trembled in disbelief to see the jumbo mammoth talking.

'How…how could it…?' A flabbergasted Aavishkar tried to utter.

The pachyderm said, 'I can do a lot more than this, Aavishkar.'

Their heart started beating faster, the blood had run from their face. They were witnessing something their mind would never be able to erase.

'You'll be facing many more uncanny creatures if and only if you continue,' the mammoth spoke, 'otherwise the back door is open.'

Prithvi said, burying his fear deep, 'We'd like to meet your friends, actually. We like surprises.' He drew his sword silently.

The mammoth advanced to them. 'I hope you'll not regret, Prithviraj. Your decision may cast your friends into a trench of perils.'

Prithvi lowered his sword, looked thoughtful.

Kanak spoke, undaunted, 'He will not as *this story depends on wisdom and overcoming fear.*'

Samrat was totally of one mind with her. 'His friends always stand for him against all odds.'

'We've gone through a lot, and we can together prevail against anything,' said Kabeer, giving Prithvi an encouraging grin.

'Together?' The mammoth added, 'We've seen your phenomenal teamwork. It's time to do something singly.'

Before they could decide on a course of action, a new danger stared them in their face.

As Prithvi blinked, he found himself alone surrounded by dense layers of mist. The view was blurred. He closed his eyes, exhaling. '*So fast*, mammoth.'

His thoughts were broken as the ambience rang with a penetrating voice but it was neither of his friends nor of the mammoth.

'*I will keep my fidelity. I will let you win for the eternal loss.*'

Prithvi stepped, straining to determine the direction of the voice, his eyes looked guarded. 'Who's it?'

He realised the fog dwindling and saw a shadow sweep in the distance, a hazy movement. 'Kanak?'

He darted towards it. All of a sudden, an icy wall emerged from the ground before him and raised high in air. He had to draw up. 'KANAK...' his voice echoed.

He turned around to find himself in a place bordered by high walls of ice. An arcane place full of silence, desolation and coldness. The only sound that met his ears was his own echoing footsteps. He saw a long icy staircase fifteen metres away to the left. He was about to lift his feet to move, but he felt them wet. He looked down.

Glacial water had started to fill the place he was caged in. A nonplussed Prithvi walked back but immediately stood still as he sensed something behind him. He tried to see from the corner of his eye and turned slowly. He forgot to breathe to find a monstrous blue-ringed octopus floating before, willing to welcome him. He froze, heard his heart beat thumping. The water had filled up to his knees. He bent down his eyes steadily, taking his sword out of his scabbard.

Trailing its eight arms behind, the octopus swam to him. It stretched one of its arms and coiled it around him.

Prithvi took a deep breath. 'I liked the surprise.' He swung his sword, wounding its arm and hurried to the stairs.

The octopus rushed after him, keeping up. Prithvi ran upstairs at full pelt. The water increased its level promptly, wishing to outdistance him.

In the same deserted, perishing place built of icy walls and stairs, a lost Kabeer could hear only his own wheeze, the crossbow in his hands. 'H-E-L-L-O. Friends, where are you all?'

His face slammed against something. He was on tenterhooks, seeing a long pale blue tail hanging from the icy ceiling. He looked up and let out a gasp of shock to see a blue iguana sticking to the roof. His breaths uprooted.

The iguana abruptly left the ceiling and landed before him, only one metre away.

Kabeer's body froze for five seconds. He managed to draw himself back. 'Back off, lizard. Maintain your distance.'

He turned his neck, seeking out a way to escape. His eyes radiated hope as he found a staircase going down to his right. He oriented himself, placing his finger on the trigger of the crossbow.

The iguana edged closer to Kabeer, not taking its golden iris off him, its red tongue repeatedly coming out.

Kabeer pulled the trigger, hitting its left eye with two arrows. The iguana retreated, and he fled to the staircase.

A myriad of white-winged vampire bats was chasing Kanak climbing long, spiral and slippery icy stairs. Whenever she stepped up, an icy door came before. She opened it. Again were the stairs and again was a door.

Everyone was ensnared in an enclosed, confusing, multi-level structure, full of ferocious creatures with no entrance, no exit. It had icy identical stairs, passages, doorways and chambers.

Kabeer and Prithvi together entered a large, vaulted icy chamber through two doors opposite to each other.

'You're all right?' asked Prithvi, panting.

Kabeer nodded his head, gasping for breath. 'You?'

As he asked, Kanak ran into through the same door Prithvi came in and bumped against him. She fell down, taking him along.

Prithvi winced. '*She's* perfectly alright.'

'Someone's coming.' Kabeer heard footsteps approaching. He turned right to see Samrat come up after opening a floor door.

'Who's got you, Samrat?' asked Prithvi, standing.

'What's the most dangerous predator in an iceland, Kabeer?' Samrat was huffing and puffing.

Kabeer asked, gobsmacked, '*A polar bear* is behind you?'

Samrat nodded. 'It was *a phantom.*'

Kanak asked, 'Where is Aavishkar?'

'He might've escaped,' hoped Kabeer.

The doorways exploded, throwing ice everywhere, revealing the ferocious octopus, iguana, vampire bats and polar bear.

'Now, how do *we* escape, Kabeer?' said Samrat, receding.

'OVER THERE.' Kanak attracted their attention to a doorway on the right corner of the chamber.

They bolted towards it.

'*What!*' reacted Samrat to find it shutting.

Kabeer turned, watching in trepidation and horror. 'They're after us.'

'Don't distract yourselves. Just outrun them,' spoke Prithvi.

As fast they were approaching the door, so were the perilous creatures. The door was about to shut. They felt their heartbeat escalating. Angry and sonorous voices coming from behind filled them with a piercing chill.

First Kabeer and Prithvi, then Kanak and Samrat funnelled out before the door blocked the access completely.

'Here, the weather and scenes change like we turn the pages of a calendar,' said Kabeer, out of his breath.

It was a sombre-stormy night out there. The thunders were deafening them. The lightning was flashing the environs.

'If we were two seconds late, either we would've been squeezed between these doors or those savage creatures squashed us to death,' heaved Samrat.

Kanak asked, 'Why was the gate closing? Itself?'

'It's out of question. Everything is occurring here *itself,*' said Prithvi. 'For now, we must find Avi.'

The lightning shone again, displaying a boy before them. 'I was expecting all of you.'

'*Arjun!*' A single word came on Kanak's lips.

Four of them were transfixed. It was beyond their expectation.

Arjun stepped, some soldiers escorting him. One of them was the rangy girl they'd met near the farm of Khazanapur.

'What are *you* doing here?!' asked Prithvi, bafflement enveloped his face.

A guileless smile floated on Arjun's lips. 'I'm here to help.'

'Like you helped before?'

Kanak's words made Arjun's smile vanish. 'I'm sorry, but I was under order,' he said, his expression serious.

'Someone ordered you to betray us and you followed?' Prithvi bordered on him. 'We trusted you, Arjun. *I* trusted you.'

Arjun saw resentment in his eyes. His words sealed his lips. Somehow, he said, 'You and your friends deserve to get the Royal Weapon, Prithvi. I'm here to take you to it.'

Bewildered, Kabeer asked, 'You know about it?!'

Arjun ordered the soldiers, 'Take them to father.'

Samrat straightaway strained his arrow on him. 'We're not going anywhere with *a traitor.*'

The rangy girl drew her sword swiftly. 'Mind your words…'

'Anahita…' Arjun calmly stopped her.

She reluctantly sheathed her sword, glaring at Samrat.

'You do not know anything about me, Samrat. But I want your misunderstanding to be dispelled. So, come with us,' said Arjun. When Samrat didn't put his weapon down, he looked at Prithvi. 'I did not betray you. I was fulfilling my responsibility.'

After a pause, Prithvi asked Samrat, 'Lower the arrow.'

Samrat said, raucous, 'Prithvi, you're…'

'I want to know what *he is* exactly, Samrat,' said Prithvi.

Samrat threw his irate eyes at Arjun and moved his arrow down.

'What about Avi?' asked Kabeer worriedly.

Anahita showed a haversack. 'Do you recognise it?'

Kanak swiftly took it. 'Aavishkar…'

***

Having walked over a wooden bridge, the group crossed an ochre lake on a boat, after which stretched a straight road. Four of them had experienced so much that the water of the lake didn't surprise them. After travelling for one kilometre, they found hundreds of very long strings of pearls dangling before, making a curtain, stretching from one side to the other as far as the eye could see.

Kabeer looked up. 'Do these have an extremity?'

Arjun touched the pearls' curtain with his right palm having the Golden Armour. The compact strings broke. Thousands of pearls interspersed in air. They tore towards them and dispersed, touching them.

A magnificent and majestic red-walled fort, rising out of the darkness, stared them in the face. It sprawled over a hill above the plains of a valley drained by a turquoise blue river. It was surrounded by tall trees like great armies protecting its citadel.

Kabeer's eyes were out on stalks. 'This fort is like the one carved behind the tablet.'

'Yes, it is. Because of *that* tablet we learnt that you've come here for searching the Royal Weapon,' said Arjun, without turning to them. 'Welcome to the fort of Ananyaakashganga.' He led them to the drawbridge.

'*Ananyaakashganga*!' Samrat whispered to Kanak, 'What do you think we're on the right track?'

Kanak nodded. 'According to the riddle, we have to find out the pearls. And just now, we've passed a storm of them.'

Prithvi fell in thought, looking at Arjun's armour. 'This sun is *something* to me. I don't know why?'

They passed the barbican to enter the lowest main courtyard. As they crossed a massive stone gate flanked by six pentagonal towers, a green imperial pigeon, flying, appeared out of nowhere and sat on Arjun's shoulder. He flashed a warm smile, patting it on the back.

'Is it your pet? How many pets do you have?' scoffed Samrat.

'You've already met this pet. Don't you remember?' replied Anahita, her tone sarcastic. 'Meet Moksha.'

Four of them were confused and staggered to see Moksha like this.

Kabeer somehow asked, 'Moksha, the horse?'

'Moksha, the horse,' spoke the pigeon, turning its neck, its voice deep and resonant.

Four of them almost jumped back to see the bird talk.

It continued, 'Moksha, the Unknown. Moksha, the mammoth. Moksha, the pigeon. Any other question?'

Arjun smiled stealthily but Anahita was in stitches. Four of them stared wonderingly at the bird.

Arjun said, 'You've done well, Moksha. Now go to Gurumata and follow her.'

'As you say, friend. See you soon.' The pigeon turned to four of them. 'Goodbye, children.' And then it flew away.

Four of them did not utter a word.

They'd walked across the courtyard and headed for an impressive stairway. Four of them noticed that each and every corner of the fort they could see was well protected by armed soldiers who bowed their head on seeing Arjun.

A confused expression crossed Kabeer's face. '*Who are you?*'

As they ascended the stairs and reached a broad cobbled pathway, Arjun found a man talking to a soldier, his back was to them. '*Mamashree.*'

Four of them stood dumb-struck as the man turned.

Prithvi jumped out of his skin. '*Gajraj!*'

'It's good to see you again,' said Gajraj, smiling enigmatically. 'You all stay here,' he ordered the soldiers escorting Arjun. 'Only Anahita.'

He, Arjun and Anahita stepped ahead, four of them followed close behind.

'What's going on? Arjun and you were in Khazanapur, and now we met him here, in *Ananyaaakashganga?*' asked Samrat.

Gajraj answered, 'Just wait for a while, child.'

They walked past the next stone gateway to enter the second courtyard, more spacious than the previous. On the right stood a splendid and elegant temple. Aavishkar's friends' face gleamed to see him sitting on its stairs, two soldiers on the lowest step.

'You're alright?' asked Kanak. 'Are you hurt?'

'I'm okay,' replied Aavishkar. 'What about you all? And...and... those icy stairs and walls? A racing champion ostrich was behind me all the time. Then I opened an icy door and found myself here, inside this temple,' he said in one breath.

A voice spoke from the left, 'Don't worry. Now everything will be in light.'

All eyes turned to find a spindly man, looked to be about fifty, descending a stairway on the corner of the courtyard. He was attired in a calf-length cream tunic, a richly embroidered cobalt-blue coat longer than tunic, open at centre front and a cream pajama. He had a thick moustache and beard with shoulder-length hair. A calm and peaceful expression gave his face an intellectual look.

A soldier was escorting him, a silver box, looking exactly the same as five of them had, in his hands.

Prithvi mumbled, '*Kakashree!*' He instantly realized what he'd said but couldn't get its reason.

Kanak looked at Prithvi and then at the man with increasing curiosity.

The man continued, 'I thought if Professor Aaditya ever needed the Royal Weapon, he would send someone more qualified and experienced than *Vyom's students.*'

'You know him?' The first question was certainly Aavishkar's.

'I'm indebted of him. Anyway, how is he?' the man asked.

Aavishkar told, 'He passed away three years ago in an accident.'

'*What!*' The man was taken aback, found it hard to accept the truth.

'So *he* didn't send us here,' told Prithvi.

Arjun asked, 'Then Professor Jaywardhan did?'

'I don't think we need to tell *you* anything, Arjun,' said Samrat, getting hot under the collar. 'Why should we believe anyone of you?'

The man came next to Arjun. 'He's my son who did nothing wrong. And I, Tilakraj, am the Protector of Ananyaakashganga.'

Five of them were at a loss of words, poleaxed.

'We wanted to know about all of you. So, Arjun and Gajraj, the chief of Ananyaakashganga's armed forces, had to play their roles,' told Tilakraj.

Five of them motioned their wide-opened eyes to Gajraj who was smiling warmly.

'We had to create obstacles in your ways,' said Tilakraj. 'A woodland changed into an endless land of sand which was distorted by a cyclone, the tunnel you reached Ananyaakashganga through suddenly crumbled, the earth started quaking, a wagon brought you to an iceland from a sod. Then, you met a mammoth and few pursuer creatures.'

'*You* were behind them?!' said a scandalized Kabeer.

Intense anger surged through Samrat. 'We suffered severely because of all this. Why did you do this to us?'

'So that you could reach *here* what's impossible without us. You've come to this world first time, and it's our first meeting. I think I should show you something so *you can believe us.*' Tilakraj signalled to his escort who took a silver plate out of the box and gave it to Kanak.

Tilakraj told, 'This is a replica of *the silver tablet* you have. When you were in Khazanapur, Arjun saw the tablet with you. It was hidden by Professor Aaditya and his colleagues in 1180 inside *Iravati* river.'

Aavishkar asked keenly, 'How did you meet Professor Dhanraj?'

Tilakraj waited in silence, looking at Aavishkar fondly. 'Professor Aaditya always wanted to do something for his country and people. He travelled through time with his team in the search of a place where his inventions could be safe. He came here first time fourteen years ago through a time machine, *the chariot*.' A stellar smile floated on his lips.

Gajraj got into conversation. 'We don't want anyone to know about us or our world, Ananyaakashganga. Everything is clandestine. Our soldiers inform us about each and every incident taking place around Khazanapur. Arjun was five when Professor Aaditya came to Khazanapur first time. He asked her mother, my sister, to see the world beyond Ananyaakashganga. She took him to Khazanapur but that was the last time she'd gone out.' A regretful expression crossed his face.

'My younger brother Saketraj, aspired to be more powerful than us, had started to use his powers wrongly. And one day, *that black sheep did the unthinkable*. He knew he couldn't take us on in a direct fight so he ambushed Pavaki and Arjun to snatch his armour and weaken us. Pavaki saved Arjun but couldn't save herself.' Tilakraj placed his hand on Arjun's shoulder, tears glistening in his eyes.

He continued, 'When Saket after killing Pavaki tried to harm Arjun, Professor Aaditya and his colleagues, who witnessed that accident, wounded his right hand by laser guns that seared his body too. He had to turn tail.'

Arjun mentioned, 'When babashree came to know about everything, he brought Professor Aaditya and his friends to Ananyaakshganga. Professor Aaditya promised that he'd always stand by us.'

'What is Ananyaakashganga, actually?' asked Samrat eagerly.

Tilakraj told, 'Thousands of years ago, a parallel world to yours was created, *Ananyaakashganga*. Why? How? No one knows. It has its own rules, own way of life. Many secret powers are here. Unbelievable. Unmentionable. Unequalled.' Tilakraj looked at the sun of a scarlet armour tied on his right palm. 'When the limit of your imaginations ends, Ananyaakashganga comes into existence. There is a supreme army of Ananyaakashganga, *the Ananyasena.* Indefatigable and indestructible. The most powerful army ever present. Whoever leads it becomes invincible.'

Prithvi and Kanak had drastic thrills. The words flowed from one side of their head to another.

Kabeer asked, 'Where's it? Will you show it to us?'

Gajraj said, 'How can we show you something we haven't seen for last eighteen years?'

'Where has it been hidden?' As the words left Prithvi's mouth, he realized what he'd asked.

Arjun marvelled at his question. 'How did you know that?'

'I... that... I...' faltered Prithvi.

'Lucky guess,' said Kanak. 'If no one has seen that army for last eighteen years, it would've been hidden somewhere.'

'Yes...yes... I wanted to ask it only,' said Prithvi, looking briefly at Kanak.

Tilakraj answered, 'You're right. The Great Lady of Ananyaakashganga, *Gurumata,* hid the Ananyasena for its protection.'

'You're the protector or the king of Ananyaakashganga, so...'

Tilakraj interrupted Samrat, 'I'm not the king. But the protector, *the second in command.* Our king Yashasviraj was put to the sword eighteen years ago.'

'*What!* Who killed him?' asked Aavishkar, his voice full of bafflement.

'His elder son.'

Tilakraj's words jolted Prithvi and Kanak, tremors in their heart.

There was more than a moment's silence.

Tilakraj asked, 'So, any other explanation?'

'You never wanted to harm us, did you?' asked Samrat. 'You wanted us to reach here, I believe.'

Arjun breathed deeply and beamed. 'Thank God, *you believed.*'

Kanak found Prithvi staring into the distance. 'Prithvi... Prithvi...'

A distracted Prithvi looked at her, catching her voice. 'Something appears a dream to me, Kanak, but I know it's more than that. Something... related to us.'

Kanak laid her eyes on him. 'What?!'

***

Chapter 21
The Royal Weapon

Anahita led Prithvi and his friends to a separate three-storey building in the southern part of the fort. Proper and highly advanced medical treatments were provided to them.

'Don't you people have such power that could heal our wounds instantly?' asked Aavishkar, looking at a bandage tied on his forearm covering the wound he suffered during his run in the labyrinth of icy doors and stairs.

'I'm sorry for that,' said Arjun, standing at the door of the room. 'If we had, father would've saved my mother,' he sounded inconsolable. 'Some losses cannot be recouped.'

Prithvi said, 'If you don't mind, can I ask something?'

Arjun's lips broke into a weak smile. 'I'll be glad to answer.'

'Why do you people wear this piece of armour having similar carving but different colour?' asked Prithvi, gesturing his head towards Arjun's right hand. 'The reason behind your powers is this?'

'Yes. They're *Dhruva Armours*. High-ranked and highly skilled people have the honour to wear them. Colours indicate how powerful they are. *The Golden Armour*, my armour, is the most powerful Dhruva Armour. My grandfather Raviraj, a master of creating these armours, made it for me and gave it to my mother. She before dying transferred her armour's powers into it,' told Arjun. 'Since my father is the Protector of Ananyaakashganga, he has scarlet armour, much more powerful than silver and bronze ones. We're not royalty so we have palm armours. The royals have their jewelled circlets having a golden sun in the centre. As far as the Ananyasena is concerned, it can be led only and only by means of a diadem, *the Surya Diadem*. Safe and secure with Gurumata.'

Arjun's words evoked a firm, male voice in Prithvi's mind.

'My son Yagya, the heir of Ananyaakashganga, the most competent king of our world, who deserves the Surya Diadem more than anyone, will now lead Ananyasena.'

Arjun's question yanked an utterly perplexed Prithvi back to reality, 'You're alright?'

'I'm good.' Prithvi rallied his disturbed mind, exchanging glances with Kanak.

'Whatever happened with us, those incidents, they were too much weird. The same powers were behind them?' Aavishkar wished to dispel his doubt.

'Yes. The existence of our world is based on these powers. Ananyaakashganga is disparate from your world, *absolutely different*. People of your world don't believe in these powers. They don't know that many such worlds full of secrets are around them but beyond their reach.'

Samrat asked playfully, 'How do you feel to carry the most powerful armour of your world?'

Arjun smiled. 'It's not the most powerful but the most valuable possession for me. It has my mother's blessings.' A conflict of emotions ran through his face. 'As long as she was with us, my uncle could never do what he wanted. That's why he killed her. And after that, he invaded us with *Yugant's* help.'

Prithvi went white. 'Whose help?'

'Yugant's. Our king's elder son,' told Arjun. 'That patricide killed him only and only for the Surya Diadem. He wants to rule over every powerful world similar to ours. He wants to finish us first for that. That's why, my uncle attacked us. His powers wanted to subdue ours. But we came off in putting him to the worse with the help of Professor Aaditya and his fellows. Father told me that Professor Aaditya had worn my armour and faced him. Uncle understood that his Vindvans powers were nothing before the Golden Armour and our unity, so he took to his heels.'

'What powers?' asked Kabeer, listening intently.

Arjun answered, 'Vidhvans powers mean destructive powers which create darkness. There is a constructive power too. *Nakshatras*, our powers which spread light everywhere.'

A soldier entered the room and told, 'The Protector needs all of you downstairs.'

Prithvi overcoming his emotions came to Arjun. 'Sometimes we've to go through hell, sometimes even worse. We're taught not to lose hope, not to be discouraged and not to give up *at all*. We must continue fighting to the end.'

'As you all fought and proved, *this story depends on wisdom and overcoming fear*,' beamed Arjun.

***

Saket, a violet dirk in his hand, cleaving through the darkness strode into the moonlight. He looked all around, muttered some words and impaled the ground with it. A stream of water jetted out of the surface and layered to an extent. The reflection of his face turned up in water.

He communicated, 'I did my job, my king, and he will do ours. He thought I made his work easier by giving him my armour.'

'Well done, Saket,' his reflection spoke with a different voice as if it was of another person. 'How fool Raviraj was that he thought I could never reach the palace.'

'Now what to do, my king?'

'At this moment, just wait.' The reflection had straight face. 'Saket, many times I wanted to cross *the Forbidden Line,* but I don't want to dice with my life and powers. But now, it's compulsory to remove it.'

Saket's reflection was replaced by a chiselled face wearing a jewelled circlet, a golden sun in its centre. 'I've been trying for last eighteen years, and *now* I'm getting the desired outcomes. My Vidhvans tell me that Gurumata will bring the Ananyasena into existence very soon.'

Saket asked curiously, 'Why, my king? Is it he? The heir?'

'Never say it again, Saket. *I am the heir of Ananyaakashganga*, not

Yagya,' the reflection flied at him, consumed by envy. 'If you're talking about his unfortunate comeback then yes, I'm also waiting for him badly.' The face flashed a firm intention that couldn't be concealed by the flow of water. 'I have to know where the Surya Diadem is, and I need someone for that. Someone, who can sacrifice himself for me.'

***

Tilakraj, Arjun and five of them were descending a spiral underground staircase. Several flaming torches, hung on the dense red-stone walls, lit the paths perfectly.

'Where are we going?' asked Aavishkar.

Arjun grinned. 'I hope you want to see it, don't you?'

Kanak asked, her eyes wide with excitement, 'You're taking us to...?'

'Yes.' Tilakraj descended and moved to a passageway on the left, followed by the rest of them.

Armed guards were standing at small distances, bowing to Tilakraj and Arjun.

'I couldn't understand one thing.' Kabeer asked, 'Why did you create those dangerous situations throughout our journey?'

Tilakraj said, 'Suppose you have a precious thing, Kabeer, and you have to give it to someone. Who would you choose?'

Kabeer had the answer. 'The one who will use it rightfully, who will deserve it. If it's possible I can scrutinize one. I won't give it easily.'

Tilakraj smiled at his quick reply. '*Absolutely right*. This is the answer of your question, son. When I came to know about all of you, it was outré for me that why Professor Aaditya sent you. But you had the tablet proving that you belong to Vyom. So we wanted to examine you, wanted to see that after facing the difficulties, would you give up? Would you go back thinking you couldn't confront the challenges?' Tilakraj verbalized, 'But you all went through fire and water, and who moves continuously towards one's goal through thick and thin, deserves an unforgettable victory.'

He stopped, a huge metallic door on his left, four guards on either side. 'How do you all imagine the Royal Weapon?'

'It might be a spear or a trident,' replied Prithvi.

Aavishkar figured on, 'A pistol or a rifle?'

'May be a bow and arrow,' visualised Samrat.

Tilakraj enlivened the introduction of the Royal Weapon, 'If you think so, be prepared for *one more surprise.*'

Two guards opened the door. They entered first of all and started lighting up a series of flaming torches.

It was a small room. A doorway exactly opposite to the entrance led them to a corridor which ended with a narrow staircase going down. The guards continued to light up the torches. Some on the walls, some hung from the ceiling, which revealed a very large vault, gradually sparkling in a shining yellow glow.

Wherever five of them from upstairs moved their eyes found umpteen outsize metal racks, glass cases and stone cupboards of different heights, various surreal inventions enhancing them. Big, small, futuristic, ancient, quite distinct, beyond the imaginations. They felt excitement running through their body. A truly breathtaking sight had left them awestruck.

'The Royal Weapon is the name of this cellar,' told Tilakraj, descending.

Five of them followed him with astounded eyes, seemed to suppress the ecstasy.

It was an oval chamber, made up of massive walls of red stone. A circular passageway linked all the racks, cases and cupboards and provided access to the inventions. In its centre stood a three-metre high marble table having two side drawers. A glass case, keeping a crimson shield and a taupe sword, was placed over it.

Aavishkar asked, touching the glass, 'Why is this sword here?'

'The sword and the shield are collectively called as *Pratham*, the first of all the inventions of Professor Aaditya...'

'*He* made them?' Prithvi interrupted Tilakraj.

Arjun looked confused. 'Professor Jaywardhan didn't tell you anything?'

'No... we didn't get the chance to ask him.' Kanak expatiated how they reached 1180 and then decided to find out the Royal Weapon.

Arjun said, 'It meant he didn't know that you've come here.'

'We'll talk about it later, Arjun. For now, I should introduce the Royal Weapon to them.' Tilakraj revealed,

'These 295 unique and powerful inventions were created by Professor Aaditya. In Vyom, they would've been insecure sooner or later, but here they're completely safe. In the beginning, we took the responsibility to protect this sword and its shield. Each year Professor Aaditya used to come to Ananyaakashganga through Mrityunjay Time Machine and store his inventions here. He requested me never to come to his world for some reasons, that's why I'd been awaiting him for three years and now I learnt that...'

There was more than a moment's silence.

Tilakraj's thoughts were distracted as Samrat asked, 'Why are these inventions unique?'

'You want me to enlarge on them thoroughly? It'll take days, child,' said Tilakraj, smiling tenderly. 'But I have another option.' He opened one of the two drawers of the marble table and took a thick and old book out. 'It contains all the answers, Samrat.'

'You're talking to the wrong person,' said Kabeer, advancing. He flipped the pages of the book. It was a collection of hand-written pages with diagrams, observations and hypotheses. The last fifty-sixty pages were blank. He looked up with a slight smile. 'It's in Sanskrit!'

Arjun said, 'Professor Aaditya himself wrote it but he didn't provide the translations.'

'It's okay. I understand Sanskrit,' told Kabeer.

Arjun and Tilakraj looked impressed.

The book gave detailed demonstrations about all the inventions. A ruthenium-niobium rod could make someone invisible for about five hours. A mocha crystal could dry a small water body by generating controlled heat. A spectrum obtained from a sarcoline prism could give precise information about uncommon cosmic rays and events of human universe. A bulky piece of greyish-brown rock, considered to be a meteorite, with few chemical changes could make anything weightless.

Kabeer read as many pages as he could before getting distracted by Aavishkar's question.

'Binoculars?' Aavishkar pointed to a tawny instrument kept in one of the cupboards.

It looked to be about six inches long, had two hollow cylinders attached to their parallel sides.

'It's *Agnikendra*,' told Tilakraj. 'When it is activated after focusing it on someone's eyes, the person goes blind for some time.'

Aavishkar asked, 'And what about this sword and its shield?'

Tilakraj took the sword and the shield out of the case. 'You can see a rectangular narrow opening in the centre of the shield. The sword is inset half into it, and then this ruby over its hilt is turned. As soon as the sword is pulled out, a blue radiation comes out of the shield which creates a particular mutation into its receiver's body making it very powerful, physically and mentally. These transformations help it to access or you can say to absorb all kinds of energies around, like heat, light, any type of compatible radiation, and then it can harness them as desires.'

'Can the body restore its original form?' asked Prithvi, curious.

'Yes, if it's exposed again to the same blue radiation.' Tilakraj breathed deeply. 'I think this much is sufficient for you. Now, we'll have to do something to send you all to Vyom or to bring Jaywardhan here.'

Kabeer asked, 'Could I borrow this book?'

'Of course but you've to finish it fast. You can't take it to Vyom,' said Tilakraj, a note of amusement in his voice.

A broad smile swung on everyone's lips.

***

It was around midnight. Four time machines, double in DTM's size, appeared near the farm of Khazanapur Prithvi and his group had landed. A group of around twenty people emerged from each time machine. Four groups joined together, forming a bigger one led by Jaywardhan.

'Mr Chancellor, if Samarth has Aavriti, its twin is indicating that he went to north-east direction,' told Samriddhi, a watch looked like Aavriti in her hand.

'Thanks to Arunima that she could build Aavriti's twin in only sixteen hours,' said Sagar, giving an admiring smile to Arunima standing next to him.

Kushal's face was devoid of any approval. 'It wasn't a difficult task for who could control Supernovae, was it?'

Jaywardhan sensed the bitterness in his voice but didn't say anything. Arunima averted her eyes downward with a repentant appearance.

'If we fight Vikrant, we'll have to be prepared,' said Prayas. 'According to Farhan, he has many exceptionally well-trained men who are adept at handling weapons.'

Jaywardhan said, stepping forward, 'First of all, we have to find Samarth.'

Jaywardhan, Sagar, Kushal and Arunima accompanied by Vyom's S.T.F. walked for two miles, laying low, reaching the public eatery.

'Who are you?' A voice came from the left, surprising them.

Everyone turned sharply to see Gajraj standing with his troop. The commandos loaded their guns as soon as they found Gajraj's men lifting their right hand to them.

Jaywardhan asked, 'Put the guns down. I hope they know us.'

Gajraj's eyes narrowed. He didn't command his soldiers to lower their Dhruva Armour.

Jaywardhan continued, gesturing to Gajraj's hand, '*Dhruva Armour*. Professor Aaditya told me about it.'

Gajraj realized that he'd seen Jaywardhan, Zaheer and Vikrant in the photo Professor Aaditya showed them once. He wanted to confirm, 'Jaywardhan Rathore?'

Jaywardhan nodded.

Gajraj's perplexed expression vanished, no longer feeling dubious about him.

***

Chapter 22

The Gory War

Arjun was standing quietly on the balcony of his room.

His thoughts were broken as he heard Prithvi's voice, 'Hope I'm not disturbing you?'

Arjun turned to see him and Aavishkar at the door. 'No, you are not. Come in.'

'Why are you still awake?' Aavishkar was with his questionnaire undoubtedly. 'You're a human, aren't you? You sleep?'

'Yes, I do. Anyway, your friend isn't with you? Princess Kanak?' grinned Arjun playfully.

'Shhh...' Prithvi hushed him. 'I'd told you. Don't call her princess or you'll be in the deep water.'

Arjun's eyes held a glint of humour. 'She'll throw *me* down, too, seven times.'

Prithvi corrected him, 'It's eight now.'

Aavishkar interposed, 'You're making fun of her, aren't you?'

'You think, Avi?' sniggered Prithvi. 'You're right then. You have any problem?' He guffawed.

Arjun joined him.

'Don't do it, Prithvi. She will shoot you,' warned Aavishkar.

'She always does it with her *ruthless* tongue. It carries so much charge. I tell you, Arjun, she's a deadly current. You touch her and say *hi* to death,' said Prithvi, pulling a funny face.

Aavishkar's eyes caught something behind him. 'Today is your hapless day, Prithvi,' he mumbled.

When Arjun's eyes fell on Kanak folding her arms at the door, his smile vanished.

Prithvi continued, 'Arjun, one day I'll delineate you *her crackbrained stories with quintessence.* Every time she overeats my grey matter. She's very adroit no doubt but always pugnacious.'

Arjun tried to give a quick signal to him, moving his eyes.

'I'm talking about such an interesting girl. What's wrong with you?'

'Mr Malhotra?' Kanak's voice gripped Prithvi's speedy tongue.

Prithvi closed his eyes. '*OH NO...*' He opened them slowly. 'I think she's heard crackbrained stories thing?'

Arjun just shook his head.

Prithvi exhaled deeply and turned back.

'I think she's heard everything,' said Aavishkar in a low voice, 'I'd warned you but you didn't listen. Apologize to her immediately.'

'Thank you for the suggestion,' grumbled Prithvi.

Kanak walked up to him. 'Keep prattling, Mr Malhotra, that....'

'I was just telling Arjun about your merits.' Prithvi modulated his voice, 'How intelligent and good you are. In the institute, you're the *golden girl.*'

Kanak asked, 'Really? And what about charge and current?'

'Current...? I was describing some science facts that...that if electric current flows through someone's body, it'll be deadly,' giggled Prithvi.

'But I guess you were describing some *Kanak's facts.*' Kanak's countenance changed. 'You were right. I'm *a deadly current.* So just stay away from me.'

Aavishkar said as usual the punch line, 'Please Kanak, don't ask Prithvi to do something he cannot.'

Prithvi's face bore an ecstatic smile. 'Good one, Avi.'

Aavishkar found Kanak glaring at him. 'I meant... Arjun... what's that? So many torches?' He asked, looking beyond the balcony towards a place far from the fort, trying to save himself from her fury.

'That's a battlefield,' told Arjun, turning about. 'About eighteen years ago, a catastrophe occurred there. A terrible war.'

Prithvi, Kanak and Aavishkar walked up to the balcony to find a large area rimmed by hundreds of intense flames overcoming the darkness of the night.

'Near the field, Ananyaakashganga's palace was situated. Since the Ananyasena was in its court, Gurumata made it disappear to hide the army. Our soldiers always guard the field. Enemies can invade us anytime.'

The silence of the night was disturbed. A blare roared, drawing everyone's attention to the lowest main courtyard. They hurried to the gateway of the fort, now scattered in pieces. They boggled to see Vikrant, with an army contained his men and hundreds of soldiers, standing at the entrance.

'If I'm not mistaken, *you five* had limited me.' Vikrant neared Prithvi and his friends. 'See, I couldn't reach DTM till now.'

Tilakraj came in between. 'How did you reach here, Vikrant?'

'You will not believe me.' Vikrant showed his right hand, his palm wearing a silver armour.

Totally shocked, Tilakraj said, '*Impossible!*'

'It was impossible to reach here. But Saket helped me to stand against you by giving me his powers and army,' he said, gesturing to the soldiers behind him. 'So, just give what I…'

Samrat fulminated, 'It was never yours and will never be.'

'You've done enough, kid. Now stay away,' snubbed Vikrant. 'Don't force me to….' he stepped aside to reveal Tilakraj's twenty soldiers under his men's gun. One of them was Anahita, blood running down her nose. 'We found them while coming here.' He said, glaring at Anahita, 'And this girl… is tough, killed my three men. Then I figured out that a silver armour is more powerful than a bronze one. Now it's up to you, Tilakraj. You give me what I've come for or want me to kill your loyal people?'

One of the guards standing in a tower next to the perimeter wall tried to attack Vikrant through his armour. An aware Vikrant neutralised the red beam emerged from the guard's armour by the purple beam emitted from his and then quickly hit him with the same. His lifeless body fell and smashed against the ground, making the blood gush from his broken head.

Vikrant's eyes flashed warning. 'If this sagacity is repeated, these twenty soldiers will have to say goodbye to their life, too.'

Nobody made a second move from Tilakraj's team sensing gravity of the situation.

Vikrant's eyes fell on Arjun. His eyes desperately scanned his right palm. 'You're Saket's lovely nephew, aren't you? Why does he want *your* armour?'

'You're not going to do this, Vikrant. You don't understand what he wants from you,' said Tilakraj in a voice that trembled a little. 'He sent you here because he cannot enter Ananyaakashganga. He's just *using* you.'

'I'm not here to do your little brother's work, Tilakraj,' spoke Vikrant in a cold, calm tone. 'What if *I* use the Golden Armour to rule my world as well as yours? Saket is armourless now. He can't do anything. Look, I don't have any bad blood with you. But if something goes wrong, you can't imagine the consequence. Choice is yours.'

Vikrant's armed men besieged the courtyard. Tilakraj's soldiers were at clear command. *Don't take any action until our fellows are rescued.*

Tilakraj said gruffly, 'Arjun, bring Pratham.'

Arjun objected, 'Babashree....'

'Just bring it,' repeated Tilakraj loudly.

Arjun seemed to catch the patent message his eyes delivered. He threw his livid look at Vikrant and left the courtyard to move to the broad cobbled pathway.

Vikrant's face brightened at seeing Arjun coming back after a while holding the sword and the shield. '*Eventually.* Professor Aaditya had told us about their powers. Now, I construct such machines, which will magnify their strength.'

Arjun demanded, 'Release the girl.'

Vikrant scoffed, 'And why do you think I'll do that?'

Arjun sounded rasping, 'My one man is dead. We didn't do anything because we don't want more casualties. And you'll release Anahita because you know who's more powerful here. *Silver or golden.*'

Vikrant's expressions became intense. 'Set the girl free.'

Prateek lowered his gun. Anahita walked up to Arjun, and Arjun handed the sword and the shield to Vikrant.

Vikrant wanted to use Aashutosh as a guinea pig. He inserted the sword into the shield, turned the ruby and then took it out. The shield suddenly ejected a blue ray that hit Aashutosh in the chest and sent him flying backwards. He hit one of the pentagonal towers and pitched forward, senseless.

Vikrant turned about. 'This is Pratham, the first invention. What about the others?'

Tilakraj barely suppressed his shock and disappointment.

'I wouldn't stake *everything* only on this sword. I knew you people would never let me enter that cellar. What if I release your one man and you hand one invention over to me? Fair trade?'

Before Vikrant could continue, Arjun, Prithvi, Kanak, Samrat and Anahita attacked his men to rescue their nineteen soldiers. Vikrant immediately paid attention to them. A purple beam emerged from his armour but Tilakraj didn't let it swallow anyone else's life. He counteracted it with his armour's red beam.

'This is not *your* power, Vikrant. Why don't you use yours?'

Tilakraj and Vikrant's army had announced the outset of the war.

Kabeer took position in a banquette to the south of the next courtyard. As he utilized all quarrels of his crossbow against his enemies, the muzzle of a gun touched his right temple. He could not breathe.

'Put the weapon down, boy,' said the man holding the gun.

No sooner did Kabeer hold up his one hand in defence than the man fell to the ground, the gun left his hand.

A stunned Kabeer looked down to find two arrows ripped through the man's limbs. He exhaled but then burst out, 'You again broke Vyom's rules.'

Samrat with his bow standing at a distance frowned. 'He'll survive. By the way, you're welcome.' He turned to leave and said, 'That's why I need a new partner.'

Kabeer glared at him. '*I would see* how you get a new partner, Samrat Chopra.'

Each troop was trying with tooth and nail to beat off its opponents while suffering many casualties. There was a counterattack for every attack. Clanging of steels and roaring of guns assured that this bloodbath wouldn't end soon.

Prithvi and Arjun standing back to back, covering all the directions of any possible attack, were fighting four men. A fifth man, a machete in his hand, advanced to join them.

Kanak from behind caught his wrist before the blade injured anyone. She, twisting his wrist, forced him to leave the machete. He tried to stamp his foot on her, but she saving it spun around to face him. He lashed out to kick at her face. She parried his attack with her hand and smashed her fist into his jaw. Blood gathered in his mouth. He fell down, now unfit to battle.

Arjun's opponent cut him fiercely across the shoulder. He, flinching, pushed him back with his shield and slashed his throat. The man collapsed to the ground, motionless.

'You killed him?' said Prithvi, finishing with his rival.

Arjun asked, amazed, 'What did you expect me to do?'

Kanak said, battling another man, 'He's not in Vyom, Prithvi.'

Kabeer had teamed up with Anahita who gave him cover to move into the palace area, the highest and most secure region of the fort. A narrow defence pathway near the eastern tower led them to the underneath staircase to the cellar.

All energies from both the sides were directed at wining this struggle. Swords cut through flesh, bullets pierced bodies, blood spilled on the ground.

Tilakraj and Vikrant were skillfully parrying each other's attack with their armour. No one had any weakness that could be exploited. One time purple rays consuming red ones. The other time red beam neutralizing its anti.

'BABASHREE…' a loud voice came from behind Tilakraj.

Tilakraj and Vikrant found Kabeer standing with Agnikendra. Kabeer was waiting for Vikrant to look at him. He'd rotated the central focusing wheel to focus Agnikendra's objective on Vikrant's eyes. As soon as Kabeer rotated the eyepiece in its mount, two orange streams emitted from both the cylinders and struck Vikrant's eyes.

Vikrant felt as if these were on fire. He bellowed in pain. Rubbing his eyes, he fell down. His vision began to flutter. 'NO…' he cried and targeted Kabeer with his armour.

The energy came out of it welted Kabeer's chest. He collapsed, instantly unconscious.

'Kabeer…' Tilakraj ran to him. He sighed after checking his pulse.

It took hardly five seconds for Vikrant to lose his eye sight. One of the soldiers thumped him on the top of the head and made him insensible.

Tilakraj closed his eyes and communicated mentally through his Dhruva Armour to Gajraj. He wanted to stop this futile fray with no end in sight.

Aavishkar accompanied by a group of soldiers was busy in protecting a two-storey building, *the ordnance depot*, near the temple. His opponent was up to the challenge. He swung his combat knife but Aavishkar moved aside swiftly to avoid the thwack. He brought his dagger up to fend off another attack from the man. He swerved right and rammed his elbow to his ribs. The opponent hit the ground, blood spewed out of his mouth.

Aavishkar didn't notice another attacker at a dangerously close distance who was ready to stab him but he suddenly arched forward as an arrow had buried deep into his back. Aavishkar turned to see him falling down. His eyes followed the direction of the arrow and found Samrat grinning, standing in the outer courtyard of the temple. Aavishkar smiled back.

'STOP,' roared Vikrant, in all his senses, aiming Tilakraj through his armour. 'I said stop it or I put him down.'

Tilakraj's companions stood still. No one's attention was to Vikrant, thinking him out of the war.

'I'd warned that I didn't want any tussle but you people didn't agree. Be prepared for the punishment then,' thundered Vikrant, seething in rage.

'If you touch him...' Arjun stormed to him.

Vikrant said, lost in his anger, 'Stay back. Do not force me to cross my limit.'

Arjun unwillingly receded.

All of a sudden, two bullets punctured Vikrant's right hand, making him unsteady. His incensed eyes saw Jaywardhan with a rifle standing just before the massive stone gate.

'Otherwise?' a voice from the left attracted Vikrant but before his neck could turn, Kushal put a gun on his temple.

When it seemed Vikrant would win, the war moved in favour of Jaywardhan and Tilakraj. Vikrant ran his eyes from one corner to another to find Vyom's S.T.F. besieged his men. Before he was shot, Jaywardhan's team had crossed the ramparts and motioned into the fort on the sly.

A familiar voice spoke, 'I hope it's shocking to see me alive.'

In his periphery, Vikrant spotted Arunima standing beside Samriddhi.

Vikrant scoffed, 'I'd expected it, Anushka. You proved that you're Kadambari Raghuvanshi's daughter.'

'I have killed that Anushka,' yelled Arunima.

Vikrant made no attempt to hide abhorrence in his eyes. 'Good. Otherwise I have to kill her.'

Arunima was stunned into a blank expression.

Jaywardhan blew a fuse. 'She's your daughter, Vikrant.'

'NO,' cried Vikrant, shutting his eyes, his face contorted in wrath. 'She was a warrior who was supposed to win this war for me. But she's failed me because she chose *you*, Jay.'

'Let's finish this war then,' Aashutosh's voice spoke aloud.

All eyes turned to see a stronger, more focused and aggressive Aashutosh standing unharmed next to the pentagonal towers. He punched one of them. The debris flung. Jaywardhan speedily moved but two commandos of the S.T.F. became the victims.

'Well done, Aashutosh. *Finish them off*,' shouted an enraptured Vikrant.

The war hadn't ended yet. Once again, chaos, noises and shambles seized the fort. Tilakraj's army stood its ground without losing heart.

Vikrant wounded Jaywardhan's hand through his armour, making the rifle leave it. When he tried to attack him second time, the armour didn't eject any energy. He tried again, but no positive result. An astounded Vikrant stared at his palm. He, refusing to retreat, picked a sword up lying on the floor and moved rapidly to Jaywardhan who'd already drawn a sword.

An unruly Aashutosh had started using Pratham's incredible powers against his opponents. His body absorbed the heat of the surroundings resulting in a sudden decrease in the temperature, introducing his strength to everyone. Seven men around him froze to death.

The accumulated heat while leaving Aashutosh's body transformed into numerous fireballs and showered on the people. Those deleterious embers didn't distinguish between Tilakraj's men and his fellows, engulfing everyone and everything coming to their way. He'd concocted his own way to kill his foes, using his body as a thermoelectric generator. He soaked up the heat energy voraciously from the people what killed them and then converted it into lightning and electric currents which became the path to hell for many more people. His hands, behaving like conductors, passed excessive electricity to his opponents' body, when he touched them and burned their internal organs. To kill a distant target, the lightning sparks emanating from his fingers were sufficient.

No any strategies posed any real threat to him. He was killing a lot of birds with a single stone.

Tilakraj had ordered his two soldiers to take a fainted Kabeer into the palace area. After coming to his senses, he stood for his people again.

Two men en masse attacked Kanak battling on the broad-topped walkway of the southern rampart. Two more appeared to join the other two. They charged her all at once. She fought back bravely, continuing her relentless assault.

A knife slashed a deep cut across the man's chest trying to gash her stomach. The remaining three attackers stood still, their eyes pointing towards her back.

'Why do you cowards do it?' Prithvi emerged from the right. 'Although she can kill you all.'

Two men out of three charged upon him. Stepping back and jumping to his left, Prithvi brought his swords up, one in each hand, blocking the strikes from them. He swung them viciously, slitting the shoulder of one man and the leg of the other. They cried in pain, falling back.

The last man fighting Kanak, filled with dread, took an immediate action. He flung a knife at Prithvi. It lacerated his arm. Kanak turned about to see a wincing Prithvi. The man had saved himself. He retreated.

Kanak grabbed the knife and pulled it out quickly. 'You...you're alright?'

'What did you think?' Prithvi's lips broke into a faint smile, his eyebrow raised slightly. 'You aren't getting rid of me so easily.' He edged closer to her, looking into her eyes.

'What?' asked Kanak, uncomfortable.

'Your eyes are dark brown?! They used to appear black to me,' said Prithvi. 'Actually the nectar you tongue showers, overshadows your other qualities.' The playful smile returned to his face.

Kanak pushed him aside roughly and headed downstairs.

Prithvi grimaced. 'You're leaving me wounded?' He followed her, rushing. 'You should request Kabeer to give his other half cotton-girdle and help me like *I did*.'

Jaywardhan and Tilakraj's teams were straining each nerve to win this war. Aavishkar and Kabeer with impatient eyes were searching someone, standing on the top step of the staircase on the corner of the second courtyard, the Pratham sword in Aavishkar's hand. Both of them together had fought Vikrant's men to get it. They wanted to terminate Aashutosh's powers so they knew what to do.

Kabeer's eyes flashed hope as he saw Kanak downstairs fighting two men singlehandedly. 'KANAK…' he called. 'Fit it again into the shield.'

'Go. Do it,' said Anahita, battling next to her. 'I'll handle them.' She, adept at the art of war, engaged those men.

Aavishkar hurled down the sword at her. Kanak caught it with no mistake.

'Not so fast, girl.' Aashutosh appeared at a distance, carrying a portcullis over his head. He speedily threw it at her.

Terrified, Kanak ran away to be out of its range. Although she couldn't, it didn't touch her. It'd hung in air, a red sparkling light enveloping it.

Aashutosh furiously turned to see Arjun lifting his right hand. His armour's energy tossed the portcullis and slammed it against the ground.

Kanak saw Prithvi, beyond Aashutosh, signalling her. She quickly lobbed the sword at him. As Aashutosh jumped high to catch it in mid air, a stream of arrows pierced his body. He shrieked in agony and fell down. The sword was successfully caught by Prithvi.

'*Fantastic!* Your crossbow did a great job, Kabeer,' shouted Aavishkar in a merry voice.

'PRITHVI, here it is,' shouted Samrat from a distance, carrying the Pratham shield.

Prithvi rushed to Samrat but couldn't reach him. Aashutosh zoomed and grabbed him from behind in mid way. The sword left his hand and slid across the floor.

Aashutosh locked his neck in a chokehold, stifling him. 'As you're enfeebled, it'll invigorate me.'

Prithvi struggled against the hold but it became tighter. Aashutosh began absorbing his body's energy through his hand.

Samrat cried, moving to him, 'PRITHVI...'

'No...do-n't c-ome,' said Prithvi in the confined voice. 'Ge-t the sw-o-rd...'

'Do as he said,' Kanak called out loudly.

Arjun picked the sword up and took the shield from Samrat. He fit the sword into the shield and turned its ruby.

'You get that sword out, the rays will hit your friend, boys,' said Aashutosh, tightening his lock.

Samrat gestured to Prithvi with his eyes. He quickly drew his bow forward and unleashed an arrow straight at him. Diving through the air, it pierced Aashutosh's hand. Prithvi's neck loosened from his clutch. He belaboured him, his elbow to his ribs. Aashutosh staggered.

'GET DOWN.' Arjun pulled the sword out.

Prithvi ducked in a blink. Aashutosh was irradiated again. The blue rays made him cannon into the wall behind him.

When Vikrant saw a senseless Aashutosh, he blew his top. He, roaring in fury, tried to strike Jaywardhan's shoulder. Jaywardhan brought his shield up to block the attack and swiftly kneeled to rip his thighs. Vikrant stumbled, the sword left his hand.

Jaywardhan put his sword on his neck. 'I wish I'd nipped you in the bud.'

Vikrant said, glaring to Prithvi and his fellows, 'I wish I could slaughter these children.'

Jaywardhan swiped him. '*Stop this barbarity*. I won't let you wave your ruthless tongue. I just want to send you to hell,' he said, bridling at his tone. 'My children, my companions already suffered a lot because of *you*. I have to cast you towards a dire death, Vikrant. *I have to*.'

'Like what I did to Ali and Samarth?' snarled Vikrant, wiping some blood off his mouth.

Jaywardhan was thrown into a chasm of woe. It had left him momentarily paralyzed. He looked dolefully at Prithvi and Kanak. Their face overwhelmed with grief told him everything.

Jaywardhan's shoulders drooped, his eyes wet, 'It... ca..cannot...'

'What level have you sunk to, Vikrant?' Sagar lashed out in anger, losing control over his composed disposition. 'How many more will have to die for your desires?'

'Many more.' An abomination flashed in Vikrant's eyes. 'One day you'll see how I get what I want,' he scorned. 'One day I will smash Vyom...'

Jaywardhan broke in angrily, 'It isn't going to happen. This has to end. Once and for all.'

He gestured to Prayas and Samriddhi with his eyes. They loaded their firearm.

Vikrant's expression showed fear rising from loathing. 'You cannot do this, Jay. You cannot kill me. You have to answer Vyom.'

'I have to answer myself, Vikrant. I cannot betray myself by leaving *you* alive. Not this time,' said Jaywardhan, booming and clear. 'You're going to stop breathing, *permanently*.'

'No...no, Jay... NO...'

The guns roared. The bullets changed Vikrant's voice into a scream.

The spirit of his army had finally broken. His men were either killed or arrested. Each and every corner of the fort witnessed a terrible war. A war began with someone's greed. A war caused by someone's scheme. A war fought to preserve peace.

'This war is not over. Not yet.' Arjun came to Vikrant covered in blood. He released red rays from his armour which hit Vikrant's right palm, vapourising Saket's armour.

***

Chapter 23

Captured in the Smoke of Doom

Jaywardhan reached five of them who were badly bruised but still smiling.

'You all put your shoulders to the wheel to find the Royal Weapon. I'm proud of you, my children.' Jaywardhan's face was covered with a genial smile.

Aavishkar looked up. 'What's that?'

The sky was turning black with a veil of uncanny gyrating smoke. It, in no time, collided against the ground near Arjun and started encompassing him, without giving anyone a single chance to grasp anything.

'What's happening?' Tilakraj quickly entered the black smoke to find no one inside. Only darkness and a whirling sound welcomed him. He exited from the other side without Arjun. 'He's not in there.'

Everyone was stunned into silence, conveying their deepest fear.

Arjun *was* inside the smoke eddy, out of Tilakraj's reach. When he tried to come out of it, he felt as if it was bordered by something solid.

Saket appeared behind him inside the eddy. '*Like father, like son. Always try recklessly.*'

Gajraj was rooted to hear his voice. '*Saket!* How could he be in Ananyaakashganga?'

A fazed Tilakraj said, staring at Vikrant's palm, 'The Forbidden Line has vanished for him.'

'Nothing will be wrong. This smoke...'

'Don't do anything. It's not ordinary,' said Tilakraj, deterring Gajraj from using Dhruva Armour.

Overwrought, Prithvi asked, 'What is it?'

'*God!*' Gajraj's eyes widened in realization. 'Is it *the smoke of doom*?'

'Generated by Vidhvans. Arjun is inside with Saket. If we use Nakshtra powers, it will neutralise itself, annihilating everything inside it,' told Tilakraj.

The eddy twirled turbulently, became so denser and higher with every passing moments that voices could not penetrate it now.

'I have waited *so long* for this moment.' Saket put his hand on Arjun's shoulder. 'I spent fourteen years to *touch* you.'

Arjun removed it insolently. 'How could it happen? Grandfather had drawn *the Forbidden Line* around Ananyaakashganga for you and Yugant. You cannot cross it.'

'*That thing* forced me not to meet you, Arjun,' said Saket. 'You always left Ananyaakashganga with Gajraj and your bodyguards. But I didn't give up. I didn't kneel down before your *respected...*'

Arjun shouted, 'Not a single word against my father.'

Saket sneered, 'Your father is the reason of *everything. Your father* cast me out but King Yugant bore out my importance.'

'You know why Yugant supports you. He wants Ananyasena,' said Arjun. 'Did he forget about the *true* heir of Ananyaakashganga?'

'And you think the *true* heir will overpower us? It's just a chimera. King Yugant walked over him once. Certainly, the heir will arrive, so will King Yugant, and I've come here to erase the Forbidden Line for him,' said Saket. 'I began amassing Vidhvans powers with his help. Although it took a long time, look at the outcomes. *This* smoke of doom, and *that* Dhruva Armour whose powers were exactly similar to mine.'

Arjun's face discoloured. 'So you...?'

'Absolutely right. I *wanted* you to obliterate it. My armour is extant,' told Saket, showing his right palm. 'I'd been biding my time for Vikrant like greedy man. I knew that he couldn't stand for long before your powers, and you'd surely destroy that armour after finishing him.' He continued, reading Arjun's thoughts, '*Only a protector* can draw and erase the Forbidden Line but there is one more way to efface it. *If the source of power of the banished is destroyed by a Nakshtra,* what you did. You destroyed that armour, thinking you were avenging your mother's death, didn't you?' His laugh was deep.

Arjun swallowed his anger.

'I think Tilakraj didn't know about it. Actually our father, *the ex-protector*, Raviraj didn't have time to tell him. He was breathing his last.'

Arjun said, fuming, '*You* had killed him?'

Saket's dark eyes were fixed on Arjun. 'I killed everyone who came between *me and your armour.*'

Arjun asked, not leaving the eye-contact, 'Don't you think you closed the path to get the spell reversed for your *King* Yugant by killing the creator of the Forbidden Line?'

Saket attempted a sardonic smile. 'Pay attention, Arjun. I didn't say the protector who drew it is the only one can remove it. I said *only* the protector can do it. You tell me who's holding this rank nowadays?'

Arjun comprehended his words. 'Father will never do it.'

'Unless we involve his son into trade.' Saket's smile broadened scornfully. 'I always wanted your armour, Arjun, but when I met King Yugant, I realized that *you* are more precious than any armour.'

Tilakraj, disconcerted and distraught, was concentrating on his Dhruva Armour, his eyes closed. His people stood silently, haunted, wan with fear ridden eyes, feeling helpless, praying for Arjun.

'What if that armour ravages the source of your trade?' Arjun was about to touch the eddy with his armour.

'No son, no. Do not even try. If you do it, you'll certainly be safe but your companions, your own people outside it will be turned into ashes. As much as I know, you'll never want it.' Saket played on Arjun's nerves. 'That's why Tilakraj and Gajraj haven't attacked it yet to save you. Because if it's done, you'll be imperilled. This is the smoke of doom, son. It has its own rules.'

Arjun was in dilemma. 'He's right. Father had told me about this type of smoke,' he thought.

Something occurred to Saket. 'And yes, I forgot to tell. Do not think of attacking me with your armour. My powers have created this smoke. I'm safe here. But your armour will do *something* to it and what's next, you know it very well.'

'I got a spell,' said Tilakraj, opening his eyes.

A white smoke emerged from his armour and enveloped the smoke of doom. But soon, the black smoke devoured it, remaining unaffected.

Saket's smile mocked Arjun, 'What happened? Caught in thought?'

'Yes, the smoke of doom has its own rules. It can't be broken from inside or outside. But if it can be ejected from a Vidhvans,' said Arjun, gesturing his head to Saket's armour. 'It can be caged into a Nakshtra.'

Saket's face abruptly lost its smile. 'You're not going to do this. Think about it, Arjun.' He grew white with sickening anxiety. 'Come with us. Be part of us.'

Firm determination flashed in Arjun's eyes. 'I'm not in that queue people sell their psyche. I'd rather go to hell.' His armour expelled out a sparkling red beam creating a curtain between him and Saket.

'NO…,' shouted Saket.

The red curtain acted as a solid wall for him. He could only knock it but not access Arjun.

Arjun, without losing a moment, touched the black smoke with his right palm. His armour started dragging the eddy into itself. Saket did the same to save the smoke but his armour misfired. Terror crept into his heart.

People, standing outside, were frightened out of their wits. Their face blanched, their eyes widened in horror, seeing the smoke waning and the eddy shrinking.

'I wish I could always be a part of this fight, babashree.' Arjun closed his eyes.

BOOM...

A blast took place with a bang. The black whirl vanished. A dreadful silence followed, quaffed every sound of the vicinity.

'He's... gone...?' said Gajraj, despondent. 'It is impossible!'

A petrified Aavishkar asked, 'What happened? Where is Arjun?'

Tilakraj was silent, his eyes downcast.

'Arjun wanted to save us, and the only way was to neutralize the Vidhvans,' spoke Gajraj, somehow. 'Did he use his armour against the smoke of doom, Tilakraj?'

'NO...' Tilakraj's cry resounded loudly. 'How could he do this to me, Gajraj?' His knees were too weak to hold him up, his voice plangent, his soul shattered.

'We understood him a traitor and couldn't apologise for it.' Aavishkar's cheeks got wet.

An intense poignancy enfolded Prithvi's face.

Everyone had broken down, inconsolable in their grief. They weren't ready to accept the bleak vacuum Arjun had left behind.

***

'Friends, I've got something.' A large hall in *Angad Bhavan,* where *Music* class was about to start, echoed with Abhyuday's loud voice. He was standing at its door. Happiness irradiated his whole face. 'Mr Chancellor has gone to the past.' As soon as these words shot from his mouth, he realized he was in the class.

'For them?' asked Paridhi, rushing to him.

A fretted Jessica said, 'Tell us quickly. I'm having a foreboding.'

'Yes. For them,' replied Kavya, appearing behind Abhyuday. 'With the S.T.F. Rajput sir told they'd return very soon.'

'*Hurray*! Our army is coming back,' whooped Narayani, drawing attention from the other students. 'Sorry. You all do your singing.' Apologising, she turned to Abhyuday.

Paridhi's eyes crinkled in a smile. 'You did a great job. Thank you so much, Abhyuday.' She touched his arms gently and left.

Abhyuday's blush deepened.

Kavya whispered under her breath, 'Well done, Abhyuday. You stole the show.'

***

It was early hours in the morning. Prithvi had left the fort, bathed in blood, to distract himself. He walked silently up to the battlefield Arjun had told about. He could see a wide and extensive expanse of land rimmed by hundreds of soldiers. He didn't notice Kanak following him.

She gently laid her hand on his shoulder. 'What are you doing here?'

'He was right. *He was* fulfilling his responsibility but I...,' said Prithvi, his face clouded with regret. 'I made a mistake, Kanak, and I didn't get time to correct it. Every time I think of him, I feel more burdened.' Tears spilled out of his eyes. 'But no matter what I think or do, he's not coming back.' He shut his eyes and lowered his head.

Kanak withdrew her hand quietly. Her eyes released the tears she'd been holding back.

'Welcome to Ananyaakashganga, Yagya,' a female voice echoed through Prithvi's ears.

A saturnine Kanak stared at him as she heard it, too.

They turned around but couldn't find its origin. Then they looked into the distance to find a golden sun, its dazzling long rays blazing out in all directions. The colour drained out of their face.

'Why are they always lost so we've to search them,' said Samrat to Kabeer, coming to them.

Prithvi and Kanak exchanged decisive looks, held each other's hand and darted to the glaring sun.

'Where are they...?' Kabeer couldn't finish as Prithvi and Kanak suddenly disappeared from the sight.

A breathtaking incident for Samrat and Kabeer.

The same morass was faced by Prithvi and Kanak. The scene before them was at once replaced by a new view. The place became ghastly silent. Their feet went motionless. They hardly believed their eyes. When they turned back, there were neither the soldiers nor the fort. Nothing appeared far and near in that endless field.

'Be careful,' said Prithvi, stepping ahead.

Kanak nodded.

Hardly had they walked twenty steps when Prithvi halted and saw Kanak's hand he was holding. 'You're bleeding!'

'What!' said Kanak, flabbergasted. She looked at her right palm. A cut across it, leaking blood.

Prithvi looked amazed. 'How did it happen?'

Kanak asked, pointing weakly with her finger behind him, 'What's that?'

Prithvi turned to see a prodigious palace at a distance, built entirely with white marble, topped by three large and eight small domes. The centre dome appeared to have the same colossal golden sun. His breath caught for it was the same palace he'd seen in Amrit city.

Samrat bustled, followed by Kabeer, to the place both of them had vanished into air. He hit something and fell backwards.

'Company impinges on *you* the most.' Kabeer held him up, making neither head nor tail. 'What happened?'

Samrat told, 'Here is something I collided with.'

'What!' Kabeer scrabbled and felt something solid. 'Yes. Something is here, like a transparent wall.'

***

'It looks familiar?' Kanak was standing just in front of the palace.

'Not to you?' Prithvi was next to her.

They entered without giving answer. The magnificent architecture of the palace left them wonderstruck. Elaborately carved pillars supported the ceiling of white marble, dazzling jewels inlaid into them. Domes worked with tracery of incised painting while walls painted in contrasting colours creating geometric patterns. Walkways used regular and semi-regular tilings.

They passed door after door, looking at all sides. They felt as though every corridor, every pillar, every room was having a relation with them, a connection that couldn't be quelled by the thick layers of time. When they walked past a large door in a corridor, it opened. They entered. Many nebulous pictures became clear, flashing through their mind.

It was a royal court. Long and huge white pillars stood, forming a passage to a throne. A majestic jewelled diadem with a golden sun manifested in the centre was placed over it. Red curtains hung from the ceiling, developing a royal look. Countless soldiers, each wearing a golden body-armour shaped like a sun around their chest, were standing around, closing their eyes.

'Welcome to your own world.' The long silence broke with these words.

An attractive and graceful woman appeared at the door. Togged up in a white shimmering sari, she had long dark hair braided in plaits with silver ribbons. An incredible glow was on her face, an eternal calmness in her eyes.

Only a single word struck Kanak and Prithvi's mind, '*Gurumata!*'

***

'*The Shrewd barrier!*' said Tilakraj, touching the transparent wall with his right hand.

Jaywardhan, Gajraj, Sagar, Samrat, Kabeer and Aavishkar stood behind him.

Jaywardhan asked, 'What barrier?'

Gajraj told, 'A wall that judges what should be concealed or revealed, what should be in secret or in light.'

Tilakraj closed his eyes and muttered a spell.

Gajraj's face lit up. He could see the palace gradually appearing. 'They.... they came back, Tilakraj. Both of them... they've returned.'

***

'We're upbeat to see both of you, *anew*,' Gurumata broke the ice, her unspoken emotions gushed forth. 'For eighteen years, we'd been awaiting you, Yagya and Raksha.'

Prithvi and Kanak said together, 'What?'

'These were your names. Now, Prithvi and Kanak?'

Both of them nodded.

'Come with me,' said Gurumata, leading them to the throne. 'Your face has been changed but you're my Yagya-Raksha.' She gestured to the diadem. 'I hope you know what it is.'

'The... Surya... Diadem,' Prithvi tried to recall, 'after wearing it, one can lead Ananya...' he broke off and turned towards the innumerable soldiers. 'Is it Ananyasena?'

'Yes, Yagya. It's *your* Ananyasena. Because of it, your elder brother Yugant killed your father and both of you. Because of it, eighteen years ago an apocalypse, a horrific carnage betided here.' Gurumata put her hands on Prithvi and Kanak's head. 'Just close your eyes, children.'

As Prithvi and Kanak closed their eyes, a view flashed.

Two men, one in his late forties and another looked to be around twenty, were having an argument.

'Father, how could you do this to me? The Surya Diadem is rightfully mine. I am older, not Yagya,' the younger man spat.

'The Surya Diadem does not choose the older but the worthy, Yugant, and it's chosen Yagya. Gurumata told me when Yagya touched it, then only its sun glittered,' the father put across.

The boy said aggressively, 'It's inequitable. The Ananyasena is mine, only mine.'

The vision changed, showing a boy and a girl talking to Gurumata.

'Why did you do it, Yagya? Why a duel with a patricide?' asked Gurumata.

'I don't want more bloodshed,' said the boy. 'He'll continue to hurt people if I don't do it. If the Surya Diadem is everything for him, he must get a chance.'

The girl asked, 'What if he uses his circlet?'

*'We'll fight without any armour or circlet. The combat between us will be based on honesty. But if something goes wrong, I want Guru*mata *to protect the Surya Diadem,' said the boy.*

Prithvi and Kanak opened their eyes, thrilled with the live experiences, enveloped by the waves of memories.

Gurumata said, removing her hands from their head, 'Yagya never wanted his responsibility to be the cause of two brothers' relationship going bitter.' She looked at Prithvi. 'You loved Yugant more than anyone. He was your brother, your own blood, but he betrayed you. He turned the duel into a war to kill you, Raksha, Tilakraj and many more.'

Everything was crystal clear for Prithvi and Kanak, every fact afloat in their mind.

'Gurumata, you can always protect the Surya Diadem and the Ananyasena then…' said Kanak, as if reading her mind.

'Not always,' Gurumata's tone was pensive. 'I could've done worse with that fratricide for killing you and Yagya, but I wanted to give him a lifetime punishment. I ceased the existence of the Ananyasena along with this palace, and Arjun's grandfather Raviraj drew the Forbidden Line around Ananyaakashganga, but we cannot protect *everything* forever. Sooner or later, Yugant will hunt this palace down.' She took a deep breath. 'That's all I wanted to tell you. Remember one thing, my children, some truths are revealed with the passage of time. Everything in its own moment.'

***

'Is it possible, Tilakraj? They've come back after dying?' Jaywardhan blinked hard.

Tilakraj's eyes sparked with faith. 'We should believe in what we're witnessing.'

'Chronologically, they've returned *here* after eighteen years but they were reborn after *hundreds of years* of their death,' Sagar's voice was startled.

'I still don't believe that Prithvi was a prince!' said Samrat, feeling hard to swallow whatever Tilakraj told them.

Aavishkar asked, 'And what about Kanak? Who was she, actually?'

'Princess Raksha was our king Yashashviraj's friend Pulkeshin's daughter. After her father's death, king Yashashviraj brought her with him. She's a very important person of our lives. She is *the Awaker*,' revealed Gajraj.

***

'Why have the soldiers closed their eyes?' asked Kanak, moving to Ananyasena.

'They've been asleep for eighteen years,' told Guramata. 'You don't remember how to rouse them, Raksha?'

Kanak saw her right palm having the incision.

Gurumata said, 'Yes. Only *your blood* can wake them.'

Kanak drew the sun on the floor with her blood. No sooner did she place her right hand over it than it glared. Its golden rays enveloped the court. The soldiers stirred, their body-armour gleamed.

***

Chapter 24
The Unfinished Business

'Here's someone else who's been awaiting you for a long.' Gurumata looked left. 'He's already met you but…'

Prithvi and Kanak turned to find the man, who'd taken the tablet and then disappeared, standing at the door.

'Glad to see you, *once again*,' he said, approaching.

'Moksha, the…the Unknown?' said Kanak, puzzled.

'Moksha, Arjun's friend, belongs to a rare species named *Atharva*. He can transform himself into any mortal,' told Gurumata. 'Moksha never fails to perform his duties. Duty to be with Arjun. Duty to be with me. He buries himself to help us.' She smiled gratefully.

Moksha conjoined her.

'I like *Moksha, the Atharva,* better than any other Mokshas,' grinned Kanak.

At once, Moksha turned to the door. 'A man of Vidhvans is coming.'

Prithvi said, 'He will definitely be brother.'

***

Twenty battalions of infantry, fifteen regiments of cavalry and eight regiments of horse archers, stretching as far as the eye could see, appeared marching to the palace.

Tilakraj said, '*He's come.*'

A distressing thought entered Jaywardhan's mind. 'We must go for their help.'

Gajraj said, 'It's not possible to cross this wall.'

Every eye turned to the palace to see Prithvi and Kanak come out.

There was a prayer on everyone's lips who were standing behind the wall.

'*Dear little Yagya,*' said a powerfully built man, dismounting a bay horse. His thick muscles could be seen hidden under his brownish-golden body-armour, his face veiled by a brown mask shaped exactly like a human face. 'You're more handsome now.'

'What can I say, big brother? It's hereditary,' smiled Prithvi with his panache.

The man's deep voice mocked him, 'You didn't change a bit.'

A scrambled Prithvi said, 'Eighteen years passed but it seems like I heard your voice yesterday only.'

The man stepped without giving his words any thought. 'So, you've returned with your partner,' he said, staring at Kanak with his large black eyes, only visible parts of his face. They scoured her from top to bottom, lingering on her right palm. They widened in realization.

'We have to finish the unfinished business,' said Prithvi calmly.

The man laughed. 'Mr bellicose, you don't need to put on a brave face. You're making matters for yourself. I want peace.'

Kanak snapped, 'These words are coming from a man whose hands are stained in his own brother and father's blood.'

'And I believe these courageous words are not coming from you because of *the Ananyasena* hidden there,' said the man, gesturing towards the palace. 'You can wake it up, Raksha, but Yagya cannot lead it. He doesn't have the Surya Diadem. Does he?' he asked eagerly. 'No matter how hard we scouted, we couldn't get it as *an impenetrable Nakshtra* had concealed it. Moreover, that *Moksha. Master of disguise.* He bothers us, spies on us, always attempts to spoil our plan.' The man's voice conveyed irritation. 'The Surya Diadem has been hidden for you, Yagya. But we will reclaim it after finishing your story of reincarnation, after you die, *again.*' His eyes flashed a desire for vengeance that burned in his heart.

Suddenly the man recoiled in horror to see hundreds of soldiers marching out of the palace.

Moksha was in the vanguard. His strides long and determined. His eyes sanguine. He came next to Prithvi, his hand holding the thing the man was yearning for.

As soon as the man's eyes caught the Surya Diadem, they shone with rapturous satisfaction.

'I'm not going to kill you like this, brother,' Prithvi's voice intruded into his thoughts. 'I'm not *you*.'

'Then let's fight.' The man looked desperate. 'Winner gets the crown as it was supposed to.'

Kanak said, anger burning through her, 'It was supposed to be finished with honesty, not with butchery.'

'Let's not dwell on the past. Let's finish the unfinished business,' said the man, pulling his shoulders back.

Kanak looked at Prithvi with an apprehensive expression. 'It's very risky. Think about it.'

Prithvi flashed her an amused smile. 'Is it concern I see in your eyes?'

Kanak said, raising an eyebrow, 'Actually I want to end your saga. So, kindly don't get yourself killed.'

'If I die, you find a new partner, and if I survive, we'll together celebrate my hundredth fall,' grinned Prithvi, drawing his sword. He took a shield from Moksha and marched up to Yugant.

The man drew his sword and unmounted a shield from his back.

'Prithvi will duel with him?' said Samrat, his face a mixture of surprise and fear.

Prithvi and the man moved in a circle, gauging each other's defences, making no move. The man, holding his shield high, looking confident that he could handle everything, swerved suddenly to the left. He was able to slash Prithvi's chest but Prithvi brought his shield up to block the blow and moved swiftly to the right to face his opponent again.

The man tried to lacerate Prithvi's neck but Prithvi dodged and sliced him across his thigh. The man retreated, snarling in pain. He quickly rallied and swung savagely to slash off Prithvi's head. Prithvi sidestepped to the right, and the blade passed a few centimetres away from his neck.

The man didn't give him any moment to breathe. He again swung, and his sword hunt Prithvi's arm. Prithvi staggered, blood gushed from his flesh, his sword still in his hand.

A wretched grin split the man's lips. 'Try harder, Yagya. I don't want to kill you *like this,* too.'

Prithvi dipped and weaved right, reaching the practised combatant. The man parried Prithvi's attack with his sword. The two swords flashed in the sunlight.

The man pressed the sword closer to Prithvi's face. Prithvi brought his shield down hard on his wounded thigh. The man staggered, slipped sideways and fell on one knee. He looked up, flinching. His eyes glowered with the terrible anger seething inside. Within a moment, he jumped high and swung from the elevation, severing Prithvi's shield arm. Prithvi's shield left his hand. The cut appeared to hurt him.

Kanak shut her eyes, her fists clenched tight. Prithvi's well-wishers gasped in dread.

The man, thinking his rival badly injured, relaxed his stance. Prithvi suddenly leapt to the left. The unprepared man straightened, holding his shield higher. Prithvi's surprise attack had slowed his charge. Prithvi veered and slitted a deep cut across his sword arm, making the sword leave his hand.

It brought hope back in Kanak's heart.

'Very good, Prithvi,' cried Aavishkar, dancing in delight.

The man's eyes were scrunched up in anger. He left his shield, showing himself ready for a hand to hand combat.

'Prithvi, don't do this. Just finish him,' shouted Samrat, even knowing that Prithvi couldn't hear.

Kabeer said, 'You're saying like you don't know him.'

Prithvi accepted the challenge, disappointing Samrat.

The man positioned himself and swiftly tried to punch Prithvi. Prithvi blocked it and planted a sock on his face, stunning him for a brief moment. Blood spurted from his mouth.

Prithvi moved again, this time quicker, and kicked, but the man blocked with his hand. The man with a furrowed brow suddenly counterattacked with a knock. It jarred Prithvi's bones.

Prithvi's friends let out a collective wince.

The man charged again and whacked him in the stomach. He ranted, 'You are no match to King Yugant.'

'Do something, Prithvi,' cried Kanak, her eyes aghast.

The man lashed out to punch Prithvi's jaw. Prithvi caught his hand and wrenched him around. He kneed him in the ribs. The man staggered, a groan escaped his lips. Prithvi used a series of offensive moves against him. He punched his stomach twice, bringing him to his knees. A final smite slammed his face into the ground. He was at his weakest.

Prithvi, bleeding profusely, picked up his sword. He raised it high with both his hands and brought it down to end this single combat. His bloodied hands halted an inch away from the man's chest as soon as he noticed him shut his eyes. He stood quietly, his chest heaving.

The man opened his puzzled eyes. 'Do it, Yagya,' he exclaimed. 'Scared of killing your brother?'

Prithvi left his sword. 'Killing a brother is not *my* forte.'

Kanak said to Moksha, 'It's time.'

Moksha came to Prithvi and crowned him with the Surya Diadem. He said, 'As you wished, Yugant. Winner got the crown.'

The sunlight bounced off the Surya Diadem, and its sun glared.

Prithvi ordered Ananyasena, 'Do your job, soldiers. Set your world free from Yugant's sins. CHARGE…'

As the man saw Ananyasena march towards him, he got up. He once looked at Prithvi and Kanak and ordered his army, 'BE READY…'

Ananyasena obeyed Prithvi's order instantly. The powerful refulgent golden rays emerged from soldiers' body-armour and petrified the entire legions. The man was now the leader of thousands of deaf, blind, stone statues.

It was Moksha's turn to work. He transformed himself into a giant eagle and breathed out fire, fluttering. His lethal breaths cremated the man's army. Stone statues turned into debris and then reduced to ashes. The battlefield witnessed the consequences of greed, betrayal and hatred.

The spectators beyond the Shrewd Barrier were gleeful, leaping up in excitement.

Kanak spoke, 'You had everything what a person dreamt of but that wasn't enough for you, was it?'

'King Yugant's downfall is impossible. He's ceaseless,' the man broke his silence, drawing a violet dirk. 'No any power present in any world known and unknown can outface him. He can die but he cannot lose. It's not in his blood.'

Prithvi, Kanak and Moksha were bemused to find the man incise his right palm with the blade. He dropped his blood on it. In no time, the blade absorbed the blood.

He looked up at Prithvi, his voice cold and unfeeling, 'I may have lost, Yagya, but you have not actually won.'

As he pierced the ground with it, very high and bright purple flames flared around him.

Prithvi and Moksha receded, staring at the rising flame. Those blazes were so fierce that they devoured the layers of dust the field was strewn with, furling into themselves. The man's mask flew out of the flames to Prithvi's feet. When the firestorm died out, the man wasn't there but a heap of shiny violet ashes.

'He's gone!' said Kabeer, boggled.

'*Aahuti,*' Gurumata's voice came from behind Kanak. 'This heap of ashes is the sign of the oblation, *Aahuti.*'

Dumbstruck, Kanak asked, 'He sacrificed himself! For what?'

Gurumata told, 'Yugant always served Vidhvans. He never wanted to be killed by a Nakshtra.'

'I didn't expect such end of him,' said Prithvi.

'Some people do not deserve an end, Yagya. They always suffer, trapped in their selfishness and delusion.' Gurumata sighed deeply.

'I think it's time to say farewell. I know you have to go back to the world you belong.'

Prithvi returned the Surya Diadem to her. He turned to Ananyasena, his voice strong, 'This world is yours, soldiers, and you are to protect it. Keep our Ananyaakashganga and our people safe.'

Gurumata embraced Prithvi and Kanak warmly. 'I believe I'd see you again, my children.' With one last look at them, she turned and walked to the palace, leading Ananyasena.

Moksha once saw both of them with wet eyes and then followed Ananyasena. As he entered the palace, it vanished so did the Shrewd Barrier.

***

'I never believed in such powers like Nakshtra and Vidhvans,' revealed Samrat.

Kabeer laughed stealthily, sitting next to him on the stairs of the temple. 'Just now, you shared your first secret with me.'

Both of them looked left to find Prithvi, Kanak, Aavishkar, Jaywardhan, Sagar, Kushal and Arunima step down the staircase led by Tilakraj.

Gajraj, followed by Anahita, entered the courtyard and informed, 'Time machines are ready, Jaywardhan.'

The emerald glass sphere in Gajraj's hand attracted Kanak's attention. 'It...it's...'

'Yes. It's the same orb you had,' told Gajraj before she finished.

'We'd found it in our bag,' said Samrat.

'It is *Pradarshak*. It helps us in a predicament, showing us a felicitous path,' clarified Gajraj. 'We'd like to give it to you.' He extended the sphere to Prithvi and his friends. 'We believe you'll use Pradrashak for the welfare of your country and people as what Vyom teaches you.'

'We've already got a lot of things from Ananyaakashganga,' said Kanak gratefully.

Tilakraj smiled plaintively. 'It's Arjun's. He'd kept it in your bag for your help. We can't take it back.'

Prithvi's face lost its brightness.

Tilakraj stepped forward and hugged him.

'I wish he...' Prithvi's voice broke, and a tear slipped down his cheek.

Tilakraj said, patting his back, 'You fought very well, Yagya. I want to tell you one thing what I shared with Arjun too.' He withdrew from the hug. 'Any war of any world can be battled through *the power of goodness* but it can be avoided through *the power of love.*' He turned to Jaywardhan, smilingly. 'We'll be awaiting your next arrival.'

Jaywardhan nodded, returning the smile.

Everyone walked up to the lowest courtyard where DTM and other time machines stood. Jaywardhan and his team bid Tilakraj and Gajraj and entered them.

'May God be with them,' prayed Tilakraj, an expression of peace and calmness descended upon his face.

***

'Why haven't they returned yet, Zaheer?' A tensed Damini was shuffling back and forth in Saptarishi lab.

'Don't worry...' Zaheer stopped in mid sentence.

God had heard their prayers. The time machines had arrived.

As soon as Jaywardhan came out of DTM, Zaheer asked, 'Everyone is okay?'

Jaywardhan's nod relieved him.

'I'll tell you everything. For now, I have to talk to them,' said Jaywardhan, turning to Prithvi and his friends. 'You all are expected not to tell anybody about Ananyaakashaganga and the Royal Weapon.'

'You can trust us, Mr Chancellor. We will not let you down,' said Kanak, confident and respectful.

Sagar smiled warmly. 'Today, everything is safe and secure because *we trusted you.*'

A discontented Aavishkar handed Aavriti over to Jaywardhan. 'Mr Chancellor, I think its black button doesn't work.'

'Any one of you had pressed it?' asked Jaywardhan.

Aavishkar replied, 'Yes, twice. But nothing happened.'

'It meant it was pressed thrice,' said Arunima. 'First time, Samarth may have pressed it to connect DTM to Saptarishi. Within half an hour, when it was pressed second time, Aavriti disconnected DTM from the lab hence DTM didn't come back. And third time, Aavriti reconnected DTM to Saptarishi.'

'That's why when I and Aavishkar tried to get DTM, it was present down there,' recalled Kanak.

'You don't wish to meet your friends? They are so much worried. And Abhyuday, that boy is *terrific.*' A grin blossomed on Zaheer's face.

Kushal said in a humurous tone, 'Don't leave without changing your traditional costumes. Otherwise your friends might think they're facing your ancient versions.'

***

Tilakraj stood silently, gazing at the place the smoke of doom had vanished from.

'What do you think where he is?' asked Gajraj, appearing behind him.

His question changed Tilakraj's countenance.

'Were you not with me when we learnt about Arjun's end? Don't you know how the Golden Armour bearer can die?'

Tilakraj spoke, without looking at him, '*A Nakshtra or Vidhvans more powerful than the Golden Armour can kill its bearer.*'

'And there is only one thing more powerful than it. *The Surya Diadem. Yagya's diadem.*'

Tilakraj stared at him. 'I hope *you* haven't forgotten the excruciating history of Ananyaakashganga. About *the Unretrieved Surya*

Diadem.' He paused for a moment. 'Saket had created the smoke of doom with *Yugant's* help, Gajraj.'

'Yugant never knew about the Unretrieved Surya Diadem.'

'We were never sure,' said Tilakraj. 'You're letting you emotions cloud the truth.'

'Why don't we let that hideous history die? Eighteen years ago whoever came in our life, neither he nor his army exists. We wanted him to be *a blessing* for Yagya but he's lost somewhere,' said Gajraj, ignoring the question in Tilakraj's eyes. 'You're Arjun's father. How can you believe that...?'

Tilakraj shut his moist eyes. 'Because I can't see him as *Half Dead.*'

'What!' Gajraj was unable to control his astounded dismay. 'No, it can't be.'

'I'm that unfortunate father who wants his son to be dead rather than *cursed.*' A tear slid down Tilakraj's grief-stricken face. 'If somehow the Golden Armour saves him, he will not be the same Arjun we know.'

Gajraj's choked throat refused to utter a sound.

***

'This time Abhyuday couldn't dig up correctly, I guess,' said Mayur.

Ibrahim sniggered. 'Yes. It's in the air that they're returning.'

Paridhi spoke up, 'Why didn't you and your friend dig up something then, Ibrahim? All you do is brag and your friend...,' her eyes motioned to Mayur, '...just... forget about it.'

Abhyuday masked his surprised ecstasy with a grateful smile.

Shikhar said, 'What if Mr Chancellor hasn't found them yet?'

Jessica's troubled gaze ran over Paridhi's face. 'What if any wild animal...?'

Kavya placed her finger on her lips. 'Jessy, if you don't think good, *don't think at all.*'

Some students of Buddha group were on the stage of *Ashvagosha Auditorium,* rehearsing a dance drama for Vyom Institute's Annual

Function. Some back stage, preparing costumes and decorative materials. Some, in Light and Technology department. The others were handling scripts, lyrics and musical instruments.

Paridhi's eyes glittered as she saw Prithvi, Kanak, Samrat, Kabeer and Aavishkar walking across the aisle towards them. 'No, Shikhar. Mr Chancellor *has* found them.' She shouted, racing down, '*PRITHVI...*'

Abhyuday felt a hand squeeze his shoulder lightly. He, bottling his feeling up, turned with a broad grin to find Kavya.

'The king has returned,' said Kavya unable to hold back her smile.

Abhyuday said with a slight wink at her, 'And his commander too.'

Kavya followed his gaze and had a big laugh, looking at Samrat.

Abhyuday put his arm around her shoulder. 'Let's go, *partner*.'

Hardly had Prithvi reached the stage when an overjoyed Paridhi hugged him tightly. 'I was so much worried about you.'

Samrat nudged Kanak. 'They've met after a hundred years? Look at Prithvi. I can see only exaltation in his eyes.'

Kanak gravely stared at them. 'Who cares?' Her tone didn't match her expression.

Prithvi's face contorted in pain. 'Yes, Pari... yes. I'm...I'm absolutely fine,' he faltered, withdrawing from the hug and laid his hand on his bandaged arm.

Kavya's eyes ran across the bruises five of them suffered. 'What happened with you all? You look *terrible*.'

'You're alright, Prithvi?' asked Paridhi, a concerned look on her face.

'It's just a superficial cut,' replied Prithvi, smiling weakly.

Jessica asked, 'Why did you take so long? You'd lost in the past?'

Samrat told, 'Yes, we had. Some maniac soldiers caught us. Then this is what happened. But the S.T.F. found us in time.'

'I'm sorry, friends,' a low voice came from the left.

They turned to see Dhairya looking down with guilty eyes.

'Why did you do it, Dhairya? Because someone dragooned you into it?' Aavishkar opined, 'Nobody can force us to do something wrong. It's our choice.'

Samrat mumbled, '*That was catchy.*'

'We're friends. Just let bygones be bygones.' Kabeer hugged a tearful Dhairya.

'But I'm not going to leave *him* so easily,' said Kanak, glaring at Shaurya who was arranging sets on the stage with Saif, Urvashi, Alexander and Lara.

Shaurya had noticed them but averted his eyes.

'They're hurt. And Prithvi, he's…,' said Urvashi, a trace of agitation in her eyes. 'At least we….'

Saif turned crimson. 'Are you out of your mind?'

'Listen to me. Let it be...' Prithvi tried to stop an enraged Kanak going on the stage.

'Go ahead, Kanak. Show him what you are,' shouted Shikhar effervescently.

Prithvi said, frustration crinkled his eyes, 'Stop it, Shikhar.' He ran after Kanak, followed by Samrat.

'I've to ask him why he did this to us,' said Kanak, her voice loud and threatening. 'If he wants to fight, fight. But don't use our friends.'

'Mind your blood pressure, Kanak. First, he's *my* brother and then someone's bosom friend,' Shaurya broke his silence, looking at Dhairya standing downstairs, his voice composed. 'And what do you think? That I wanted you all to visit the past? Then my answer is *no.*'

Samrat was quick off the mark. 'And we should believe you? Then our answer is *no.*'

'You're beyond the pale, Samrat,' said an infuriated Lara. 'We're not here to watch your attitude.'

'Then why don't you do it what's expected from you?' shouted Kabeer from the downstairs with a grin that summoned his dimple.

Saif said frostily, 'What do you all want? We apologise otherwise you'll tell about it to Mr Chancellor?'

Kabeer studied Urvashi's expression.

Urvashi looked unsettled and sympathetic, looking at their injuries. Her eyes fell on Kabeer noticing her. She quickly looked away.

Prithvi said, 'I don't want this wrangle to go on, Saif.'

Shaurya came closer to Prithvi. 'I did not want to harm anyone of you, but *I don't care* what you want.'

Urvashi stepped in, 'Shaurya, let's drop it.'

'Mr Chancellor won't be happy to learn about any fight among their students,' said Alexander.

'This fight will always be going on, Alex,' said Shaurya, continued to stare intensely into Prithvi's eyes. 'You don't see? Prithviraj Malhotra *never* believes us.'

'*Dear little brother…*' No sooner did Prithvi turn to the voice than Prarthana clasped him in the arms. 'Thank God, you're safe.'

Prithvi clung to her. 'I missed you so much.' His smiling lips suddenly shrunk. 'I'm lucky I have *you*.'

'You're the luckiest, actually.' Prarthana's large eyes were bright and expressive. 'Oh yes...' She turned back, withdrawing from the hug. 'Shaurya, I couldn't thank you and your friends for helping us.'

'It's okay,' reacted Shaurya. 'You don't need to do it.'

'The assembly is about to begin,' shouted Narayani from the balcony.

'Let's go, everyone.' Prarthana walked ahead.

Prithvi and Shaurya stared at each other and followed her.

***

'I express my heartiest gratitude to Mr Mittal, Mr Solanki, Mr Siddiqui, Mrs Rathore and their entire team for saving hundreds of lives,' addressed Jaywardhan, gesturing to Sagar and Devraj sitting to his right, and Zaheer and Damini to his left in Vyom Hall. 'I want all of you to give a standing ovation for them.'

Everyone stood up. Clapping echoed through the hall.

'But it wasn't possible without Buddha group and Mangal group's students who surmounted a dire situation without losing hope.' Jaywardhan beamed with pride.

All heads turned to Buddha group and Mangal group. A cheer erupted for them.

'Vyom is proud of them. Their courage, determination and wisdom are behind this perfect teamwork. As I say, *a best team engenders a best plan*,' articulated Jaywardhan. 'But we have lost our many friends in this battle, and no any victory can take away the gloom of losing someone. I just want you to keep in your mind that those sacrifices must not go in vain.'

***

'I'm feeling blissful,' said a buoyant Aavishkar, sipping his favourite drink, *Kesar Milk,* from a kulhad. He was sitting with his friends in *Aahaar*, a canteen in *Sanrachana* for the students.

Kabeer headed for a water cooler in a corner and saw Urvashi pouring water into a glass from one of the taps. Urvashi had already registered him from the corner of her eye.

Kabeer cleared his throat. 'We're alright, by the way,' he said without looking at her.

Urvashi did not react.

'You seemed concerned there, so I...'

Urvashi turned sharply and gave him an icy look. 'So what, Kabeer? What do you want?'

Kabeer tried to say something, but he was at a loss of words.

Urvashi noticed someone behind him. After delivering a clear message through her eyes, she made for the exit.

'*I* also want to know what you wanted from *her*,' Samrat's voice surprised Kabeer, who was standing just behind him. 'She's in Shaurya's team. Don't you know?'

Kabeer cast an annoyed glance at Samrat and went back to his table, where Prithvi and Kanak had declared *the Armageddon*.

'You should thank God that he saved you today from *the ninth fall,* Mr Malhotra.' Fury turned Kanak's face bright red.

Prithvi's eyes flashed angrily. 'But He couldn't save me from *you,* fighter plane.'

Samrat said, coming on the scene, 'Friends, don't start your strong language again.'

'Because it's time to have fun and a good time together.' Abhyuday turned up, smiling with his eyes. Accompanying him was Kavya.

Kavya grinned with delight. 'We're going for a PICNIC.'

***

Two intense eyes were staring at the battlefield which had witnessed a victory of Nakshtra over Vidhvans. They belonged to the same chiselled face that had replaced Saket's reflection when he was communicating to someone through water, but this time it wasn't bearing the jewelled circlet which had a golden sun in its centre.

A muscular and well-built man in his late thirties appeared, standing on a brink of a cliff to the south of the battlefield.

A man in a long grey robe spoke from behind him, his voice deep, 'He did sacrifice himself for you, Yugant.'

'That's why I'm here, My Lord. In *Ananyaakashganga.*' The muscular man looked pleased. 'Yagya defeated *him,* and *we* won.'

The man in the robe turned about, darkness enveloping his face. 'So, the Surya diadem and the Ananyasena are inside the palace with that lady as we expected. And she couldn't learn that it wasn't you but your man.'

'The credit goes to *you*, My Lord. If Yagya has Gurumata, I have you,' said the muscular man gratefully.

'Prepare yourself, Yugant. THE WAR HAS JUST BEGUN.'

***

- Tripty Bhardwaj

About the Author

Tripty Bhardwaj is a script writer, an anchor, a newsreader and a teacher. She is a Master's degree holder in Physics and a Bachelor's degree holder in Science as well as in Education.

She has worked with Doordarshan as a script writer and an anchor in the shows 'Geet Bahaar' and 'Geet Gunjan' for two and a half years and as a Newsreader in an agriculture-based show 'Krishi Darshan' for three years

Tripty has always been a voracious reader of variety of literature especially science fiction, mythology and thriller and mystery. Being a creative and self-motivated writer, she always tries to formulate her writing in a meaningful and logical manner. She successfully turns her framework of mind into simple and understandable language.